OFF SEASON

NASHVILLE FURY: BOOK 3

CHELLE SLOAN

OFF SEASON PLAYLIST

I love putting together playlists for my books. Sometimes they are songs that fit the vibe. Sometimes they fit the scene. Take a listen to the Spotify Playlist for Off Season

- Drink You Away - Justin Timberlake
- Break Up in a Small Town - Sam Hunt
- Kiss You Tonight - David Nail
- Here Comes Goodbye - Rascal Flatts
- Wildest Dreams (Taylor's Version) - Taylor Swift
- Love Me Like You Do - Ellie Goulding
- Ride - Chase Rice, Macy Maloy
- Better Man - Little Big Town
- Again - Janet Jackson
- My Boo - Usher, Alicia Keys
- Perfect - Ed Sheeran
- Kiss The Girl - Brent Morgan
- It's Your Love - Tim McGraw, Faith Hill
- All Cried Out - Allure, 112
- Bless the Broken Road - Rascal Flatts

To Julia.
Thank you for making sure I never gave up.

PROLOGUE

BRYCE

"Goodbye, Bryce. Go be amazing."

I jolt up from the bed, a cold sweat covering me as I try to catch my breath, as I try to figure out why she continues to haunt my dreams every night. I look to my left to see Cole still asleep in the second bed in the hotel room as I roll off my bed and stumble to my duffle bag where I pull out a half-finished bottle of whiskey and my cell phone. Yes, it's the night before a game. No, I'm not supposed to be drinking while staying in the hotel, which the team mandates we do the night before games.

Frankly, I don't care. If they want me to be any sort of a functioning quarterback tomorrow, then they want me to finish this bottle. It's the only way I'm going to fall back asleep and make sure I don't dream of her again.

I quietly slide open the door to the small patio and fall into the chair as I down a healthy swig of the burning liquid. I look at my cell phone, hoping I can find something on here to take my mind off the dream I just had. Instead, I see a text message from my father. Fucking wonderful.

Dad: Don't fuck tomorrow up. I have a lot riding on this game. Ten grand to be exact.

I squeeze my phone until it nearly breaks because it's better than throwing it over the balcony. Instead, I take another drink from the bottle.

"Why?" I say to no one. "Why can't I stop dreaming about her?"

I've been having some sort of version of that dream for what feels like every night for the past nine months.

Sometimes I'm watching Lucy get married, and I can't do anything about it. I'm just sitting in the back of the church, wondering why it wasn't me she was pledging to spend the rest of her life with.

Sometimes I'm kissing her before she's pulled away from me.

Tonight I dreamed of the last time we were together. It was during my rookie season a year ago, and I was a wreck. The transition from college to pro football was more than I could handle, and my play was paying the price.

And, just like always, Lucy made it better. She silenced the doubt in my brain and got me back on the right track. I really thought that the next time I saw her, we'd finally be starting our life together, that it was finally our time.

Until it wasn't. Until I found out she moved on. That she got engaged.

When she told me goodbye and to go be amazing I never thought they were going to be the last words she said to me.

She's gone. My rock. My first love—the only person in this world who knows how to fix me when things get bad—is out of my life for good.

She's someone else's now. I was too late.

So, I'll just sit here on this balcony, drink the rest of this whiskey, and do my best to forget her.

Too bad there isn't enough whiskey in the world to ever make me forget her.

But that won't stop me from trying.

———

"Donald. Coach wants you."

Fucking fantastic.

Not only am I still nursing a hangover from hell after last night's whiskey-on-the-balcony bender but also now I'm going to have to get chewed out by my head coach. If only that last jackass reporter wouldn't have asked me the stupidest question in the history of press conference questions I'd already be out of here. But no, because of that dip shit, I'll have to listen to Coach McAvoy drone on about how we need to fix the offense and how it's my job to do it.

No. It's his job. I'm doing mine. Not my fault his offense can't hang with me.

I toss my bag into my locker, and if I didn't know better, I'd swear that every one of my teammates was watching my progress across the locker room toward Coach McAvoy's offices. It's like I'm getting called into the principal's office or something.

"Hey"—Cole's hand on my shoulder stops me mid step— "whatever happens, I'm here for you. You know that, right?"

It takes all I have not to roll my eyes at my teammate and lifelong best friend. Because what he just said? That is the most Cole shit I've ever heard.

"How many times do I need to tell you I'm fine?"

"And how many times do I need to tell you that I don't believe you?"

"Whatever, man," I say, shrugging away his hand and making my way to Coach McAvoy's office. I don't have time today to listen to Cole's latest spiel about how I need help and should talk to someone. I don't. I'm fine. And the quicker I get this meeting over the quicker I can get to the bar tonight. If I have my way, I'll be forgetting about today's loss with a blonde or two.

Coach McAvoy is standing next to Coach Davis when I walk in, which is fucking wonderful. He's been on my ass more than McAvoy has. I swear, the man feels like it's his personal mission to be my counselor.

Or worse. My friend.

I don't need either. I need to be left the fuck alone.

"Bryce."

"I know. We sucked today," I say before either of them can say anything else. "Your shiny new wide receiver can't catch any of my passes. He needs work."

"Dexter has nothing to do with this," Davis says. "It's not his fault that he ran the correct route and his quarterback underthrew him by ten yards."

Of course, he'd say that. In his eyes, everything that goes wrong with the offense is my fault.

"Like I said, the receivers need to be where I put it. Not the other way around."

Why is it so hard for these two to get that? Hell, McAvoy was a quarterback. He should know. I don't understand why they aren't comprehending this.

"Who the hell are you?" Coach McAvoy asks.

Here it comes. The attempt at the intervention.

I'm Bryce fucking Donald. I'm the former number-one draft pick and best up-and-coming quarterback in professional football. My contract was the largest for a rookie in the history of the league. My face is on billboards all around Nashville. The city might be known for its country music, but since I arrived and led the Fury to the playoffs last season, it's my town now. I can get into any bar, club, or restaurant. I see a woman I want? She's mine. I'm living the life every twenty-four-year-old dreams about.

Though, by the looks that McAvoy and Davis are giving me, they don't care about that.

"I'm being serious, Bryce," McAvoy continues, his tone conciliatory and calm. "You aren't the guy we drafted. You aren't the player who led us to the playoffs last year. You aren't the leader of this franchise like you're supposed to be. This guy . . . I don't know this guy, and I don't want to."

"No one says you have to." I stand and turn to leave. I'm over this conversation. "Just leave me alone and let me play football."

"We aren't done," Davis says, pushing me back into my chair. "You want to play football? Then start fucking playing football. What you showed us today was pathetic, so quit the partying, get your priorities straight, and get your head back in the game."

"Here we go again with the partying," I say, sounding as bored as I feel. I don't have a fucking problem, yet he's acting like I'm drunk twenty-four hours a day. "What I do outside of this facility is none of your damn business."

"It is when it affects your play," Coach McAvoy says, his voice growing sterner. Uh oh. Good cop is getting mad. "And it is. Bryce, you're a liability right now. Today's loss? That is all on you. Until you can prove to us that you are the leader and player we drafted, you're benched."

I have to shake my head a few times because I clearly didn't hear him correctly.

I'm the starting quarterback. The future of this team. The face of the franchise.

I don't get benched.

"I'm what?" I demand, still not believing what I've heard. "You can't bench me. I haven't violated anything in my contract."

Coach McAvoy laughs. He fucking laughs. The asshole.

"Damn right, I can. And I am. I never thought I'd have to do this again after last year, but here we are. Maybe this time it will work. As for your contract? Consider this me helping you to make sure you don't break it."

I start pacing in circles. My hands grab pieces of my hair and if I'm not careful I might pull some out. They can't do this to me. I won't let him.

Then I catch Coach Davis out of the corner of my eye.

Him. He's the reason McAvoy is doing this.

Well, this isn't going to fucking happen. Not if I can help it.

"Fuck this! This is all his fault!" I yell, pointing at the fucking traitor who calls himself my offensive coordinator. "This fucker has been on my ass since the summer. He tell you to do this?"

"While I take all recommendations from my coaching staff into consideration, this decision is mine," Coach McAvoy says. "If you can't clean up your act on your own, we will demand you go to a rehabilitation center to get treatment."

"Treatment?" My teammates are starting to gather outside the office, but I don't give a shit. Let them hear what our coaches are doing to me. "I don't need fucking rehab. I'm fine. Why can't you just get off my ass?"

"We're on your ass because despite what you think, we care about you and we don't want you to run your career into the ground," Davis says. "This is for your own good."

I laugh, though there is no humor in my tone. "You know, it's funny that you've been telling me to clean up my act all summer. Like you have the right to fucking talk."

Davis's face gets red. Apparently, I touched a nerve. Good. I have him right where I want him.

"What is that supposed to mean?"

"Last year, you were partying with us. The fun uncle coach, isn't that what they called you? Now I hear you knocked up McAvoy's sister-in-law?" Yeah, I know I'm throwing Davis's own drama in his face, but ask me if I care. He's over here acting as if he's a fucking saint when, this time last year, he was asking us what bar we were hitting up. "Real responsible, Coach. Great role model. Maybe take your own advice and get your shit right before you come after me."

My eyes are locked on Davis, and I see the minute he snaps. Good. Serves the asshole right for getting me benched.

I don't flinch as he charges toward me, and he probably would have landed the punch I know he's dying to throw, but Coach McAvoy got to him before he got it in.

Too bad. I would have loved to have told the owners that a coach hit a player.

"You need to go. Get the fuck out of here and get your head straight."

Cole's voice takes me by surprise. When did he get in here? And when did he place himself like the brick wall he is between me and the coaches? I swear, this man is fucking everywhere. He's almost as bad as Davis.

"Shut the fuck up," I yell, shoving my apparent former best friend in the chest. If he's telling me to go, that means he's on their side and he's no friend of mine. "How many times have I told you to mind your own fucking business? You aren't my father."

"And how many times have I told you I'm not fucking going anywhere," Cole says. "When we were kids, I promised you that I'd protect you. And that's what I'm doing. Do what coach says. Get out of here. Go home. Get help. Do something."

I look up at Cole, and for the first time since we met when we were six years old, I'm staring into the eyes of a stranger. My best friend wouldn't side with coaches over me. He would have my back. He's always had my back.

He turned on me. Lucy turned on me. Everyone has fucking turned on me.

"Go," Cole says again, putting his hand on my shoulder, which I promptly shove off.

I look at the three sets of eyes in the office, ones that are all trying to show sympathy.

Fuck their sympathy. They have no clue what it's like to be me.

Fuck Cole. Fuck the coaches. Fuck all of this.

They want me gone? Fine. I'll leave.

I don't need them.

I don't need Cole.

I don't need her.

I don't need anyone.

CHAPTER 1
BRYCE

ONE WEEK LATER...

"The Nashville Fury win their first game of the season, and they do it without franchise quarterback Bryce Donald, who will be out for the remainder of the season."

Wait, what?

I blink a few times. I was just about to take my daily afternoon nap so I'm not sure I heard the announcer correctly. Did he just say that I'm out for the season?

If so, my agent has a hell of a lot of explaining to do.

I grab the remote from the coffee table and turn up the television as I grab my phone. And here I thought it was a good idea to turn it off for the game so I didn't have the temptation to see what was being said about me on social media.

Instead, I watched my team play the best they had all season. My backup looked like a starter. Dexter caught every pass, and the defense played out of their minds.

All I could think about during the entire game was that I should be with them. We should be celebrating our first win of the season together. I shouldn't be watching it from my mother's couch in my small hometown in Southwest Ohio because I've been benched for the season.

"According to Donald's agent, Dean Braxton, who released a statement in conjunction with the Fury at the end of today's game, the second-year quarterback out of Clemson has been placed on injured reserve to focus on his mental health, which is the first time we've seen this happen in league history."

I mute the television and shake my phone, begging it to turn on faster. When it finally comes to life, there are seven voice mails from my agent. There are thousands of social media notifications, and a handful of texts. Three from Cole, two from my sister, and one from my father, which I'm sure is telling me that I'm no son of his now because he can't make money off me.

I don't have a chance to search for Dean's number before I see his name flash across my screen.

"I'm done for the season? This how you normally deliver news to your clients?"

"Only ones who make it their goal to be a pain in the ass."

"I'm your highest-paying client." I stand, needing to pace because all of this is too much to deal with sitting down. "You should have told me before the rest of the world found out. And mental health? I don't have a mental health problem. Where the hell do you and the team get off saying that without my permission?"

"I tried. Seven times. But it couldn't wait," he says, a long and frustrated breath following. "So we released the statement, and your tweet about taking the season off just posted."

"My what?" I shout, putting the conversation on speaker as I navigate to Twitter. And just like he said, a picture of a statement that I didn't write is there for the world to see.

"Fans, thank you for your support. I haven't been in a good state of mind for many months. My off-field actions have carried over on to the field, and that isn't the player I want to be. I owe it to the Fury,

the fans, and my family to make sure I am the best version of myself. Mental health is an important topic today, and I hope that you will respect my privacy as I work on becoming the best version of myself. I'll see everyone next season. Go Fury!"

I re-read the tweet. When Dean told me that, from time to time, he or someone on my PR team would be tweeting for me, I didn't think anything of it. But this? Admitting to my fans— and to the professional football world—that I've been having mental health problems? How fucking dare they.

I'm fine. I'm definitely not crazy. I'm fine. How many times do I have to tell people that before they start to believe me?

I swallow my anger. "I don't have mental health problems. I'm not crazy."

"No one said you were," Dean says, his voice trying to soothe the anger that is pouring from mine.

"Apparently, I did. And you did. And the team did. Without my consent, may I add."

"We did what we thought was best. It's important that you get help, which you need, so that you avoid a potential suspension after the shit you pulled with Davis last week. It's the smartest solution for everyone involved."

The last week has been kind of a blur to me—I was so mad I was being benched I couldn't see clearly. I remember throwing words at Davis. I know that Cole and McAvoy had to keep us apart. Next thing I knew, I was walking out of the facilities to find Dean waiting for me in a non-descript car with tinted windows. Roughly four hours later, we were pulling into the driveway of my childhood home.

Dean told me to lay low and keep out of trouble until he and the Fury could work something out. Apparently, that answer was to tell everyone I was nuts.

I feel my face getting redder the more and more it seeps in

what my team and my agent did. "So, instead of suspending me, this is what they are doing? Putting a stamp on my forehead that I'll wear for the rest of my life?"

"You can't look at it like that," Dean says. "Just because you are working through mental health issues doesn't mean you're crazy. Mental health is just as important as physical. Only for mental health, we can't send you to the trainer at halftime and have you ready to play in the second half. You need to talk to someone to help you through this. And that's what you're going to do because, whether or not you're ready to admit it, there is something going on with you that no trainer or coach can fix."

I try to listen to Dean, but I'm too angry. How dare they? How dare he? Especially when I'm fine. I've told everyone this for months but no one will listen to me. I don't need to talk to some shrink.

Everyone just needs to leave me alone and let me be.

"So what? Am I stuck here in Ohio?"

"You aren't stuck."

"My apologies. I should have asked if I'm being held hostage here."

I hear the exasperated breath from Dean. At least we're both over this conversation. "No one is holding you hostage. The Fury and I just don't think Nashville is the best place for you right now. That is, unless you can promise us you won't end up shitfaced drunk in the nearest bar."

I'd be lying if I said I hadn't thought about doing exactly that. Shit, that was the first thing I thought of when I got to Laurel Heights last week. The bars here might not have the same ambiance as Nashville, but I'm sure they still pour a stiff drink.

And maybe I could have found a girl from high school who wanted to live out a fantasy from the past.

I was told under no circumstance was I to drink or even leave the house. And not only was I told it but also my mother was told as well.

There's no security guard quite like Pamela Donald.

"So, that's it? I'm done for the year?"

"Yeah. Yeah, you are," Dean says. "Listen, it was either this or they were going to start looking into legal avenues. So, keep your head down, stay out of trouble, and go talk to someone like they asked you to. I have three sports psychologists lined up when you're ready. Two of them offer online appointments or you can drive out to Cincinnati for a face-to-face; I don't care which you choose, but you have to pick one. If you don't, then you might not have a team to go back to next year."

He hangs up the phone, and I fall back into the couch.

The phrases *mental health* and *out for the season* roll through my head as I process everything Dean just told me. When I arrived in Laurel Heights last week, I really thought it was only going to be for a few days, but now it looks like I'll be stuck here for God knows how long.

During which time, I will no doubt end up seeing her.

I let out a laugh that has absolutely no humor in it. The Fury think they have everything figured out. They really think sending me to Laurel Heights will be the key to fixing me, when the person who broke me is right around the corner.

"I DIDN'T KNOW there was a new landscaping company in town. Do you have a card or should I just find you on Facebook?"

Each day in Laurel Heights, I get another reminder of how I was whisked away like a thief in the night. Right now? I realize I don't have any headphones to drown out the sound of my twin sister's voice.

Note to self: Order some online and pay for overnight shipping.

"What brings you by Brenna?" I ask, raking the last of the leaves into a pile.

"Can't a girl come by and visit her mom and brother? A brother she hasn't seen in months?"

I don't even need to use my twin telepathy to know this girl is lying out of her ass. "She could, but that's a bunch of bullshit. And don't lie and say it's for pizza night either."

It's been two hours since it was announced to the world that I was done for the season to focus on my mental health. When I got off the phone with Dean, I was so pissed I almost punched a hole in my mom's living room wall.

I wanted a drink, but then remembered that Mom cleared the house of any alcohol when I got here.

Then I looked outside and realized that her yard could use tending to. Figured I might as well burn off some of this energy in a more productive way than stewing on the couch, or trying to resist putting holes in walls.

"Fine. I watched the game today and heard the announcement. Sue me if I wanted to come and check in on you."

"I'm fine," I say through clenched teeth. "It's what the team needed to say."

"Who's spewing bullshit now?"

"What's that supposed to mean?"

I throw down the rake and stare at my sister, who is returning my glare right back. Brenna Donald has never stepped down from a fight or challenge. Apparently, she's not going to step down now.

"It means maybe, just maybe, they know what you need more than you do right now."

"So, you're on their side?"

"No. I'm on your side," she says, taking a seat on the steps leading to our front door. "No matter how bad you fuck up, or how many times I want to smack you on the back of the head, I will always be here for you. I might not agree with everything you do, but I'm always on Team Bryce. However, if this is what needed to happen to get my brother back, then I'm going to side with them."

"So, you are on their side. You think I'm crazy?"

Brenna lets out an inaudible grumble as she rubs her temples. "I don't know who said you were crazy, but it sure as shit wasn't me. I do think you need professional help to figure out a better way of dealing with life without Lucy's help. Oh, and Mr. Jack Daniels is not an acceptable replacement."

"You have no clue what you're talking about." I turn my

back from my sister in the act of looking for trash bags to shove the leaves into. What I'm really doing is hiding the fact that she hit the nail on the head.

Though I'm not ready to admit that to anyone.

"I think I do," Brenna says. "The quicker you realize that none of us are out to get you, the quicker the old Bryce can come back."

I want to laugh at the thought of "the old Bryce." The old Bryce thought he had the world in front of him. The old Bryce thought that once things got settled in his life, he'd have it all —the career, the fame, and the girl.

Obviously, that's not going to happen.

"Maybe the old Bryce is gone. Or maybe this Bryce was the real Bryce all along."

"Nah," Brenna says, walking up next to me and taking the trash bag from me and holding it open. "He's there. He's just lost. The real Bryce isn't the guy who parties every night and leaves with a different woman each night. The real Bryce doesn't blame his teammates for losses. That's not my brother. You're not that guy. That guy is a stranger to me. And frankly, from what I can tell, he's a fucking douchebag."

I let her words hang in the air and drop my gloves to the ground. I'm not replying because she's right. Though, I'm not ready to admit it yet. Frankly, I'm over this conversation. Actually, I'm over this whole fucking day.

I try to walk past Brenna, but she grabs my arm to stop me.

"I know she hurt you," Brenna says, her voice soft as if trying to comfort me. "But she did nothing wrong. Neither did you. You guys just grew up and your lives took you separate ways. Don't ruin your life—don't ruin your career—because it didn't turn out the way you wanted it."

My blood turns cold as I shrug away from my sister's hold.

"You think you know a lot more than you do Brenna. Just stay the fuck out of it."

"I know a lot more than you're willing to admit. Remember who was here for her all those years. It wasn't you, Bryce. It was me."

Brenna is now toe-to-toe with me, well, as much as she can be for someone who tops out at five-foot-four.

"You might have been here for her. But you don't know what it's like for me out there. A spotlight always on you. Every decision, every play, every waking moment under a fucking microscope. Your own father texting you about how you cost him money because of one pass or play call."

"Fuck Dad. You should just block his number."

"That's not the point Brenna. The point is you have no idea what's it's like to walk in my shoes. So, until you do, don't try to pretend you know what it's like. Because you don't. No one does."

I turn and storm past Brenna, really needing this conversation to be over. Actually, I need this whole fucking day to be over.

"So that's it? You're just going to hole up here?"

I turn back and look at my sister, who looks as over this conversation as I'm sure I do. "That's the plan. Got a problem with it?"

She shakes her head and gives a shoulder shrug. "Nope. It's your life. You've made that abundantly clear."

"Hey. Do me a favor?"

She raises an eyebrow, which I don't blame her for. It's not like I'm in the best position to be asking for favors right now. "What?"

"Don't tell her I'm back in town. Don't tell anyone."

"Bryce, people are going—"

"I know they're going to find out. Just . . . let's try to keep it hush for a minute."

Brenna lets out a defeated breath. "Fine. I promise. But you have to promise me something."

I should have known my words would come back and bite me in the ass. "And what is that?"

She gives my arm a playful punch. "Find the old Bryce. I miss him."

CHAPTER 3
LUCY

"IT WAS GOOD SEEING YOU, Lucy. You tell your mom and dad hi for me."

"Will do. Have a nice day, Mrs. Latimer. Congrats on the new car!"

"Thank you, dear. Oh, and you make sure that wedding invitation of mine doesn't get lost in the mail. I bought a new dress for the occasion and everything!"

"Mm-hm." That is the only sound I manage to get out before a coughing fit like no other overtakes my body.

"Oh my goodness, dear!" Mrs. Latimer says, running to grab the bottle of water from my desk and handing it to me. "Are you okay? This is so adorable. Just the thought of your wedding gets you all choked up!"

I take a big gulp of the water and nod my head, praying that the worst of it is over. "Something like that."

When she's convinced that I'm not going to die, and at this point, I'm considering it as an option, Mrs. Latimer exits my office at the bank and I fall back into my seat.

I really thought these coughing fits were over. It had been almost two weeks since my last episode. That was when I went for my dress fitting and the seamstress told me that, the next time I was in, I'd be taking the dress home with me. Then there was the time before that when the florist reminded me that I needed to make a decision because my wedding was just a few months away.

Now, here I am, six weeks before the big day, still getting fits every time someone brings up my wedding. And yes, as a former mathlete, I realize that the common denominator to all of my coughing fits is my wedding.

The wedding that my family has been planning since my birth.

The wedding I have yet to send the invitations out for.

The wedding the entire town is talking about.

"It's about time they realized they were meant to be together!"

"I heard their mothers started planning this wedding when they were in the hospital right after they gave birth. How adorable is that?"

"It was meant to be. Luciano and Lucy? They have their own celebrity name! They are LuLu!"

I take another sip of water before my thoughts send me into another coughing fit.

This is normal, right? Doesn't every soon-to-be bride have near panic attacks every time her wedding is mentioned?

God, I hope they are normal.

Though I've never been called normal in my entire life, so there really isn't any point in aiming for it now. I'm the smart girl. The girl who is just slightly on the weird side of things. The super-analytical, loves-math-and-anything-with-numbers girl.

I'm also now the coughing-when-thinking-about-her-wedding girl.

I slouch back into my seat in my office at the bank, thankful it's in the corner. No one can see me unless they look but I can still hear and see everything. It makes days like today great because, after that episode, I need a few minutes to myself.

Maybe the coughing bouts are because I'm ready to get it over with and just be Mrs. Luciano Tripoli. I mean, I *know* I'm not coughing out of excitement, but lying to myself and saying that is better than admitting the alternative.

Don't get me wrong, I'm excited for the day, but I was never that little girl who had her whole wedding planned out with a color-coded binder. I couldn't tell you the difference between a gardenia and an orchid. All I know is that they cost a lot of money for something that is just decorative.

Honestly, it all seems very impractical when one could buy a brand-new car for what it cost to throw a wedding.

Maybe that is the source of the coughing fits?

Yeah, keep telling yourself that. Maybe one day you'll believe it.

"Heard this one almost took you out. You know if I have to do CPR, you might not get back up."

"Ha, ha," I say as Megan, my assistant manager, sits in the chair across from me. "Your humor is too much for me to handle. Really, you should go on the road with that act."

"You're being sarcastic. Something must be wrong. Tell me all about it."

I consider lying and telling her that I'm fine and it is no big deal, but I know better than that. The woman can sniff out a lie a mile away.

"I'm fine. Just hit me out of the blue."

"Are you ready to talk about why you start coughing every time someone mentions the wedding? Or are we still ignoring that? Just tell me which one we're doing, and I'll make sure I follow suit."

"Don't all brides get jitters?" I ask, hoping to play this off.

"They do," she says as she stares into me, likely trying to assess my level of bullshit. "I was nervous as all hell before Joe and I got married. Then again, I was pregnant with the first one, and I was hoping that no one could tell. But you? This isn't just normal jitters."

"I didn't know there was a difference in pre-wedding jitters?"

"There is when the bride doesn't want to go through with it."

Did she just . . .

"What? Of course, I want to go through with it!"

She tilts her head, and all of a sudden, I feel like I'm a criminal being interrogated. All she is missing is the lamp. "Between you and me, are you sure you want to do this? It's okay if you don't."

"Yes!" I say, probably a little too loudly. "Yes, I want to marry Luciano. He makes me happy. He's a good man who loves me. One day, he'll be a good father. He's the man I'm going to marry."

The most important thing is that he puts me first. It doesn't matter how busy he is with the restaurant or with his obligations around town, at the end of the day I'm what matters most to him. It's a crazy concept for the man I'm with to want me more than anything else in life. For a while, I thought that was only a myth. It's not, and I'll never have to worry about being second when it comes to Luciano.

So, what if he doesn't make me feel butterflies? Who cares that the few times he's kissed me I didn't feel a spark in every part of my body?

Butterflies and sparks are overrated.

Stability. Stability and commitment. That's what matters the most.

Just when I think I've convinced Megan that what she said was preposterous, the silence that she lets sit between us allows for the chatter in the bank lobby to filter into my office.

"I heard he's back in town."

"Heard the same thing, but no one has seen him."

"I heard he got kicked off the Fury for partying too much."

"I heard he's been cooped up at his mama's house. Won't even step foot outside."

"Too bad. That boy had such potential."

No. It can't be. They can't be talking about . . .

"Bryce was something special to watch on the field. No one ever played like him."

He's special off the field, too; though, no one chooses to see it.

"Remember when he led that ninety-nine-yard drive in the state championship game?"

I do. I was wearing his jacket and was so proud of how he played. After the game, he kissed me like we had a forever full of kisses to look forward to.

"That was a good season. No other Laurel Heights football team is ever going to be that good again."

And no other man is ever going to make me feel the way he did.

"There!" Megan yells. "That look. That's the look you need to have when you're about to marry someone. The look that tells anyone who sees it that nothing else matters besides you and that person. How have I never seen that look on you before? Hell, I was at your engagement party."

All I can do is shrug. She's right. She has never seen this look on my face. Megan is five years older than me and only knows me as an adult. She never knew the girl who fell in love with the hometown hero.

"I looked like that because I was thinking about the date Luciano has planned for us tonight," I lie, straightening papers on my desk that don't need to be straightened. "You're reading too much into things."

"If you say so," Megan says as she stands. "Otherwise, you have a lot to think about."

I shoo Megan away from my office, praying my face doesn't give anything else away.

Shoot. That was close.

As soon as Megan is gone, I hurry and grab my cell phone from my purse. If what I heard in the lobby is true, someone has a lot of explaining to do.

> Lucy: Is there something you want to tell me?

> Brenna: Whatever do you mean?

> Lucy: Cut the crap. Is he here?

> Brenna: Before you get mad at me . . . I wasn't allowed to tell anyone.

> Lucy: BRENNA! How could you not tell me?

> Brenna: He's not leaving the house so I was kind of hoping you wouldn't see him. Or hear that he was home. In my defense it was a great plan and would have totally worked if the gossip mill in this town wasn't on paparazzi level.

> Lucy: It's Laurel Heights. You think that Bryce Donald being home was going to stay a secret?

> Brenna: It was worth a shot. I'm sorry. I really am. But I told him not to contact you. That you're happy and he needs to leave you alone.

I toss my phone back into my purse and resist the urge to scream in frustration at the top of my lungs. When I look back up, the picture of Luciano and me at our engagement party on my desk is suddenly all I see.

I pick it up and look at it, maybe really looking at it for the first time. We're smiling at each other, but I can't remember if it's because it's natural or if the photographer told us to smile. While his arm is around my waist, I wouldn't say I'm pressing into him, dying to be closer.

No, that isn't our relationship. Yes, I love him, but I learned a long time ago that love with sparks only burns you. The love Luciano and I have? The love that's built on friendship and respect? That's the one that will last forever.

That's the one who will always choose me first.

And that's the one I'm choosing to spend the rest of my life with.

Butterflies be damned.

CHAPTER 4
BRYCE

BRENNA WAS RIGHT.

I hate saying that, but she was right about so many things. Yet, there are only a few right now that I'm ready to admit.

The biggest one is that she said I couldn't hide in Mom's house forever. There's only so much television you can watch without going stir crazy. It's why, when Coach Roberts texted me, I jumped at the chance to come down to visit my old high school.

It isn't just getting out of the house that brought me to my old stomping grounds, it's also that Nick Roberts will always give it to me straight. The man isn't a teddy bear, but he's not a dick. Once I tell him my side of what's going on in Nashville, I'm sure he'll agree with why this mental health bullshit is just that, bullshit.

When I enter the doors that lead toward Coach Roberts's office and the weight room, a flood of memories come rushing back to me. It doesn't help that as soon as I walk into the facility, there is a huge trophy case with the championship trophy we won my senior year prominently displayed. Next to the trophy is a framed photo of Cole and me celebrating our win. Shortly after that picture was taken, Lucy came running toward me, wearing my jacket, with tears falling from her eyes as she leaped into my arms. That photo might not be hanging, but it's one I'll never forget. I can still feel her arms squeezing my neck.

"Seems like just yesterday."

I give my head a little shake as I hear Coach Roberts walking up next to me. "Can't believe it was seven years ago."

"A lot can change in seven years. For example, the best player I ever coached could go from rookie of the year to water boy in a matter of months. Oh wait, that didn't take that long at all."

I whip my head to my coach, who is far too focused on the trophy case. "Not you too?"

"Not me what?" he asks, signaling for me to follow him into his office. "Did I misspeak? Did my former star player go from top of the league to sitting at home on Sundays watching his team on television? Or do I have you confused with another player?"

I take a seat across from him at his desk. A lot might have changed in seven years, but not this space. Coach Roberts's office is exactly the way I remember it. Yes, it might have a few extra trophies, but that's it.

"I really thought our days of having to have a come-to-Jesus talk were behind us," he says as he takes a seat.

I let out a small laugh. "What can I say? I missed your words of wisdom."

Coach Roberts takes in a deep breath, his gruff demeanor seemingly melting just a bit. "I talked to Cole."

"Of course, you did," I say, annoyed that yet again Cole has taken it upon himself to try to fix things in my life. "What did my locker-room Dad have to tell you? Does he think I'm crazy too?"

"He never used the word crazy, so we're going to come back

to that. He did say that you're partying until all hours, fucking anything that walks, and coming to practice and playing hungover."

My blood starts to boil just like it does every time someone tries to tell me that I'm fucking up my life. Why is everyone so concerned about what I'm doing off the field? "What I do with my life is nobody's business but my own."

"That may be true, but when it spills over onto the field, then you lose that privacy."

"It's not affecting—"

He slams his hands on his desk. In all my years of knowing this man, I've never seen him this angry. "Bullshit it's not. I watch you every week, and I can't believe the young man I knew has turned into this. I love you like a son, but damn it, boy, you are fucking up everything you've worked for. Now, I want you to watch this and tell me everything is fine with the way you're playing."

He fires up his old DVD player that he still uses to watch game film. The man does not care that everything is available online. Nope. He refuses to get rid of his trusty DVD/television combo that he's had since 1999.

"Are we really going to break down my film? Coach, while I appreci—"

"I said watch."

Feeling like I'm back in high school, I sit back and do what he says. If this were anyone else, I probably would have gotten up and left. But Coach Roberts is more of a father to me than my own ever really was. This is the man who made sure I kept my grades up to get into Clemson. He has always had my best interest at heart and never texted me to see if I'm going to cover the spread.

He was who introduced me to Lucy.

Don't. Don't think of her. Thinking of her does no good.

I shake my head and sit back, knowing what play is about to happen. Another pass to my would-be star receiver, Dexter Smith. I do my part right, I drop back, roll right, and I launch it to Dexter.

Only, he is ten yards short, and I overthrow him. Luckily for the defense, they have a safety there who catches my pass and runs it back for a touchdown.

"What happened here?" Coach Roberts asks.

"Smith stopped short. Pass got intercepted."

"Did he?"

Confused as to what he's asking, I watch the next play. Only this isn't from the last game I played. This is a game from last season because Coach McAvoy is calling the plays, something he doesn't do now that he's head coach.

I watch the play develop, and it's the exact one that Smith fucked up last week. I drop back, my receiver rolls out, and . . . stops exactly where Smith did.

I found him with a perfect pass.

What the hell?

"What are you showing me?" I ask, confused even though I know what I just saw.

Coach Roberts fast forwards the DVD to the next play. "Just watch, Bryce."

If the person who edited this video together wanted me to feel like a piece of shit, they succeeded.

Holy hell, is this how bad I've been playing all year?

It's like a bad 80s montage of the worst playing of my career. Bad passes, not looking for all my options, rolling right when I should have gone left. I overthrew targets I haven't missed since I was in middle school. I've seen all of these plays before. I've watched them ad nauseum with Coach McAvoy and Coach Davis, but it's like I'm seeing it with a new set of glasses.

Probably helps that I'm sober.

Just when I think the video is over, the video zooms in on me as I break the huddle in last week's game. It's worse than any bad play I've been shown.

All I can see are my eyes under my helmet. My bloodshot, tired eyes that are barely open. When I don't think it can get any worse, a video flashes on the screen of me dancing on a bar with three girls. I lick salt off one girl's chest and then another one pours tequila into my open mouth.

That wasn't all I licked that night.

"Fuck..."

It's all I can say as I slump down into the chair as the video goes black. Ten minutes of concise footage perfectly outlining the train wreck that is now my career and my life.

"I'm sorry I had to put it out there like that, but someone had to."

I sit back up, lean forward and drop my head into my open palms. "I didn't think it was this bad."

"What's going on with you, Bryce? I know I'm not there to see this, but from what Cole told me, and from what this shitty video showed me, this isn't the player... this isn't the man you are. You are better than this."

"There is nothing going on." I have to force the words out of my mouth. I've been asked what was wrong with me more times in the past nine months than I ever have in my entire life. My answer is always, "Nothing," or, "I'm fine."

I'm not fine. Nothing is fine.

She broke me, and she's the only one who can put me back together.

"Bullshit," Coach Roberts says, his voice louder than it's been all day. "You know it, and I know it."

"You don't know shit," I say, growing angry—at him or

myself, I'm not sure. All I know is that the walls are starting to close in on me and I need to get the fuck out of here.

"I know the team said you were dealing with mental health problems, and I don't think they're wrong. Never use the word *crazy* because that's not it, but that doesn't mean you shouldn't talk to someone," Coach says, standing and rounding his desk. "Have you talked to Lu—"

"I said I'm fine! Thanks for the intervention, Coach. Don't quit your day job."

I stand and stride out of his office. I need air. I need to feel like the walls aren't closing in around me.

I mean to run to my truck. Away from this school and one of the few people who can see through my bullshit. Away from the memories threatening to puncture my brain.

But because karma is a devious bitch, I don't end up in my truck. Or even outside.

No, somehow, I run right to the place it all started.

CHAPTER 5
BRYCE

"ARE YOU BRYCE DONALD?"

I bite back my grimace and ignore the girl's voice as I delete yet another message from someone I've never met. He isn't the first guy to reach out and tell me all about how great their old college's football program is, and he won't be the last.

It doesn't help that he caught me on a really shitty morning. Coach Roberts told me that, until further notice, instead of lifting each morning with the team, I'm to come to the library to work with a math tutor. He said her name was Lucy and that I was to listen to her or else. I didn't know what "or else" actually meant, but I could read the look in his eyes that said he wasn't messing around.

When I look up at this girl, who I'm guessing is around my age, she looks thoroughly annoyed. "I'm not happy being up this early so please just answer my question."

"I am. Can I ask who you are?"

My question isn't to play the role of dumb jock. I honestly don't know her, which is odd considering my graduating class is going to be seventy kids. It's not hard keeping everyone straight when you've known them since kindergarten.

From the way she is looking at me, she doesn't know me either.

"Yes, of course. I'm Lucy. Your math tutor."

My eyes grow wide at her introduction. "You're the math tutor?"

I never expected a girl who is . . . well, she's gorgeous. She's not one of those model types who guys my age go ga-ga over. But she's beautiful in her own right. Her long brown hair and black-rimmed glasses make her stand out from the crowd. She's not wearing anything flashy like some girls here who try to show off with expensive clothes, but that doesn't make her any less beautiful.

And I can't stop staring at her.

She takes a seat across from me, clearly unfazed by my confusion. "Yes. I am. Ready to start?"

I blink a few times, trying to decipher if this is real life or if I'm still sleeping and this is some really fucked-up dream.

I wish it were a dream, but the longer I sit here watching Lucy take out books and notebooks, the more I realize that no, this is real life. I'm also definitely feeling things below the belt as my apparent tutor pulls her hair up on the top of her head in that messy way girls do.

Why is that so hot?

"I'm sorry . . ."

"Lucy."

"Yeah. Lucy. Listen, I'm sorry you woke up early for this, and I'm not sure what Coach Roberts told you, but I don't need a tutor."

"Why would he tell me you did if you didn't?"

Damn, she's right. I can't think clearly. I want to blame it on being up and at school before six thirty in the morning, but it's really her big brown eyes. They are making me stupid.

"I know what I'm doing in trig," I begin, trying to figure out how to word this without sounding like a complete dumbass. "I just . . . haven't done it."

What I'm not going to say is that I'm barely passing because I've been too busy to study or do homework. In my defense, I've had a lot going on. Like football and trying to decide where I'm going to play football in college and working out for football. Oh, and there is also the constantly deleting of emails and messages from crazy fans.

Though if I don't pass trigonometry, I don't play. If I don't play, there's no chance for a state title and my scholarship offers will be out the window. But I'll pass. The teachers always make sure I do.

Lucy stops fiddling with her textbook and looks up at me. "So, you know what you're doing, but you just aren't doing it? Does Uncle Nick know this?"

"Yes. No—wait, who is Uncle Nick? And while we're at it, who are you again?"

She smirks and then tries to stifle a laugh.

"Yes, let's start over. My name is Lucy. I moved back at the beginning of this year, and Uncle Nick to me is Coach Roberts to you. He's my mom's brother."

"Coach Roberts has a niece?"

"He does."

"And you just moved here?"

"Technically, I just moved back," Lucy says matter-of-factly. "I was born here, but then my family moved to Indianapolis. Now we're back. So, here I am."

"Here you are."

I don't mean for it to come out sounding creepy, but I can't stop staring at this girl. She has a blush creeping up on her cheeks that stands out against her ivory skin, and I can't help but hope that blush is there because of me. I internally slap myself for letting my head—both of them—think like that. I don't date during football season because I need to stay focused. I barely talk to girls during school just to resist temptation. Little did I know, the biggest temptation of all would come in the form of a five-foot-nothing math tutor.

"Why haven't I seen you around school?"

She shrugs, her messy ponytail bouncing around on the top of her head. "I'm going to guess we don't exactly have the same friends."

I lean forward on my elbows. "You didn't answer my question."

She gives me a look that suggests I'm dense—or, at least, that's what I assume it is. Brenna gives me that look all the time.

"You're Bryce Donald."

"We've established that."

"Do I really have to say it?"

"Considering you haven't answered my question yet, I'm going to say yes."

She lets out a frustrated breath. "Fine. I'll say it. You're the captain of the football team, you broke Ohio's high-school record for yards passed in a season, you have your pick of which college to play for, and you are on the trajectory to be a top draft pick when you go pro. Based on high-school stereotypes and assumptions, I'm going to guess you date the head cheerleader and you're most likely to be voted homecoming king. Then there is me—captain of the mathletes and newest member of the debate team. I don't care if this is a small school, the captain of the football team doesn't hang out with the mathletes."

While everything she just said may actually be true, I like to think I'm an approachable guy. Still, high school is what it is. The jocks pal around with other jocks. The band kids stick together. If she's smart enough to be tutoring math, I'm going to guess she's in the honors classes. I'm in the classes where kids go just to pass.

"You're right."

Her eyes go a bit wide with shock. "I am? I mean, I know I am. I just didn't expect you to admit it."

I shrug, leaning back in my chair. "Can't argue with facts. Just takes one look at our cafeteria to know that. Though, I must point out that you weren't completely right. You did get a few things wrong."

"And what may I ask was that?"

I lean back forward and get the slightest whiff of her perfume. Something floral. Hmm . . . Miss Math Wiz didn't strike me as a perfume wearer. Good to know.

"I don't date the head cheerleader," I say. "First of all, she's my twin sister. And second of all, I don't date during football season."

She tilts her head, almost as if she's studying me. Usually, when I say that I'm single, I can tell the moment a girl decides it's her mission to try to lock me down.

But Lucy? That look never comes. She just studies me as if I'm an equation she can't figure out.

"Interesting. Not what I thought I would have got wrong. Based on the size of the population of the school and town, it would have been a more than forty-six percent chance that—"

"Is everything a math problem to you?"

My interruption takes her off guard. "Math is everywhere. A football player should know that."

"Touché, Lucy. Touché. Now, let's dive into this math stuff. Teach me your ways."

Ten minutes ago, I wanted nothing to do with a tutor. I still don't think I need one. But thinking about spending a few mornings a week with her? I think I can handle it.

Plus, I don't date during football season. No one, not even this girl, who is throwing me for all sorts of loops, is going to change that.

CHAPTER 6
LUCY

COUGH DROPS. That's what I need, cough drops.

Honey lemon. Cherry. Menthol-lyptus. Give me all of them.

I put two of each flavor into my basket, scanning the rest of the aisle to see if I need anything else. Right now, talk of my wedding only makes me cough, but who knows? The closer it gets, the worse the reaction might get. I might start breaking into hives.

I pick up a box of Benadryl, some Midol for good measure, and then head to the checkout counter, only to pull to a sudden stop.

No, no, no . . . Please, God, let that not be him.

I could ask every holy being in existence not to let that be Bryce Donald, but unfortunately, they'd all let me down. It might have been more than a year since I've seen him, but I could go fifty without laying eyes on him and I'd know that profile from a mile away.

Stupid chiseled jawline and perfect features.

Bryce has always been good looking. In high school, he was your stereotypical teen heartthrob. Light brown hair that was never purposefully styled but always looked good. A muscled frame that made every girl lose their mind. Blue eyes that sucked you in from the moment they made contact with you. And don't get me started on his smile that, when he aimed it at you, made you feel like you were the only girl in the world.

But the Bryce who is standing thirty feet from me isn't the boy from high school. No, he is all man. His hair is just as messy but a little longer that he used to wear it. The muscles he had back then are nothing compared to the ones he's sporting now. I believe the term Brenna uses is "arm porn." Though she wasn't talking about her brother because that would be weird.

The longer I stand and stare at him, the more I feel like I'm being stabbed with a thousand knives that are slicing open old hurts.

I miss him so much.

I want to hit myself for thinking that because it's ninety levels of wrong. I'm engaged. I made my choice, and that was to spend the rest of my life with Luciano. I decided to quit waiting for it to be the right time in Bryce's world for him to finally be with me.

I'd be a liar if I didn't say I missed him, though. I miss our talks. I miss the way he made me feel. I miss the way he'd look at me, like he's looking at me right now.

"Shit!" I yell, realizing that in fact he is looking at me and I was caught staring. So, I do the only logical thing a grown woman can do—I turn around, run to the back of the store, and hide behind a display of potato chips.

With any luck, he'll finish checking out and then leave. There is no reason for him to come looking for me, and if he does, my hiding spot is fantastic. He'll walk right by—

"Hiding from me now, Lulu? I knew you weren't talking to me, but I didn't know hiding was also a part of it. Should have figured though."

I jump at the sound of Bryce's voice, knocking down six

bags of potato chips in the process. I don't want to look at him not only because I'll have to have a conversation I've been putting off for months but also because I can hear the pain behind the arrogant tone he's trying to project.

He has every right to be mad at me.

"I wasn't hiding from you," I say as I begin to pick up the mess.

"Sure, you weren't."

The last time I looked Bryce in the eyes was the last day we were *us*. Whatever that means. I lied to him that day. Well, I didn't lie. I just didn't tell him the whole truth. I didn't tell him I was engaged. I didn't tell him that I was done waiting for him. I let him believe there was a future for us.

It was the most selfish thing I have ever done. I knew it was the last time we'd be like that, and I wanted as much time as possible. Had I told him, things would have ended far worse than they did.

And now that act of selfishness is about to bite me in the ass.

"Oh, for God's sake, Lulu, stand and look at me."

"Don't call me that," I say, reluctantly standing. "And I'm not avoiding you."

Wow, I haven't gotten any better at lying to him.

When I finally manage to look at him, I want to flinch and turn away. He's looking at me in a way I don't deserve—full of longing and hope—and I wish he would stop. I deserve his ire and mistrust.

"Oh really? You aren't avoiding me? Then what is this? Or did you mean when you wouldn't answer my phone calls after I found out from my mom you were engaged? Which time are we talking about? Cause I'm starting to lose track."

His voice is angry, and honestly, I don't blame him. But I had to dodge his calls and cut ties with him. It was the only way I'd survive. I had to make a clean break or the cycle I've come to coin as the Bryce and Lucy Saga would have just continued.

It was the same thing every time. Bryce would tell me that the season was almost over and then we could finally be together. I would wait for Bryce. The season would end and then something would happen in Bryce's life that would make this not the right time for us. Bryce would ask me to wait again, and I would. Then the cycle would start over again.

That had been my life since senior year. I had to break it. My heart couldn't handle it anymore.

I square my shoulders, doing my best to try to seem the confident woman I've become. "I'm sorry, but it was for the best."

"The best for who? And don't say it was for me because, in case you haven't heard, I'm pretty much a train wreck these days," he says bitingly.

He might as well have punched me in the heart, but his inability to handle his own life isn't really my problem. It used to be, sure, but he's an adult. It isn't fair that he would blame me for his own terrible choices. I want to be so indignant that he would do that, but I'm too full of my own guilt for doing what I did in the way I did it. He may have hurt me on a fundamental level, but that doesn't mean he doesn't deserve an explanation.

Only . . . I can't. I can't hurt him even more than I already have. I can't say the words. So, I make the second most adult decision I've made today.

I drop my basket and run.

Before the cough drops and Benadryl even hit the floor, I'm making a beeline for the exit. I know Bryce is behind me, but I have to get out of here. I may never be able to have this talk with him, but if that moment comes, it won't be at five o'clock inside the town convenience store with ten or so people watching us. It's not the place to air out our dirty laundry.

"Lulu, Stop!"

I stop and turn to find Bryce inches from me. "Don't call me that. Not anymore."

"Why? Why can't I call you that?" His face is so close to mine as he silently begs for answers. He might be trying to come off as intimidating, but my heart says otherwise having him this close.

"Because I hate it."

"Liar."

"I didn't lie to you!" I yell, knowing we're causing a scene. I feel the eyes of Laurel Heights on us.

"Yes, you did. You did then and you are now."

"I did what I thought was best."

"So you've said." His voice drips with disdain.

"I can't do this. Not now, and not here."

"Then when? When are you going to give me the explanation I deserve? Coincidentally, it all started right after you decided I wasn't worth having in your life anymore."

Tears are burning in my eyes, but I push them back. I know I owe him an explanation, but I'm not ready.

Every time he's low, he needs me to pull him back up. Every time there is a hard decision or his dad decides to pop back into his life, I'm there to talk him through it. And, as much as it kills me not to help him, I can't. He has to learn how to navigate his problems without my help.

"Yes, you can. You've always been able to."

"Is that a joke? In case you haven't seen—"

"Oh, I've seen," I say, taking a fortifying breath. "I've seen it all. The headlines. The pictures. The games. But Bryce, you've always been able to. I've been your crutch for years, and I can't be that anymore. I'm sorry. I can't be the girl who you go to when things get hard and then leave behind with empty promises of a future that is never going to come. It's not fair to me, Bryce. It hurts me too much."

"But it was finally time!" he yells, his hands gripping my shoulders. "It was time for us."

I laugh, but there's no humor to it. "What made that time different?"

My question silences him. If he's honest with himself, he knows that's just another promise he wouldn't have kept.

I use the silence to shrug away from his hold and race to my car down the street. Thankful that I left it unlocked, I hurry and get in, immediately locking it and firing up the engine.

When I look back toward the front of the store with tears streaming down my face, I don't see the man who has been on the front page of every tabloid in America.

I see the lost boy I first fell in love with.

CHAPTER 7
LUCY

"BRYCE! EARTH TO BRYCE! HELLOOOOO!!!"

I know I shouldn't be yelling in a library, but I don't feel bad considering he and I are the only ones here.

And he is currently asleep.

"Bryce!" I yell again, giving his arm a nudge.

"What?" he says, jumping a bit, which would be funny if I weren't so annoyed that he fell asleep.

"I know morning tutoring sessions aren't ideal, but the least you could do is try to stay awake."

"I can't help it," he says mid yawn. "This is boring, and I was up late last night."

"I don't care if you think it's boring. You have a test tomorrow, and you aren't ready for it. What were you doing up anyway? Don't tell me studying because I know that's a lie."

"You wound me." He puts his hand over his heart. "If you must know, I was going over college brochures."

I have to blink a few times because that was not the answer I was expecting. I was waiting to hear something football related. In the month I've known Bryce, I have come to learn that the man eats, sleeps, and breathes football. I suppose it's why he's so good. Though, I can't imagine one thing taking up so much time of my life. I mean, I love math and all, but I'm not up at two in the morning simplifying equations.

"Really? You don't know where you are going yet?"

He just shrugs, pulling the textbook back in front of him. "I have a bunch of offers, but I haven't been able to figure out which school is going to be best for me. So, I figured maybe if I looked at the colleges a little more it could help my decision."

I'm pretty sure my mouth is open a bit.

"What?" he asks

"I'm just surprised."

"Why?"

"Because I didn't think of you as the guy to go through college brochures to help make your decision on where to play football."

"And why is that? Because I'm the dumb jock who needs trig tutoring?"

"No. I didn't say that," I say, closing the textbook. "I never said you were dumb. In fact, I don't think you need me at all. It's just that, in the time I've known you, every decision you have made has had football as the deciding factor. I figured you would have already made a decision on school."

He seems to calm down a little and slouches down in his chair. "Thanks. Too bad it was a waste of time. I can't figure anything out, and I need to make a decision soon."

"Says who?"

"Everyone."

"Who is everyone? Because by the definition of everyone, I would be included, and I can guarantee you I am not waiting on pins and needles for you to tell me where you're going to college."

That makes him smile, which makes me feel . . . well, I

don't know how to describe this feeling. Maybe it's as if a family of butterflies have taken up residence in my stomach.

"Fine. Everyone is Coach, my parents, and Cole, who is insisting we honor a blood oath we made when we were ten and swore we would play football on the same team for the rest of our lives. Fans, recruiters, and even other quarterbacks around the country who are waiting to see what I do so they don't commit to the same team I do. It's . . . it's just a lot. How do you make a decision that pleases everyone when it can make or break your entire future?"

I take a second to look at him and don't see the football player who walks the fine line between confident and cocky.

I see a teenage boy who is just as confused about life as the rest of us.

"Is there anyone you can talk to? Maybe someone can help you make a pros and cons list? Uncle Nick? A guidance counselor?"

He just laughs and shakes his head. "Every person thinks I should do something different. Mom wants me at Ohio State because she wants me close to home. Coach thinks I should go to Auburn because of their track record of putting quarterbacks in the league. Dad wants me to go to Alabama, but I'm pretty sure a booster is padding his pockets so he'll talk me into going there."

"What?" No way I just heard him right. "Fans are paying off your family to get you to go to their school?"

"I think. I'm not sure," he says, the defeat clear in his voice. "I can't figure out another reason why my so-called father, who barely cared to come watch my high school games, is so intent on me going to a school I haven't even visited."

"Wow," I say. "College football is a whole other world."

"Tell me about it," he says, starting to doodle in a notebook. "I just I wish I knew the right answer. I never thought I'd say this, but I wish it were like trig. Only one right answer."

I pause and wonder if I should point out that he never once said what he wanted to do. He only outlined what everyone else wanted him to do. He is trying so hard to please other people that he is putting the most important person's wishes on the back burner.

His own.

"You want this to have a right answer? Then let's figure it out," I say as I grab the notebook from under his hand.

"Lucy, I appreciate it, but there is no—"

"Shh. Who is the tutor here?"

This earns me another smile. "You are."

"Then let me help you figure out this problem. First, where do you not want to go. Don't think about anyone else. Just you."

"But, Lu—"

"Nope," I say in my best no-nonsense voice. "This is your decision. No one else's. While you respect their opinions, you have to figure this out on your own. This is your career. Your future. So, let's start with the places you cannot imagine playing a day of football."

"But they are all good—"

"Are you listening to me, Donald? Shut off the brain for five seconds, and then, on the count of three, I want you to tell me the one school you'd rather quit playing football than to play for."

"You'd be a great football coach," he teases.

"You aren't doing it."

"It's not going to work."

"Humor me."

"Fine," he says reluctantly.

"Ready? One . . . two . . . three."

"Ohio State."

His eyes grow wide, and his hand immediately covers his mouth.

"See? It worked."

"My mom is going to be so mad, and it's my in-state school. Fans are going to go ape shit."

"Who the heck cares what the fans say, and your mom will be fine so long as you're happy," I say, ripping off a piece of notebook paper. "She might like you to be close, but at the end of the day, she wants you to be happy. And those fans? They only want you for how far you can throw a football. They don't matter. Now, let's keep going."

For the next half hour, Bryce and I write a pro-and-con list for every school that has made him an offer. We quickly eliminate the state schools. Any schools with snow are a no. I don't blame him. A chance to get away from snow sounds amazing. We also cross off Alabama just in case his dad is getting paid off.

Five pieces of paper later, he writes down one word: Clemson.

"Is that it?" I ask, hoping I didn't rush him. "Is that where you want to go?"

He looks at the paper and back up to me with confidence back in his eyes. "Yeah. Yeah, it is. I love the atmosphere. They have a great rate of turning players pro. I can win a championship there. They want Cole just as much as they want me. It's . . . that's it. That's where I'm going to go."

I grin and clean up the papers I've strewn over the table. "See? That wasn't so hard, was it?"

He laughs, also gathering his stuff as the first bell of the day rings. "Who knew a good pro-con list was what I needed?"

"I find most life decisions can be made with a solid pro-con list."

I start to walk out of the library when I feel his hand on my arm. When I turn back around, I see a look on Bryce's face that I've never seen before.

It's . . . happy. Relaxed. Free.

Before I know it, Bryce's arms are wrapped around me. I'm too stunned at first to return the embrace. It's not like I've never been hugged before. I've even shared hugs with guy friends. It's just that, as I wrap my arms around his waist, I realize that being in this position with Bryce is like nothing I've ever experienced before.

"Thanks, Lulu. For everything."

His words are a whisper against my ear and send a shiver down my body. It's probably why I don't realize for a few seconds that he called me . . . Lulu?

"What did you call me?"

"Lulu," he says, and even though I can't see him, I know there is a smile forming on his lips. "Is that okay?"

"I guess so?"

"Well, get used to it. From now on, to me, you're Lulu."

"What if I don't like it?"

"Too bad."

I've never had a nickname. Well, my real name is Lucia, but no one calls me that except my mom and the Tripolis. It's always just been Lucy.

For some reason, the thought of having a name that only Bryce calls me . . . well, it makes me feel the same way it does when I make him laugh or smile.

Like a million butterflies are fluttering in my stomach.

Though, I'd never tell him that.

"Come on," he says, taking my books from me. "I'll walk you to your next class."

FOR THE SECOND week in a row, I watch my team win without me, and it feels just as bad as it did the first time.

Though, it's not just because I've been told I'm done for the season.

Last week, I hadn't seen Lucy. Last week, I hadn't been reacquainted with her big brown eyes or her floral perfume. I had almost forgotten what it smelled like.

Almost.

It took all I had not to try to wrap myself in her orbit, where everything is always okay.

She's my safe space. My calm when things get too loud.

At least, she used to be.

The diamond on her hand reminded me that she's no longer my Lulu. She's someone else's. I don't even know who she's marrying. When I found out, I didn't ask because the only thing that mattered was that it wasn't me.

"Well don't you look like a ray of sunshine."

I glare at Brenna, who is walking into the house with my mom, grocery bags in tow. "Have you ever thought of giving up teaching for comedy?"

"Nah. People aren't ready for my brand of humor," she says

as she begins to unpack the bags. "What did you do today? Wait. Let me guess. You watched your team play football without you then moped instead of working on getting reinstated."

"Brenna, be nice to your brother," Mom says, her tone the same one she used when my sister and I fought when we were kids. "He's working through things, and that doesn't happen in a few days."

"Thank you, Mom, and I'm not moping," I say, doing my best not to sound like I am. "I'm lying low, which is what my agent and the coaches told me to do."

Brenna puts the last of the groceries away and takes a seat on the other side of the couch. "I'm pretty sure they didn't mean for you to come here and do nothing. If I were to guess, I would say they meant for you to work out your shit so you can go back and play the game they are paying you millions to play. Have you set up an appointment with any of the therapists your agent recommended?"

I haven't, which I don't admit. I'm not ready to talk to anyone about what's been going on in my head or admit I have issues I need to work on. After this past week, though, it's getting harder for me to deny it.

It's hard opening up to someone, especially when I used to have a person to talk to about that stuff and that person is gone.

"You know you can stay here as long as you'd like," Mom says, taking a seat on the other side of the room. "I like having you back."

"You like having a lump on a couch?" Brenna jabs.

"He's not a lump," Mom says. "I've always liked having my children home. In fact, it makes me wish he played closer or that my only daughter didn't move out the second she could afford her own place."

"Don't start, Mom," I say because I already know where this conversation is going. "You know there was never a chance I was going to play pro ball in Cincinnati."

"A mother can dream," she says as she stands and grabs her phone. "I'm going to call for the pizza. Brenna, are you staying for dinner?"

"Do I have a choice?"

"No you don't."

"Then get one with pineapple and one without."

"Anything for my babies. Oh, I just love having you both here."

Mom leaves the living room, and I swear I see her skipping. That woman is way too excited for me to be home. It doesn't matter that I'm here against my will and for reasons no mother should be proud of.

"You think she's going to kidnap me and make me move back in?" Brenna asks.

I laugh, but only because it's an actual possibility. "I'm surprised she let you move out in the first place."

She turns off the television. "I didn't tell her. Signed the lease and was moved in before she realized my stuff was gone. It was the only way."

"You broke free. I'm proud of you, sis."

That makes it sound like Brenna was serving a jail sentence, but it was nothing of the sort. Everyone thinks their mother is the best, but ours truly is. She never missed a game when I was growing up or an event that Brenna and the cheer squad were performing at.

Then there is our Sunday pizza tradition. It started when she had to tell us that she and Dad were splitting up. She thought that if she had our favorite meal—pizza from Tripoli's—that it would lessen the blow.

Somehow, it did. It also helped that she talked to us like

adults, even though we were still three months away from our eighth birthdays. Our mom just has a way of knowing what we need even when we don't.

Ever since then, Sunday has been pizza night. What started as a way to heal our hearts became a tradition. On the weekends we spent with our dad, she always had the pizza ready for us when we came home. During high school, it was the one meal each week we made sure to eat together.

"Speaking of breaking free," Brenna says, turning to face me. "How long *are* you going to stay here? Don't get me wrong, I love that the town gossip has switched from the installation of solar panels to you and Lucy fighting in the street, but I don't think that's why the coaches sent you back here."

I groan. "Heard about that, did you?"

"Who hasn't? You should be happy I didn't call you a second after it happened. What were you thinking?"

"Clearly, I wasn't thinking at all. It was the first time I'd seen Lucy since everything happened, and I wanted answers. She owes me answers."

Brenna raises an eyebrow. "What if someone had recorded it and posted it online? I'm sure that video would have gone great right next to the one of you getting a lap dance from the cleat chaser."

Shit, I hadn't even thought of that. When I saw her hiding behind the aisle, thinking a bag of Doritos was going to mask her from me, all I could think about was that I needed to talk to her. The last time I saw her, we were supposed to have forever in front of us, and then she was gone, and I needed to know why.

"It might not have been the best move, but what should I have done? Ignore her? Pretend like she didn't exist? Not confront her with questions I've been saving for nine months?"

When I found out Lucy was engaged, I bypassed the whole

five stages of grief and went right to drinking myself stupid every night and fucking any woman who wanted a piece of me. Her absence broke me in a way I couldn't deal with, and I acted like an ass. I've been a shitty teammate. I've turned into a PR nightmare. And I've pushed away everyone and anyone who tried to reason with me simply because they weren't her.

Lucy is the only one who can. That's what she does. She fixes me. She takes the broken pieces of me and puts them back together.

Or, at least, she used to.

"You never answered my question."

I look over at Brenna, feeling completely defeated. "Which one?"

"The one about when you're going back to Nashville?"

"Not sure," I admit, my voice filled with defeat.

A silence falls over the two of us as Mom makes her way back to the living room.

"I'm going to go get the pizza," she says, grabbing her keys and purse.

"No," I say as I push to my feet. "I can get it."

Mom shoots Brenna a panicked look before looking back at me. "You sure? You said you didn't want to go out a lot. It might not be a good—"

I take her hand in mine, lowering her keys. "It's just pizza, Mom. I think I can handle a pickup. Consider this me not being a lump on the couch. Plus, I haven't driven my truck since I've been home. It will do me some good to get out."

"Bryce!" Brenna shouts. "Mom is right. I don't think this is a good idea."

"Oh, for the love of God, Brenna. It's pizza. I'm not in high school anymore. I'm not going to cause a scene at Tripoli's. There is nothing to worry about."

BENEFIT OF HAVING a fiancé who owns the town pizza place? Access to my favorite food whenever I want it.

Downside of having a fiancé who owns the town pizza place? Access to my favorite food whenever I want it when I also need to fit into a wedding dress in a few weeks.

It's been three days since I saw Bryce, and I swear I have eaten four large pies with extra cheese, three orders of cheese bread, and a whole dessert pizza. Apparently, I cough when I think about my wedding and stress eat when I think about my ... whatever the hell Bryce is.

Ex-boyfriend? I mean, technically yes. Though, we were actually together for such short a time that I doubt it even counts.

Friend? Friend doesn't really scratch the surface of what our relationship was.

What Bryce and I shared was something that can't be explained. Our friendship was a force so deep I thought it could never be broken. I was his calming voice when things got too loud. He was the one who taught me that it's okay if not everything had an exact answer or neat formula. We understood each other like no one ever has or likely ever will. I could feel him in a room before he even entered. It's like my heart knew when he was near.

He was my best friend. Until he wasn't. And yes, I may be the one to blame for that, but no one told me that the worst thing I could have done was fall in love with my best friend.

"Amore! What do I owe the pleasure on a Sunday?"

Luciano's voice pulls me from the unhealthy rabbit hole my mind was about to go down. I hurry to plaster a smile onto my lips as he comes around the corner from the kitchen.

"Can't a girl want to see her fiancé and maybe grab some dinner?"

He wipes his hands on the front of his apron before bringing me in a little closer and placing a gentle kiss on my forehead.

Oh, Luciano . . . if there is one thing I can count on about this man it's his predictability. Whenever we see each other—it could be him coming over to my house for a date night or in the middle of a crowded restaurant—I'm greeted with a quick kiss on the forehead.

Never anything more. Never anything less.

It's one of the many things that makes him, well, him. Even when we were kids, Luciano was an adult in a child's body. He was a rule follower. He was the student teachers always made line leader. It's why his parents made him a manager here when we were seventeen. It's why he's about to take the family business and grow it by leaps and bounds, leading up to a franchising endeavor that would put Tripoli's all over the state of Ohio.

He's a good, upstanding man. I may not ever get surprised with flowers just because, but I also never have to worry about what's around the corner.

"A girl can, and I know you love my pizza, but this is the third night in a row. Everything okay?"

Luciano guides me to an open booth and we sit across from each other. I would reach for his hands, but I know he doesn't like PDA, so I keep them to myself.

"Everything is fine. I'm just stressed with the wedding and cooking is the last thing I want to do. Besides, why would I go anywhere else when I can come here and get my favorite food and see my favorite guy?"

He gives me a soft smile. "I hate that you are stressed about the wedding. I wish I could do more to help."

"You are doing more than enough. You organized and planned all the food at a discount. Do you know how happy that made me? You're already the best husband ever."

He laughs softly and reaches for my hands, twining his fingers through mine.

I barely manage to stop myself from raising my eyebrows in shock.

"I want to be."

His words are so soft I'm not sure I hear them. That and I can't stop staring at our joined fingers.

"Want to be what?"

He lets out a sigh before saying, "The best husband. You deserve that. You deserve the world. And I'm not sure if I'm the man to give that to you."

"Luciano, I don't know why you're worrying. You make me happy. I can only hope I make you as happy as—"

The sound of the bell over the door has me glancing toward it. Blood rushes to my brain so fast that I might pass out as I watch the door of Tripoli's swing open.

That's the effect Bryce Donald has on me. Always has.

It happened the first day I met him when I was his trigonometry tutor. Back then, it took me almost ten minutes to work up the courage to go over and introduce myself.

It's happening now as I feel his presence as he charges toward our table.

"Bryce..."

He doesn't say anything, which is making me more nervous than if he were yelling. He just looks down at us completely expressionless.

That's when it hits me. What he's looking at. Why he's not saying anything.

I follow his eyes down to the table where my hands are linked with Luciano's. My engagement ring glinting in the fluorescent lights of the restaurant.

"Him! Out of all the men in this town and you pick him?"

The neutral-to-anger shift is so sudden it makes me jump in my booth. Though, I should have expected this reaction.

"Bryce, you need to calm down."

"Why, Lucy?" His voice grows louder with each word. I'm pretty sure the cooks in the back can hear him. "You don't want me to cause a scene? Maybe that's our thing now. Hell, I've caused plenty here over the years, why not another one for old time's sake?"

Luciano lets go of my hands and quickly stands, going toe-to-toe with Bryce. "How dare you come into my restaurant and talk to my fiancée that way."

Oh God . . . it's high school all over again.

I stand, quickly putting myself between them.

"Luciano, how about you go back and finish making our dinner. We'll take it to go."

"But, Lucia—"

I put my hands on his chest, hoping to calm him down. "It's okay. I'll handle it."

Luciano takes my hand and gives it a quick kiss, never dropping his stare from Bryce. I wish I had two seconds to be shocked that my fiancé kissed my hand for the first time in our relationship, but no, I have to deal with Bryce before he explodes.

"You. Outside. Now."

"Oh, come on, Lulu, we were just getting reacquainted."

I narrow my eyes at Bryce. "Get. Outside. Now."

Bryce laughs, which fuels my anger, but he does as I said and heads to the door, pushing it open more forcefully than need be.

"What the hell was that?" I ask the second I'm outside.

He stops and turns to me, but his face is no longer angry. It's blank. Emotionless. I think I preferred anger. I know how to handle angry Bryce. Indifferent Bryce? It leaves me floundering.

"Like a brother to you, huh?"

"Listen, I can—"

"In high school," he says coolly. "I always thought he had a thing for you, but you always said you only saw him like a brother. Something about your families being friends? Funny how that worked out, huh?"

Now, it's my turn to be angry. "That was the truth. Back then, there was nothing romantic between us."

"And now?"

I open my mouth to say something, anything, but nothing comes out.

Maybe because if I said there was something romantic between us it would be a lie. I love Luciano, just not in the romantic way. This is a marriage of convenience—at least, for me it is. I've denied that for long enough, and it feels good to admit that to myself.

Luciano was the right man at the right time when I finally realized I was done waiting for Bryce. I wanted to begin the next part of my life. I wanted to be with someone who would put me first and never make me wonder if I'd make the cut of things he'd care about that day. Yes, I could have dated and tried to find someone I loved and who was ready for a committed relationship. But I didn't. I said yes to the first man who asked me to marry him. I said yes to the first man who asked because all I wanted to do was break the vicious Bryce Donald cycle and let me move on with my life, even if I don't feel "that" kind of love toward him.

"Why didn't you tell me you were engaged? And to him? Why Lucy? Just tell me why."

I look down, unable to meet his eyes. They are too full of hurt and anger. It's too much.

"I didn't know how to tell you. When I saw you last season, you were already dealing with so much, and I didn't know how to tell you I was engaged. So, I didn't. I took my ring off and didn't tell you."

Bryce just stares at me, his face emotionless. "When did you start seeing him?"

Tears threaten at the corners of my eyes because this might be harder to tell him than anything else.

"Right after the draft."

I look up and see the moment the realization hits him. His body goes from still and stoic to looking like a volcano about to erupt. Let him be mad all he wants at the timing, but at the end of the day, he's the one who broke another promise.

He's the reason I went out with Luciano in the first place.

"How could you?"

"How could I?" I scoff. "I was *tired*, Bryce. I was tired of hearing the same lines over and over. I was tired of waiting. So, I stopped waiting."

"You could have told me. You could have told me our time ran out. Have a little respect for me."

"I do respect you."

"No you don't. If you did, you would have told me about

him. You would have told me you were engaged. You would have told me that we didn't have a chance."

"I tried!" I scream, my voice just as loud as his because, how dare he make this out to be all my fault. "I tried, Bryce, but someone—that would be you—would never take no for an answer. Every time I tried to give us a clean break, you came back with talk of next year, asking me to wait just a little longer. You were the one who refused to listen, but I was the one who fell for it. Every time you let me down, my heart broke a little more. After the draft? What we shared that day? That just sealed the deal."

"You still didn't tell me you were engaged. That we can both agree on. Why, Lucy? When were you going to tell me about that? When I got an invitation to the wedding?"

"I don't know, okay? I don't know!" I begin pacing because it's all I can do to keep from ripping my hair out. "When I saw you in Cincinnati, you were a mess. Your rookie year wasn't going as planned, and I didn't think hearing about my engagement was what was going to pull you out of your slump. So, did I withhold the truth? Yes, but I did it for you. I didn't want you to spiral."

"Well, that worked out exactly to plan," he says sarcastically. "Look at me, Lucy. You did this. If you would have just told me—"

"Oh no you don't!" I stop pacing to glare at him. "You don't get to put your spiral on me. I didn't put a bottle in your hand. I didn't tell you to become a playboy. I didn't tell you to quit caring about your career. You did that, Bryce. Do you really think that if I had told you that day, or even when it happened, you would have acted differently? No, I don't think you would have. So, vilify me all you want, but don't try to tell me your garbage choices are my fault. I was just smart enough to finally realize that there's never an offseason with you, which meant there would never be a time for us."

He doesn't say anything or try to dispute my final claim, and I'm not waiting for him to.

He knows I'm right.

I take a few steps toward him, gently placing my hand on his heart. "I'm sorry. I truly am."

His hand covers mine, and for a second, I let myself get lost in the feel of his touch. Of the feel of his calloused fingers against my skin and the warmth that soaks into me every time we touch.

Then I remember where I am and the choices I've made and quickly walk back into the restaurant.

CHAPTER 10
LUCY

"WHY DO I give a shit about how tall a tree is? When in the hell am I ever going to have to know something like that?"

I let out a frustrated sigh and redraw the equation. "Probably never, but you need to understand the equation to pass this test and play this week, so focus."

I begin to cross out what he did wrong, and Bryce reaches across the table to try to grab a slice of pizza.

"No," I say, slapping his hand. "No pizza until you correct this."

"Ouch!" He shakes his hand as if I actually hurt him, which is unlikely. I saw how hard he gets hit during a game. I highly doubt my little slap did more than annoy him. "Why would you invite me to study at a pizza joint if I can't eat pizza while I do this crap? That's pretty mean of you Lulu."

"Listen, I'm still not sure if I'm a fan of that name," I say as I push the notebook back in front of him. "And I have to work at six and you have to take a pizza home to your mom and sister. We're being practical."

"That's my Lulu. Always the practical one." He flashes me

that cocky smile before bending to begin reworking the problem, and I fight away my own.

It might be the nickname, or the fact that we now spend every day together, but I can't seem to stop smiling when it comes to Bryce. There's something special about him, and I'm not just talking about on the football field.

After he begged me to come watch him play, I caved and went to his game last week. The whole time I sat in those stands, I was in awe of what he could do on the field.

The Bryce I'm talking about, though, is one not many people get to see. I'm talking about the guy who follows me home every time we study late to make sure I get home safely. I'm talking about the guy who got me my favorite donut last week because I said on one of our now nightly FaceTimes that I liked them. He's the guy who walks me to every class even if it means he's going to be late to his own.

I'm talking about the guy who I think I'm falling for but who doesn't see me as anything more than his math tutor.

I shake my head, refocusing on Bryce working through this math problem. This is what I'm here for. Uncle Nick told me to make sure he passes trigonometry. I'm not supposed to be swooning over him like every other teenage girl in Laurel Heights.

But Bryce wasn't lying when he said he doesn't date during the football season. When he first said it, I didn't believe him. Then I watched him turn down Moriah Marks, who was very up front with him about what she would let him do to her while she was in her cheerleading uniform.

The man is focused on the game and nothing else.

"Am I right? Do I get pizza?"

"Sure. Yeah. Go for it."

"I knew you'd cave," he says, passing the notebook to me as he grabs a slice of Tripoli's famous supreme pizza.

"I was just tired of hearing you complain," I say as I check over each step of the equation. "But you would have gotten one anyways. You got it right."

"Hell yeah!" he says, pumping his fist like he just threw a touchdown. "That means another slice."

"How about another problem," I say before I start to draw a triangle. His hand covering mine stops me, and I blink at it dumbly for a second before slowly forcing my attention to his face.

"How about we take a break from math and you enjoy a slice of pizza with me?"

Honestly, no one has ever looked at me like the way Bryce is looking at me right now. It's as if there is no one else in the restaurant but us. Like life outside of this booth doesn't exist.

It's just him, me, and this moment.

"Lucia, it's time to clock in, and I believe this is for you, Donald."

Luciano drops the pizza box onto the table, and I quickly pull my hand out from under Bryce's. Just when I'm about to tell Luciano that I'll be right back there, Bryce takes back my hand.

"She'll be there in a second," Bryce says, cockiness oozing from his words. "I don't think I *really* understand this math problem yet, so we're going to be a few more minutes. But thanks for bringing me my pizza. The service here is impeccable."

Luciano stares at our joined hands with narrowed eyes before he turns his gaze back to Bryce. "You are not her job or her boyfriend. You should not be holding her hand in public. Tripoli's is her job. She needs to get to work. Lucia, let's go."

"You can't tell her what to do," Bryce says, letting go of my hand to stand as if he's about to go toe-to-toe with Luciano.

"I'm her boss," Luciano says, not backing down. "And if I

understand correctly, you are nothing more than the boy who she is helping pass math class."

I quickly stand from my side of the booth and slide between them.

"Luciano. I'll be right there," I say, pleading with my old family friend and boss to cut me a little slack. "Please let me finish then I'll clock in."

I don't move as Luciano and Bryce send each other one more round of dirty looks before he goes back into the kitchen.

"What was that?" I ask as I take my seat again.

"You know he likes you, right?"

I give Bryce a confused look. Maybe he got hit in the head last week and I didn't know about it. "No, he doesn't. It's . . . he's Luciano. He's like a brother to me and I've known him as long as I've been alive."

"Yes, he does, Lulu. His thoughts? Not very brotherly."

I feel the blush creep onto my face as Bryce reaches for my hand again.

The first time I wasn't sure what was happening. But now?

Oh my God, Bryce Donald is holding my hand.

On purpose.

Cue freak out.

"Well, he shouldn't feel that way," I say with as much confidence as I can muster. "Because we're just friends even if our moms like to joke that we are going to get married one day."

Bryce laughs. "Believe me, Lulu, he wants what your mothers want. And now he hates me because I'm the one holding your hand and he's not."

I shake my head. "Whatever. I need to go to work before he comes back out here."

I hurry and stand from the booth, but before I can leave, Bryce grabs my elbow.

"Was it okay that I held your hand?" Bryce asks softly, the cockiness and anger now long gone.

I nod. I want to tell him it was more than okay and that he can do it whenever he wants, but the words won't come.

Without letting go of me, Bryce stands. "He said something that I'm not sure I like."

"Yeah? And what was that?" He actually said more than one thing that I didn't like, but I'm curious as to what set Bryce off.

He takes my other hand in his. "He said that I'm not your boyfriend, and I don't like the sound of that very much."

I'm pretty sure if I saw myself in a mirror, my eyes would be as big as basketballs.

"But . . . I . . . I'm sorry?"

Talk about throwing a girl for a loop. Of all the things he could have said, that was the one thing I hadn't expected.

"What I mean is, when he said I wasn't your boyfriend, it felt like I was punched in the gut. Sure, it may be true, but if I were your boyfriend, I'd get to hold your hand all the time. Give you a hug and a kiss like I want to every day but I can't."

"But it's football season . . ."

I know that probably isn't the best thing to point out, but I'm in a bit of shock. Yes, I'm going to blame it on the pure shock over what he just admitted.

"I know, and while I might not be the best boyfriend over the next few weeks because of the playoffs, I can't go another day just being your friend."

Be Bryce Donald's girlfriend? I can't lie, I've thought about it. Many times. Many nights when we were on the phone, talking way too late into the night about stupid things like television shows or our favorite toys when we were kids.

"I don't want to get in the way. I know how important football is to you. I don't want to rock your boat."

He grins. "I know. That's also how I know you're it for me. You know what football means to me. So, I think I've come up with a solution."

"Is that right?"

"Yup. So, I'm going to ask you to give me six weeks."

"Six weeks?"

"Yup. That's when the state championship game is and also when the season ends."

Could I wait six, short weeks to be his girlfriend? I'm pretty sure that's the dumbest question I've ever asked myself.

When I don't answer right away, Bryce laughs softly and shifts closer to me. "In six weeks, I'm going to ask you on a date. A real one. Our real first date. Not one where you bring math books and bribe me with pizza. One where I put on a shirt with buttons and you wear something that will make me crazy and we spend the entire night together. Just you and me."

"I like the sound of that."

He smiles at me, and it's as if he just got the perfect present from Santa.

"You just agreed to a date, we're in the playoffs, and Clemson is processing my scholarship information. All my dreams are about to come true."

"That's amazing, Bryce."

He brings our joined hands to his heart. I'm thankful that his is beating as fast as mine is.

"I'm so close to finishing out my high school career exactly how I wanted. But I can't go another day without being able to sneak a kiss from you when I drop you off for English class. I want to drive you to school and hold your hand the whole way. I want you in the stands at every one of my games with my number painted on your face. Hell, I want to go to your math tournaments and make signs and cheer you on when you get the answer to a problem I don't understand."

This makes me laugh because, somehow, I'm imagining him and Cole at a math tournament with painted chests.

"I can't get you out of my head, Lucy. You and football, it's all I think about. So, right now, if you'll have me, I'd love for you to be my girlfriend. And in six weeks, when things settle down, I'm going to take you on a night you'll never forget."

"Yes."

The word comes out of my mouth before I can stop it—not that I'd have said anything different.

The smile he gives me is the biggest one I've ever seen. Then he presses his lips to the back of my hand, and yup, there they are . . . the butterflies are back.

Or maybe they are here because I just officially became Bryce Donald's girlfriend.

WHEN I FIRST FOUND OUT THAT Lucy was engaged, I got drunk. Feels fitting that I do the same thing on the night I find out who she's marrying.

Correction, I am drunk and getting drunker. With any luck, it will only take a few more beers and another shot of Jack for me to erase the image of Lucy holding hands with that pizza fuck face.

Yes, I've known for months that she was engaged, but seeing her tonight with him hit me in a whole new way.

It's real. She's engaged. She's his.

It's no longer a hypothetical thing I try to drink away every night.

"Fuck 'em all!" I yell, tossing another empty beer can from the bed of my truck toward Lake Laurel in the distance. It's called a lake when, really, it's an overgrown pond. But what do I know? I'm just the guy who can't seem to get anything right.

"That's the best throw you've made all year."

I turn and squint at the hallucination of Cole Campbell standing behind me. He's in Nashville.

Without me.

With the winning team.

"Get out of here, imaginary Cole," I say as I crack open another beer. "I betchu are here to judge me just like real Cole. Well, I don't need it from either of you! Unless imaginary Cole has more beer. Then he can stay."

Imaginary Cole laughs as his shadow—well, shadows because I think there are three of them—walks toward my truck.

"You have always been a shit drunk," imaginary Cole says, hopping up to sit next to me on my tailgate.

Damn, imaginary Cole weighs a lot. I didn't know imaginary people weighed anything, but the tailgate bounced around like real Cole sat on it.

Or maybe I'm that drunk. Probably that.

"Not a shit drunk. Imma good drunk. Except I usually don't talk to imaginary people when I'm drunk, so maybe I am a bad drunk. Imma bad quarterback. Imma bad drunk. Imma bad boyfriend. I fucking suck."

It takes me a solid five seconds to register the fact that the smack I just felt on the back of my head was in fact real. Only then do I look to my right.

Holy shit, imaginary Cole is real, and he looks pissed. All three of him.

"What are you doing here?"

He cracks open a beer and takes a drink before answering. "Early game. Bye week next week. Was planning on coming back anyway to check on you and see my folks. Then I got a text that said I should probably get here sooner rather than later. Honestly, I'm just glad I'm not bailing you out of jail."

"I'm really not a fan of you and Brenna talking as much as you do." Though I don't blame my sister for calling him. After I left Tripoli's, I texted Brenna that she needed to go get the pizza. When she asked me what happened, I hung up, turned off my phone, and drove to the liquor store before coming here.

"It wasn't your sister."

I don't have to be sober to know he means Lucy. Why she would call Cole when she wants nothing to do with me, though, is a mystery.

"So, you drove all this way to do, what? Lecture me again? To pass along how disappointed McAvoy is in me? Fine then. Let me at least get another beer before you tell me for the millionth time that I'm a train wreck. Good news. I have figured out that I'm a train wreck. To being a train wreck!"

I sway back and forth as I wind my arm back to throw my newly empty beer can toward the lake. I try to reach for a new one, but Cole rips it from my hand and throws it toward the shoreline.

I liked him better when he was imaginary.

"No more."

I try to focus my eyes but the damn world won't hold still long enough for me to do it. "You always were the fun killer."

"Someone has to be the responsible one, and God knows it's not you."

I shoot him a look. At least I think I do. I really can't feel my face. "No one ever told you that you were responsible for me. You aren't my father."

"Thank God for that."

I mostly fall to my ass in the bed of the truck, too pissed that Cole chucked my last beer to say anything else.

"Do you remember what I told you before our first game?" Cole's voice is back to even, which means he's about to go into lecture mode, and I groan.

"Which first game?"

"The very first."

I fall backward and look up at the sky as I think back to all those years ago. We were six. It was Laurel Heights Little Tigers football. I was the quarterback and Cole was my center. Later in his career he was moved to left tackle to protect my blind-side. Back then, he was the only one who could figure out how to snap the ball.

"You told me not to drop the ball."

He barks out a laugh. "The other thing, asshole."

I let out a sigh. "That you'd always protect me. That no one would get to me if you had anything to do with it."

I remember thinking that he was nuts because he was talking like an adult, but that's always been Cole—the guy was six going on thirty. We were also in Pop Warner football. It wasn't like I was about to be tackled by a three-hundred-pound linebacker.

In true Cole fashion, he kept his word. I don't think I got sacked until high school, and that was because he was out with mono and couldn't play that game.

Who knew the words of a six-year-old would hold so much truth? This man has lined up with me in every level of football, which is unheard of in this day and age of recruiting and professional ball. From what started with the Little Tigers that led to high school, which led to college at Clemson, and then to Nashville with the Fury.

The man has had my back, and my front, for my entire life. He's kept me alive—literally and figuratively.

"Whether you care to admit it or not, you need me," Cole says. "Only this time, I'm not blocking guys who want to rip your head off."

"Then who are you protecting me from?"

"Yourself, you asshole. I'm protecting you from yourself. The fact that you can't see that means you haven't figured out shit since you've been here."

He's right, of course. He's been right all along. I was just too stubborn or prideful or stupid to admit it.

Probably all of the above.

I'm spiraling. I'm out of control. I'm my own, and everyone else's, worst enemy. And it's all because, for the first time in my life, I lost. I lost her, and I didn't know how to handle it. Correction, I *don't* know how to handle it. Throw that on top of the other things in my life that I'm barely holding on to with a string, and that leads to the absolute shit show that has become my life.

"Is this the right time to tell you I'm sorry?" While I didn't expect Cole to give me a big hug and tell me everything is okay, I definitely didn't expect him to laugh. "What's so funny?"

"That you need permission to apologize. I find it amusing. Has the great Bryce Donald never done this before?"

I can probably count on both hands how many times I've had to admit I'm wrong, and most of them have been to my mom.

"What I was going to say is that I'm sorry. I was a dick to you. Not just the day I left Nashville but also over the past nine months. Ever since I . . . well, you know. You tried to help me, but I didn't want it."

"And now? Are you ready for help now?"

Isn't that the million-dollar question.

"I have no idea how to do this without her," I admit, the words tasting vile as they pass through my lips for the first time. "She was my calm. My center. You've always been there for me, but with her? It was different. I love her. I love her so fucking much I can't see straight. I waited too long, and now she's gone and there is all of this . . . this . . . shit that I've let build up. Endorsement deals are ready to drop me. The team probably hates me. My dad won't leave me alone. For the last seven years, when something like this happened, I would go to her. And now I can't. She's not mine anymore. Maybe she never was to begin with."

"You're right."

I have to blink a few times because did I hear him right or is that me making things up because I'm still pretty drunk. "Did you just say I was right?"

"Focus here, Donald. But yes, you're right. You have shit. Some of it you built on yourself, some of it comes with the price of being a professional football player. And yes, you have to learn to do this without her. It has been nine months. She's moved on. Now it's time for you to. I guess the question is, how do you plan to do that? Because it's not just moving on from her. It's also getting your career back as well."

I sit up and start to answer, except I'm at a loss for words. All that's going through my head right now are the last nine months of my life.

All the booze. All the women. All the times I treated my teammates like trash. How I treated my coaches.

"God, I've fucked up so bad," I say, my hands catching my head in defeat. "How can I even come back from all of that?"

"Do you want me to tell you or let you figure it out? If I'm the new Lucy, I need to know the protocol."

He may have known when it was time to call her, but he never understood how she was able to get through to me when he couldn't. No one can fill the space her absence has created, but that doesn't mean her method won't still work.

"Apologies. I owe so many apologies."

"That's definitely on the list. What else?"

I think about it before saying, "I should probably start working out again. Can't come back to the league if I can't throw a football."

"Also a good idea. Anything else?"

I let out a breath because I know what I need to say, but saying the words are harder than I thought.

"I need to talk to the therapist," I admit. "I need . . . I need help."

Cole gives my back a slap. "It will be hard, all of it, but I'm proud of you. You need to move on. These are the first steps."

I jump off the tailgate, which might not have been the best idea as I stumble before I catch my balance. "Do you realize that I never went home with a brunette? Always a blonde."

"I just figured you had a new type."

I shake my head, which is also a bad decision. "She's my only type. She was it. She was my end game. And it was almost time. I was almost ready. Last offseason. After the playoffs. That was going to be it. That was going to be our time. I was finally going to be able to show her how much she really meant to me."

I hear Cole's footsteps coming from behind. "I know, man, but maybe this just wasn't in the cards for you two. Hell, maybe it was and the opportunity has come and gone, but you need to take the steps to move on. You need to get back to being the Bryce I know. Only this Bryce is without Lucy. I need the Bryce who was going to take the league by storm. The Bryce I am going to win a league championship with."

A Bryce without Lucy. I don't even know what that guy would look like.

Cole is right, though. I need to take the steps and figure this out.

Starting now.

CHAPTER 12
LUCY

I THINK I'M DYING.

Well, not really dying unless I could die from too many consecutive minutes of coughing, then I probably would have keeled over seven minutes ago.

"Lucy! Are you okay? I'm coming!"

The coughing fit continues as Brenna runs up the stairs to my bedroom where she finds me sitting on the edge of my bed with my wedding dress on my lap as I gasp for breath.

"Here. Take a drink of water."

Why Brenna has a bottle of water at the ready I'm not sure, but I'm not about to look a gift horse in the mouth. This woman literally just saved my life.

I take a few sips before finally calming down enough to take a deep breath. That was by far the worst coughing fit I've had since they started.

If I'm like this just from looking at my dress, I can only imagine what it's going to be like when I'm wearing it on my wedding day, which is in five weeks.

Not that any of my guests would know that since I still have not sent the invitations.

"I came by to drop these off," Brenna says, tossing a few

bags of cough drops onto my bed. "I know I'm a few days late, but I heard you went to buy them but left before you could check out. From how you sounded when I walked in, it's a good thing I grabbed them, too."

"Something like that," I say as I finally catch my breath.

"Are we going to talk about it?"

"Talk about what?" I ask, trying to play dumb as I hang the dress up on the back of my bedroom door. "Oh! Luciano held my hand in public last night! At the restaurant. In front of customers. How exciting is that?"

Brenna plops down on my bed. "Are you listening to yourself? This should not be big news."

"I am listening, but this is a big deal. I think we should talk about that and only that and nothing else that has happened over the last week."

"Nice try," Brenna says. "While I'd love to dive into the fact that it should not be major news that your fiancé held your hand, I'm more interested in what happened between you and Bryce when he walked in on such an exciting milestone in your relationship. Or would you rather talk about how, if I hadn't shown up today, you might be dead from coughing as you held your wedding dress? You can pick."

"What if I don't want to?"

"Then I'll pick, of course. It's like you've learned nothing in the six years we've been friends."

I sometimes wonder why we're even friends. What started as just someone I knew who ended up in my freshman English class in college has turned into a friendship of a lifetime. She has been my shoulder to cry on more times than I can count. In return, I'm her shoulder when she is ghosted by another shitty online date. She's my person.

"I was at Tripoli's last night."

Brenna falls back onto the bed. "Ugh. I thought that would

happen. We tried to get him not to go in case you were, but he was insistent."

"It's not your fault," I say, falling back next to her. "He had to see us together at some point. Might as well rip the Band-Aid off."

"Was it as bad as I heard?"

"What did you hear?"

"That he and Luciano almost fought in the middle of the restaurant and that he broke the door when he left. Oh, and that he took out someone's mirror when he sped away"

I roll my eyes. The Laurel Heights Facebook gossip page will never cease to amaze me. "Partially. They did argue, but the door is still intact, as far as I know. As for the mirror, I'm not sure. I walked back inside before he drove off."

While I hate how last night went down, in a strange way, I'm glad it happened. I owed Bryce an explanation. Yes, I wish I didn't give it to him while we were screaming at each other in a parking lot, but I'm glad I got it out.

He needed to know how I felt and why I made the choices I did.

Even if I question them every day.

"Well, that explains why Cole showed up at my place at three in the morning carrying in a very drunk and very passed out Bryce."

I sit up, putting my hands to my head. "I hate that he's drinking as much as he is. I know he's responsible for his own choices, but I can't help but feel guilty—"

"No. Do not put that on yourself," Brenna says as she sits up next to me. "You did what you had to do and made a decision for your life and your future. My idiot brother's inability to figure out how to cope with adult things without a bottle of booze is not on you."

"I know," I say. "But what if I made the wrong decision?"

I don't make eye contact with Brenna as my words linger in the air. Instead, I move my hands from my head to a suddenly very interesting piece of thread that is coming undone from the bottom of my T-shirt.

"Excuse me? What did you just say?"

I stay focused on the thread, wondering how I'm going to play this.

Reverse. Reversal seems good.

"Nothing. Absolutely nothing. I said no words. Want to go get tacos?"

Brenna moves closer to me, forcing me to look at her. "Bullshit and don't you dare try to distract me with the deliciousness that is the best food in the world. You just said you're wondering if you made the right decision. Need I remind you of the pro-con list that took us five hours to make? Do I need to go find it so you can reacquaint yourself with it?"

"No," I say, though it would be nice just to look at it one more time. It was the biggest list I'd made to date—fifteen pages. Front and back.

On it listed every reason I should continue to wait for Bryce.

Pros: He was my first love and my best friend.

Cons: It will never be the offseason. Football will always come first.

Then it had the reasons Luciano would be a good life partner for me.

Pros: My family loves him. He makes time for me and our relationship.

Cons: Not overly affectionate.

There were many more reasons than those—and Brenna made an entire section of cons when she found out that Luciano and I hadn't slept together yet—but that's what it all boiled down to.

Luciano wants what I want. He's ready to start the next chapter in his life that involves marriage and, eventually, kids. I don't need to be pregnant tomorrow, but I want to get the journey started. Most importantly, I never have to wonder if he'll break promises he makes to me. I know he won't.

As for Bryce? Yes, the last time we spoke he said that he was ready to settle down and start our future. He said the same thing when we—well, before the draft. He's been saying that in some way, shape, or form since our senior year of high school. Yet, his actions have always spoken louder than his words. Actions that always leave me waiting and wondering. That was what happened the night I decided I was done waiting. So, I moved on. Even though it hurt like hell.

"List aside, why did you say it? Because if you ask me, which you kind of did, it's that you're finally willing to admit that you're marrying Luciano because you were so desperate to get over my brother that you said yes to the first man who asked."

I stand and take my wedding dress off the hook, holding it in front of me. I feel a cough, but I swallow it.

"Furthermore," Brenna yells, making sure I can hear her from where I stand in the back of my closet. "I may never have been in a relationship like you're in, but I do know that if you're going to marry someone, then you should have zero doubts. You should be counting down the days until you become husband and wife, not counting the days since your last coughing fit. If you're having any hesitations—any at all—you need to figure them out soon."

She isn't telling me anything I don't already know. The longer I let this go on, the more people this is going to hurt, and Luciano deserves better than that.

"This shouldn't be so hard," I say, hanging my dress back where it was.

"Right? Decisions like this need to come with signs from the universe. They are too big to make on our own. Even though I think you already know what to do."

I already know I can't marry Luciano. I'm not in love with him. It isn't fair to him. It isn't fair to me.

Though it would be nice to have a sign from the universe confirming that is the right choice.

Maybe lightning could strike.

Or maybe something in your closet can catch my attention after years of being ignored.

Something like Bryce's high school letterman jacket.

CHAPTER 13
LUCY

I AM GOING to kill Bryce Donald.

That is, after I find him.

I thought it was strange when he didn't show up for tutoring before my Sunday shift at Tripoli's. It is state championship week, so I thought maybe he had extra practice that he forgot to tell me about.

Then he didn't come in to pick up the pizza his mom ordered. I tried to call and text him, but both went unanswered. I messaged Cole, but he thought Bryce was with me. Same with Brenna.

So, now we're searching. Cole is checking the high school while Brenna is searching around their house. As for me? I'm going out on a limb and heading to check Lake Laurel.

It's not like Bryce not to message me back. Or Cole or Brenna. No one has heard from him since this morning, and it is already well past dusk.

I pull on to the main road that leads back to Lake Laurel, and at first, I don't see anything. Just trees and the remnants of last week's first snow. Then I turn on my bright lights and, in the distance, right in the middle of a picnic area, I think I see an outline of a gray truck.

Lucy: Found him. He's at the lake.

Cole: Tell him I'm going to kick his ass.

Brenna: Same.

I put my phone away and exit my car. It's not until I take a few steps toward the truck that I see Bryce sitting on the end of this tailgate. If he hears me, he's not reacting.

"Hey," I say as I walk toward him. "Are you okay?"

The only reason I know he is alive and not a mannequin is because I can see his breath in the cold Ohio air.

"Bryce? What's the matter?"

I look at his hand, and narrow my eyes.

"What is this?" I ask, walking in front of him and grabbing his hand. "Whiskey? Where do you even get a bottle of whiskey? You're not even eighteen yet!"

He jerks his hand away from me, causing liquid to spill on both of us. "I have my ways." At least if it's full enough to spill like that, then he hasn't drunk that much of it. "Besides, I've only had a sip of it. Turns out I'm not that big of a fan of it."

Well, that's good.

"Why do you even have it in the first place? And what are you doing here?"

I wait for him to answer even though I'm freezing and am already having to clench my teeth to keep them from chattering.

"Do you know that if we win this Friday, we'll be the first state champions in school history?"

"I do." Friday's game is all anyone in town is talking about. It's in Columbus, and the town is shutting down and renting buses to take the two-hour drive to watch the game.

"What happens if we lose?"

The question takes me by surprise. In all the months I've known Bryce, I've never heard anything but confidence in his voice when it comes to his football abilities. It's why he works as hard as he does. He talks the talk and walks the walk.

"Why would you ask that?" I ask, doing my best to ignore the cold. "You guys are undefeated this year. No one has even come close to beating you. This is your year. You've said so yourself."

"I don't know. It's just . . ." He sighs, and just when I think he's about to take another sip of the whiskey, he tosses it to the side of the truck. "We've worked our entire lives for this game. When we were ten, we had a coach tell us that if we couldn't win a state title one day, then no one in Laurel Heights could. Now it's here, and . . . and I . . . I don't feel ready."

"Why wouldn't you be? You do nothing but think about football, despite my best attempts to make you focus on math."

Usually, this kind of joke got a laugh out of him, but not tonight.

"Do you want to make another pro-con list?"

When he turns to me, the look in his eye breaks my heart. He looks . . . lost. Defeated. Tired.

"I told Mom this week about Clemson."

Oh no. I know he had been putting it off because he was scared of her reaction. "I'm taking that it didn't go over well?"

He shrugs. "She freaked out and cried. Brenna couldn't even get her to calm down. I tried to tell her all the good things about it. I even showed her the list we made, you know, to show her I put thought into it. All she could say was how far away it was and how she'd never get to see me."

I lift his hand and give it a kiss, which feels natural to do even though I'm still navigating this girlfriend thing.

"I'm so sorry about your mom. But I have a feeling that she'll come around. That she was just taken by surprise."

"I hope so. I really need at least one parent on my side."

And there it is. I had a feeling this was big, and if his dad has anything to do with it, then it's huge. Bryce hasn't told me much about his dad, except that he comes in and out of his life, usually at the worst possible times. And that when he comes in, it's because he wants or needs something.

Which, I'm sorry, is just shitty.

"Did you talk to him?"

He nods. "He called me when I was on my way in to study with you. I shouldn't have even answered it, but he's my dad, you know? How can I ignore him?"

"What did he say?"

"That he arranged a visit for me next weekend at Alabama. I told him that I didn't want to visit and that I was planning to commit to Clemson."

"I take it he didn't react well?"

"He told me I was worthless and that if I knew what was good for me I'd visit. I asked him why he cared so much about Alabama, and he gave some bullshit reason. Then I asked him if he was coming to the game this weekend, and he said, and I quote, 'why bother when I'm not going to do what he wants.'"

I'm not a violent person. I believe in trying to find peaceful resolutions to problems. But if I saw Bryce's dad right now, I would punch him straight in the throat.

"Oh, Bryce." I let go of his hand so I can wrap him in my arms. If there were ever a person who needed a hug, it would be Bryce.

His arms tighten around me, and he leans his head on my shoulder. If I listen closely, I'm pretty sure I could hear his sniffle.

All he wants to do is make everyone happy. He wants to

make his parents and his coaches proud. He wants to win a state title for the town and his teammates more than he wants it for himself. He is worrying about everyone else at a time when most teenagers—heck, most humans, would only be worrying about themselves.

"I'm sorry all of that happened, and I'm sorry it's happening now," I say as we let go of each other.

"It's not your fault, and I'm sorry I scared you. I actually came to Tripoli's to talk to you tonight, but when I pulled in, I saw pizza boy with his hand on your back. Between that and the call with my dad, I didn't trust myself in there."

Luciano did put his hand on my back briefly, but it was to guide me around a spill on the floor. I hadn't thought anything of it.

"There is nothing going on with him. I'm with you. Please know that," I say, trying again to ease his mind when it comes to Luciano. "But, Bryce, whiskey? You know that isn't going to make anything better. In fact, it will just make things worse."

"I know," he said, his voice resigned. "I was . . . I'm just all over the place. I can't focus. I can't figure out what's right and wrong. I'm . . . I'm lost, Lulu."

"Well, then let's get you unlost," I say, patting my thigh. "Come on. Lie down."

He quirks an eyebrow. "What are you doing?"

"Just trust me," I say. "Now put your head down and close your eyes."

He gives a groan but complies, laying his head on my lap. I begin gently massaging his scalp, hoping that it helps alleviate some of the tension I know he's carrying.

"That feels good," he says as he slowly relaxes.

"Shhh. Don't talk." I give him a soft smile as I continue to rub small circles around his temples. "All I want you to focus on is the game this week. That's what you've worked for.

That's what you want more than anything else right now. You've worked too hard to let everyone else get in the way. So just lay here and focus on that. Let all of the other noise go away."

I'm not sure how long we sat like that. At some point I think he might have fallen asleep. I know for a fact that my butt is frozen to his truck. But it's all worth it because soon I hear the best words I could hear.

"One week."

I can't help but smile at his words. "One week."

He slowly sits up, and the picture in front of me makes my heart swell. Gone is the lost boy from an hour ago who felt like the world was crashing down on him. Now here is the person I'm falling for more and more every day.

"Thank you."

"You don't need to thank me."

"Yes, I do," he says as I visibly shiver.

"Lulu, why didn't you say how cold you were?" He's quick to tug his jacket off, but I hold my hand up.

"No," I say, trying to refuse it. "It's cold for you too. I'm fine."

"Don't care," he says, reaching behind me so he can put it over my shoulders. "Wear it."

"Thanks," I say shyly because I secretly love how it's huge on me and how it smells of him. I have to do all I can not to bring it to my nose and sniff it.

"And I do need to thank you. Not just for tonight but also for . . . well, everything."

"I didn't do much." I shrug.

"You did everything," he says, reaching for my hand. "You get me. You know when I need to vent or when I need quiet. You know how to talk me off the ledge or how to encourage me. You're amazing."

I open my mouth to thank him or tell him that I am just trying to be a good friend.

But neither of those things happen because before I can, Bryce Donald is kissing me.

And it is warming me in every cell of my body.

This isn't our first kiss, but every time our lips touch, I notice something new. His lips are soft, which is maybe the only part of his body that is. I taste the faint hint of whiskey, and I think for the rest of my life I will associate that taste with Bryce. He opens his mouth, and I follow suit, our tongues meeting in a way that is both weird and thrilling at the same time. Bryce is the first guy I've kissed, so I find myself wondering how I'm doing, which I probably shouldn't do.

Oh God, what if I'm bad at this? What if he has kissed dozens of girls, and I'm on the low percentile of kissability?

"I can hear your brain," Bryce says, slowly pulling away from me. "What is going on in that beautiful head of yours?"

Our foreheads touch as he links our hands together.

"Promise not to laugh?"

"You can tell me anything, Lulu."

I take a deep breath, hating that I'm about to say this. "You're the only guy I've kissed."

He backs away, and his eyes grow wide. Oh geez, I've scared him off.

"I was your first kiss?"

I nod. "Embarrassing, isn't it?"

I try to back away, but he pulls me back to him. "Not embarrassing at all. In fact, I kind of like that you had never been kissed."

I give him a sideways glance. "And why is that?"

"Because now I know I don't have to beat up any other guys who have kissed you before."

I shake my head. "That's a little much, don't you think?"

He shrugs, pulling me on his lap. "Don't care. Want to know what else I like?"

"What is that?"

"You in my jacket."

I pull it a little tighter around me. "Good, because I like it too."

"Will you do me a favor?" he asks while giving me one more small kiss on the cheek before pulling me tighter.

"Anything."

"Wear this to next week's game? I feel like I could use a good luck charm in the stands."

"You don't need luck," I say, wrapping my arms around his neck. "You're Bryce Donald. You got this. You're going to be amazing."

He leans in to kiss me again, only this time I don't overanalyze it. I just revel in the feel of his kiss and his arms around me as I mentally count down the days until next week when it will just be us.

I'VE BEEN hungover a lot over the past nine months.

Some of those nights I was able to completely forget what happened the night before. Other nights, I wasn't so lucky. This is one of those mornings. My head hurts, my mouth feels like it's stuffed with cotton balls, and my stomach is revolting.

I remember everything from Tripoli's and fighting with Lucy to getting shitfaced at the lake to Cole appearing out of nowhere. The only thing I can't seem to remember is how this bruise got on my knee. Though, I do have a vague memory of trying to jump off the tailgate of my truck and not actually landing. That might have something to do with it.

I deserve it all. And frankly this hangover is making up for the times that I thought nothing was wrong.

Everything was wrong. I knew it, but I just didn't want to believe it.

But Cole is right. Hell, everyone is right. I can't keep doing this. I can't keep going down this path. I can't jeopardize my career all because things didn't go my way.

And as much as I never thought I'd admit it, the team isn't wrong. I am going through something. And it is definitely a mental problem. I'm not making the right decisions for myself or my team. I'm allowing myself to self-destruct. As much as I hated them for doing it at the time, the Fury did exactly what they had to do for me.

Step one was admittance. But what's next? I've fucked up so many things over the past nine months that I don't even know where to begin.

"Numbnuts! Are you going to wake up today or should I just plan on you being on my couch for the foreseeable future?"

I blink a few times, hating every ounce of light in Brenna's living room. "What time is it?"

"Time to drink this," she says, throwing a full bottle of Gatorade at me.

I sit up slowly, though that doesn't stop the room from spinning. "Why aren't you in school today?"

"Because it's four o'clock," she says. "And it's Columbus Day so I had the whole day off."

I fall back onto the couch. "Thanks for letting me crash here."

"I didn't have much of a choice. One minute Cole is messaging me to open my door and the next he is dropping you—literally—on my couch."

Okay so maybe I don't remember everything from last night. Now that I think about it, everything is kind of blurry after leaving the lake.

"Well, I appreciate it," I say, trying my best to sit up again. "Fuck, I drank a lot."

"So I heard," she says, taking a seat on the chair next to me. "If this was how you were when you lived in Nashville, I have no idea how you functioned."

"Denial is a powerful thing," I say, taking as big of a swig of the drink as my stomach can handle. "It makes you think nothing is wrong when, in reality, the world is crashing down around you."

"Do my ears deceive me or is my brother admitting that he does in fact have a problem?"

"What is your brother admitting?"

I look over to see Cole standing at Brenna's door. I'm starting to seriously question on whether or not he has magical powers that just make him show up at places.

"That he's a jackass," Brenna says.

"We knew that," Cole says as he sits next to me on the couch.

I take another sip of my Gatorade, watching Cole and my sister stare at each other.

Then again, the room is still spinning when I try to move so I can't trust anything I'm seeing right now.

"What are you doing here?" I ask.

"Giving you this," he says, tossing my cell phone to me. "It fell out in my truck last night. Figured you'd want it when you came back to the land of the living."

I pick it up, almost scared to see what is waiting for me. Numerous texts asking where I was last night. Most of them from Cole. Twelve missed calls from Brenna and Mom. A shit load of emails that I'll deal with later.

Nothing from Lucy.

I drop my phone on my lap, disappointed when I have no right to be.

Though I can't shake the feeling that we're not done yet. That our story isn't over. Maybe because we're in the same town? Maybe because I felt the same spark I always do when I touched her the other day?

I know she did too. I know that's why she ran.

Spark or not, she made her choice. She's marrying pizza boy. And now I have to learn how to navigate life knowing that Lucy isn't my end game anymore.

"So, what now?" Cole asks in his serious "dad" voice as he takes a seat next to me.

"I'm not sure," I say defeatedly.

"Well, are you staying here?" Brenna asks. "I mean, not here with me because I love you, but I'd kill you. I mean as in Laurel Heights."

This gets a smile out of me. "No, Brenna, I will not cramp your style. But I . . . I don't think I'm ready to go back to Nashville."

Cole pats me on the back. "If you're not ready, then you're not ready."

If I go back to Nashville now, still this raw and vulnerable, I know it would be easy to pick up the first bottle I see, or call any of the faceless women in my cell phone for a night of meaningless sex to make me try to forget. I know Cole would keep an eye on me if I asked him to—hell, he'd move in with me if he thought it would keep me above water—but I can't ask him to do that.

I need to do this myself. For the first time in my life, I need to figure out life on my own.

"How are you going to stay here—"

"Without fighting with Lucy every time I see her?"

Brenna nods. "Well, yeah, that. Or you need to figure out a way to just steer clear of her. Can't fight with her if you don't see her."

The Jack Daniels threatens to come up from my stomach because I know Brenna is right.

Hell, maybe that is why I should stay here. I can work on getting back in football shape—both physically and mentally —while also learning how to live in a world where Lucy is there, but just not in the way I'm used to. And if I stay away from her, I'll get used to her not being in my life.

"Can you do that?" Cole asks. "And don't just say that you

can because that's what we want to hear. You have to mean it or I'm dragging your ass back to Nashville and you're moving in with me."

I lay my head back against the couch and close my eyes, knowing that going back to Nashville isn't an option. I need to stay here.

Here I can't ignore that Lucy has moved on. I can't ignore that I'm not with my team. I have to work to get back to Nash-ville. I have to earn it.

And that's what I'm going to do.

"Yeah . . . I can do it. And I will."

"COME ON, Donald. That all you got? Give me five more!"

I had forgotten what kind of drill sergeant Cole was in the weight room.

My arms feel like they are going to fall off, I think I'm sweating out the last nine months of whiskey while I plot my best friend's murder.

But the pain is good. It's a reminder of what I did to myself.

It's a good reminder never to do it again.

"Three . . . two . . . one. Done!"

Cole takes the weight bar from my hands as I lie still on the bench press. "Remind me never to half ass off-season lifting again."

"Not a problem," he says as he adds more weight to the bar for himself. "How about you go fill up our waters while I knock out this set."

"You don't need me to spot you?" I ask jokingly.

"I think I got this," he says, putting up his first rep. "Maybe next time, I'll just bench you."

"I'd like to see you try."

I talk a big game, but Cole could easily bench me. He could probably do it without breaking a sweat. It's not that I'm small, but compared to Cole, who is six-foot-four and two-hundred and ninety pounds, I'm nothing.

I make my way over to the water station as I hear Cole grunting through his set. It's the only sound in high school weight room at six in the morning.

One of the first phone calls I made during the hangover from hell was to Coach Roberts. I owed the man an apology. He tried to help me the other day, and I stormed out of his office because I couldn't handle the truth when it was right in front of my face.

I also needed a favor.

If I'm going to eventually earn my way back onto the Fury, I need to get myself back into shape. I half-assed training camp and was too busy drinking and fucking during the off-season that I don't think I went to a gym once. Looking back, I can't figure out how I survived the few days of training camp I participated in, which didn't sit well with me. But I'm not about to go to the town gym where the equipment is subpar and the people will start gossiping up a storm.

Nope. I'm not about to put myself through that. So, I asked coach if I could come in before school to get in my workout. Yes, the league frowns upon players working out at non-team facilities, but I can't sit around and get even more out of shape. Plus, the equipment at my old high school is state of the art—Cole and I made sure of that the second after our first checks cleared.

Plus, I like working out in peace. Well, I will when Cole goes back to Nashville at the end of the week. It will give me time to think. To figure out the rest of my new plan.

I know what I need to do on the football field. I know what I need to do in the weight room. And Coach Roberts will help me get there if I need additional support.

Personally? That's a whole other story. The person I always had to help me with that I can't have anymore.

And I get why.

I kept Lucy on the hook for years—unintentionally, of course. I never wanted to hurt her. Hell, I would have cut off my own arm before hurting her on purpose.

Yet, that's what I did.

I just always felt like I couldn't give her what she deserved until the time was right, not even considering that my promises wouldn't be enough for her.

When my clock ran out, I only had myself to blame for not starting the play earlier.

"You done?" Cole says, setting the bar back on the rack. "Or you want to do another set?"

"No, I'm good," I say, tossing him his water bottle. "Baby steps are probably best for me at this point."

"What is that I hear? Bryce Donald making a good decision?"

I give him the finger and walk to where I dropped my gym bag. "Isn't it time for you to go back to Nashville? Don't you have other friends to annoy?"

"Nope. Just you, and you're stuck with me for another three days. Don't hate me, but I'm going to ask one more time, are you sure you don't want to come back with me?"

I take a seat on a bench across from him. "Thanks, but I'm good. I did think about it for longer than five seconds. I know you'll be there for me and you'd do whatever needs to be done to make sure I don't slip back into old habits, but you have to be with the team. Plus, there are still six away games on the schedule. I promise you, the second I am ready, you'll be the first to know."

He nods. "I'm proud of you, you know that, right?"

I laugh. "What do you have to be proud of me for? For

almost fucking up my career, being two steps away from a thirty-day program, or treating you like a piece of shit?"

"While you might have done all of those things, I'm proud because you're owning up to them. Not many people could do that. They would just keep going down the path until they hit rock bottom."

"Rock bottom isn't getting kicked off a team that thought you were worth ten-million dollars a year?"

"You weren't kicked off. You were put on personal leave for the season. There is a huge difference."

"Sometimes you can polish a turd in ways no one else can."

"It's my specialty," Cole says, standing from his bench. "Rock bottom would have been you in a hospital after a night of black-out drinking. Rock bottom would have been one of your many nameless, faceless blondes telling you that you were going to be a daddy. Rock bottom would have been getting fired by the league for breach of contract. That would have been rock bottom."

Cole is right, all of those things would be far, far worse than what I'm dealing with, but even that bit of perspective doesn't make me feel any better. It just makes me feel like more of an asshole.

As angry as I was with Coach McAvoy and Coach Davis for sending me away, I now know that they needed to. As much as I hated seeing the tape Coach Roberts showed me, I'm not sure if I would have realized how bad things were had he not done it. And I don't know if I hadn't seen Lucy with Luciano—God I hate even thinking his name—that I would have realized that she is not mine anymore.

I needed all of that. Sometimes, the truth hurts and you need it to smack you in the face so you can feel the pain.

"Well, thanks for making sure I didn't get there," I say as

we begin to walk out of the weight room. "I know I wasn't the easiest person to get along with for a while."

"Understatement of the year," he says as we walk past Coach Roberts's office just as the door opens.

"See you soon, Uncle Nick. Keep me updated on Brandon's test scores."

Lucy's voice freezes me mid-step. I knew I was going to see her around town. I knew I couldn't avoid her entirely, but I thought I would be safe at the school.

Apparently not.

"Oh!" she yelps, taking a few steps back as she almost runs into me and Cole. "Bryce . . . Cole . . . I didn't . . . I didn't know you would be here."

"No problem, Luce," Cole says as he pulls her into a hug. "Come here. It's been too long."

She lets out a breath and slowly accepts Cole's hug. I want to look away, not because my best friend is holding the only woman I have ever loved but because I know a hug for me isn't coming next. Hell, I'll be lucky if she says two words to me. She hasn't even looked at me.

"What are you guys doing here?" she asks nervously, still avoiding eye contact with me.

"Coach is letting Bryce work out in the mornings. I'm just tagging along until I go back to Nashville. What are you doing here?"

"I . . ." She releases an uneven breath that betrays her nervousness. Why? My Lucy isn't nervous. My Lucy doesn't care what the world thinks, and she says it like it is. Maybe that's another thing that has changed? "Apparently, I'm the only one Uncle Nick can find when he needs a math tutor. So, I come down a few days a week to help out a few of the players."

Of course she would because she's the type of girl who would wake up early and tutor kids before she goes to work. It brings me right back to all those mornings we spent together when I acted like I didn't know trig. All the conversations we had that changed my life. All the secret looks we gave each other as feelings we both didn't know how to handle started developing. All the times I would sneak a kiss because I couldn't help myself.

As if she's thinking about the same things, when she finally looks at me, her eyes are bright with remembrance.

"He's lucky to have you," I say as I contemplate what I'd give to have Coach Roberts bust out of his office and launch into one of his tirades about technology in football just to break the tension between Lucy and me.

"Well, I need to get going," Cole says as he backs away. "Call me later, Bryce? Good to see you, Lucy."

Cole makes a quick exit, and if I thought the silence was awkward a second ago, it has nothing on what it is like right now.

"Hey, can I—"

"We should—"

We both awkwardly laugh as we talk over each other.

"You first," I say.

She glances at her phone. "I have to be at the bank in twenty minutes."

"This won't take long," I say, guiding her to the empty locker room. I know this is my one shot at an apology, which also means I need to bury all thoughts about bringing her in my arms, kissing the hell out of her, or trying to convince her to call off the wedding.

"Cole said he was going back to Nashville," Lucy says as she takes a seat on one of the benches. "Does that mean you're going back with him?"

"Actually, I'm not," I say, taking my own seat. "I need to

figure out a few things before I head back, so I'm going to stay here for the rest of the season."

Her eyes grow wide. "You're staying here? In Laurel Heights? But what about the Fury? Your contract?"

"My agent worked it out. I'm technically on the injured reserve list. So, I'm taking the rest of the season to work through my . . . issues."

"Oh," she says, the nervous tone back in her voice. "Well, I'm glad you're doing what you need to do."

She starts to stand, but I reach for her arm. "Lucy, wait. I need to apologize."

She looks down at my hand, but she doesn't move to pull free. It's almost as if she's just as desperate for the connection as I am.

Then, slowly, she slides her arm free, and my heart sinks. "You don't need to apologize," Lucy says. "We both said what needed to be said, and that's that."

"But it's not," I say standing. "You said what you needed to say, and I deserved every word of it. I didn't do right by you for many years, and I know that now. I'm so sorry, Lucy. I never wanted to hurt you. I loved you. I still love you."

"Bryce—"

"No. Let me finish. I will *always* love you, but I know you've moved on, so I have to accept that. If Luciano is who makes you happy, then I'll support you because, before you were my first love, you were my best friend."

I wasn't expecting laughter mixed with fits of coughing that's more of a wheezing gasp, but it's what I get.

"What's so funny?"

"I think that's the first time in all these years you called him by his first name."

"I'm growing," I say as a smile forms on my lips.

"Apparently." Her smile is so brilliant that, when her phone beeps, I want to break it and snatch the moment back.

"It's the bank," she says looking at it then tossing it into her purse. "I need to go."

"Yeah. Sure," I say, walking to the door and holding it open for her as she walks out. "And, Lucy?"

She turns to look at me. "Yeah?"

"I meant what I said. If you're happy, then I'm happy."

"Thanks," she says, quickly turning and walking away. All I hear as she walks down the hallway is echoes of her coughing.

"THIS ONE IS from your Aunt Linda, and I snuck another cough drop under the bow. This is the last gift. You got this."

I couldn't have asked for better bridesmaids than Megan and Brenna. Megan made it her mission to get this shower over with in record time, all while sneaking me cough drops like a boss so I didn't start coughing. Brenna is steering the conversation away from specific wedding talk to avoid the chance of coughing fits, which is really hard at a bridal shower, but Brenna is pulling it off.

In fact, I haven't had a spell all day. The only downside is that my mouth and throat are numb and all I can taste is honey lemon.

That's fine. It's a small sacrifice to pay.

"Aunt Linda, they are lovely!" I say, as I hold up the embroidered towels I picked out. Though, Aunt Linda went a step further and had them personalized with our town nickname instead of our initials. How . . . thoughtful.

"Those are precious, Linda!" my mom says, which is what she's said about every gift I've opened, including the vase shaped like a penis that was not on my registry.

I thought Brenna was going to lose it on that one.

"I'm so happy," Mom continues as she takes the towels from me. "Guiliana, can you believe this is finally happening? Who would have thought that our babies would actually get married, just like we planned!"

Damn. We almost made it through the whole shower without this conversation. Though, someone would have been a fool not to bet on it. The math nerd in me set the odds at a hundred-to-one.

"Do you remember lying next to each other after we gave birth to them? All we could talk about was their eventual wedding. We just knew that this day was in our future," Guiliana says standing, very clearly wanting this conversation to be about her and my mom and not me and Luciano. Again, that is fine. I've never been comfortable being the center of attention anyway. "I'd like to propose a toast. To Luciano and Lucy, may your days be filled with love and ours be full of lots of grandbabies."

"You'd have to have sex with him for that to happen," Brenna whispers as she walks past, and just like that, my throat closes faster than a door being slammed. It's more from trying not to laugh than from the thought of sleeping with Luciano.

"Oh, I remember crying tears of joy when Lucy told me she and Luciano were going on a date. Lucy, why don't you tell everyone how you two reconnected?"

I look to my mom, who is looking at me like she's a child wanting to hear her favorite bedtime story.

"Well," I begin before taking a sip of water, "he had just gotten back from his internship in Italy, and I was in the mood for mint chocolate chip. We ran into each other in the freezer aisle, and *boom*, he asked me out, and I said yes."

The oohs and aahs I'm getting from the room make it sound like I just told the greatest love story ever written. I might prefer mystery novels to romance, but even I know that our love story isn't one they make movies about. Or pornos. Or anything that's not rated PG.

What I don't tell the forty people here, who are all friends of my mom's and Guiliana, is that the only reason I said yes to Luciano was because it was days removed from Bryce breaking his last promise to me. I figured one date couldn't be a bad thing. It would be a good way for me to start putting myself out there, and Luciano was someone I knew and trusted. Heck, when I was in high school and didn't have a date for the prom because Bryce couldn't make it back, Luciano agreed to take me. That night was nothing to write home about, so I figured a date with him wouldn't blow me away but it would be good enough to make me feel like I was moving on.

I was right. We had a pleasant time and had a lovely meal. We talked about our families, his time in Italy, and what my plans were now that school was done. It was bland and boring and exactly what I hoped for.

It was only supposed to be one date. Next thing, I knew it was seven months later and he was proposing at our surprise engagement party.

"I heard there was a beautiful bride who could use some help taking these gifts to the car?"

Everyone's head turns toward the door of the coffee shop, where Luciano stands holding a bouquet of red roses.

"Luciano!" Guiliana squeals, walking to greet her son. "This is for ladies only!"

He leans down and presses a kiss to his mother's cheek. "I know, but I thought my future wife could use some help after you lovely women spoiled her. Plus, I heard there was cake."

This makes everyone laugh. I even hear a few *awwws* and someone whispers, "What a lucky girl Lucy is."

"Well, this works perfectly," Guiliana says, grabbing my

mom as they make their way toward us at the front of the coffee shop. "Anne Marie and I had this game prepared for the wedding, but it will be more fun here with a more intimate crowd."

I do everything I can to hold in my sigh. "I said no games, Mom."

"Oh, you can play one," she whispers as she pulls me from my seat and rearranges it so I'm now more front and center. Guiliana does the same to Luciano, and then, somehow, they both produce notebooks and pens for us. Do they carry those around in their purses?

"Now, Guiliana and I are going to ask the engaged couple a few questions. They are going to write down their answers, and we will see for sure how perfect you are for each other!"

I can feel the color drain from my face as I frantically look for Megan or Brenna, begging them with my eyes for another cough drop, but neither of them seems to be here any longer.

"I'll start with the first question," Mom says, her voice oozing with pride. "What is Lucy's favorite color?"

I don't start writing down my answer right away, trying to look out of the corner of my eye to see what he's writing, though I can't make anything of it. Shit, I honestly don't know if my fiancé knows my favorite color, which is navy-blue.

"On the count of three, turn your notebooks around. One . . . two . . . three!"

We do as they say as a group of my mom and Guiliana's friends laugh. Clearly, the answers are not the same.

"What did you put?" I ask.

He shrugs, turning to show me his notebook. "I went with pink. It felt safe since those were the wedding colors."

"Colors my mother picked," I remind him. "It's okay. It was a safe guess."

"Next question!" Guiliana yells. "What is Luciano's favorite movie?"

Shit. I know this one. I remember because it's one of my favorites, and it was one of the first ones we watched together. I mean, a historically accurate tail of a female mathematician? Sign me up.

Until we both turn around our notebooks. Mine says *Hidden Figures.* His says *The Greatest Showman."*

"What?" I ask, really thinking I nailed it. "I remember you saying the night we watched it together you couldn't believe I liked it too."

A blush creeps over his face. "I just said that because I wanted to impress you."

"Oh," I say, a little taken aback. "Okay, let's try again."

We are asked five more questions, and five more times, we get our answers wrong. Even I can't do the math of how long it would take until one of us gets an answer correct. I really thought we were going to find out, but Brenna saved the day with an announcement that everyone needed to leave because coffee shop had to close due to an emergency.

I could have kissed her.

"It's okay, Lucia. We have the rest of our lives to learn this stuff about each other," he says before leaning down and giving my forehead a kiss. This, again, drives the women in the room crazy. All it does is remind me of how little chemistry there is between him and I.

That had never bothered me before. I chalked it up to the fact that Luciano and I have a love based on friendship and respect.

Only, I want more. I want the spark. I want it all.

Who knows when it will happen or who it will be with, but I deserve a once-in-a-lifetime love. Everyone does.

I watch Luciano walk away, heading to take the first round

of presents to the car. He's a good man, and he deserves that kind of love too. That person would know what his favorite movie is and look at him like he hung the moon.

Like how my parents still look at each other after thirty years of marriage or how Megan and her husband look at each other when they don't think anyone is watching.

Like how Bryce is looking at me right now.

Wait, what?

I shake my head, wondering if I'm seeing what I think I am.

Outside the glass window of the coffee shop, is Bryce. When I first got a glance of him, he was looking at me like I was the most beautiful woman in the world.

Now? Now, all I see on his face is conflict and hurt.

There is only one other time he's looked at me like that, and it was the day before the draft.

I can't stop looking at him. I want to run outside, bring him into my arms, and tell him everything is going to be okay. I want to scream at him because he did this before whispering that I've never stopped loving him and that I'm about to call off my wedding.

Oh my God, I'm going to call off my wedding.

I look back at Luciano and then back at Bryce, and for the first time in months, I don't feel like I'm going to cough.

DECEMBER, SENIOR YEAR, HIGH SCHOOL

I SHOULD BE on cloud nine right now.

We won the state championship game last Saturday. I played the best game of my life. Cole and the rest of the offensive line were on another level. Our defense was unstoppable.

The best part? Seeing Lucy run toward me wearing my jacket, her eyes shining with pride as our fans stormed the field. The kiss I gave her after she jumped into my arms was icing on the cake.

I'll never forget that moment for as long as I live.

And I have a feeling I'll never forget this night either.

"Bryce?" Lucy says as she walks out of Tripoli's. "What are you doing here?"

It's a fair question. It's Friday night and she had to work all night. In fact, between her work schedule and my unexpectedly busy week, we haven't gotten to see each other at all.

I missed her, but after tonight, missing her is going to be something I better get used to.

I hold open my arms, and she immediately comes into them, wrapping herself around me.

"You smell like pizza," I joke, placing a kiss on the top of her head.

"Comes with the territory."

I take her hand and guide her to my truck. "Do you mind if we go for a ride?"

She shakes her head. "No. My parents are with the Tripolis. They won't be home for another few hours."

I let out a sigh of relief as I get into my truck and rev the engine. As soon as it's in drive, I reach for her hand, needing to feel her touch.

How am I going to tell her my news, especially after I promised her that once football was over, things would be different? That I would be able to focus more on her, on us.

I really do want to be her boyfriend and walk her to class so I can steal kisses in the halls. I want to treat her the way she deserves because Lucy Valenti is the best girl in the world. She deserves everything.

Now I have to break that promise, and it's killing me even thinking about it.

"Do you mind if I turn on the radio?" she asks, already reaching for the dial.

I shake my head. "Nope. Just please no Taylor Swift."

"Hey now." She laughs. "Don't you dare speak ill of Taylor."

"I would never." I really just love to tease her about her crappy taste in music. Though, I must admit, the song that's now playing is catchy. And fitting.

It's a song about goodbyes. About tears. About heartache and heartbreak.

It's like the world is fucking with me as we make our way to the lake.

"What are we doing here?" she says as I put the truck in park.

I don't say anything as I round the truck to help her out of her seat. I take her hand in mine and walk her back to the tailgate, which is already set up with blankets.

"For some reason, when life gets tough, I always end up here," I say, helping her onto the tailgate before I join her and tug her back to my front. "Then, one day, I went missing. Neither my sister nor Cole could find me. Yet, you knew I was here."

"I took a guess," she says, snuggling closer to me. "All I could think about was that stupid conversation we had on the differences between a lake and a pond."

I laugh. "Well, no matter what, you found me, and I like to think it's because we have a connection. One that not many people have."

I know this probably sounds cheesy, and if the guys on the team heard me right now, they'd give me hell for weeks, but it's Lucy. I can always tell her the truth, no matter what.

"I think so too," she says, laying her head back on my shoulder. "But why are we here? I feel like you have something you want to say, and it's killing me not to know what it is."

How is one person able to see through me like that? It doesn't make sense.

Then again, Lucy and I don't make sense. I'm the jock whose whole life is going to be determined by how far I can throw a football. She's a smart-as-hell girl who could run the world one day if she wanted.

That's just one of the reasons I'm in love with her.

It's also why I have to break both of our hearts tonight.

"The guidance counselor called me into her office on Monday, and to my surprise, Coach Roberts and Coach Carvill were in there waiting for me."

"From Clemson? Your recruiting coach?"

I nod. "One in the same. Apparently, if I take an online

course this month, I'll have enough credits to graduate high school early."

She gives me a confused look, and I don't blame her because it took me awhile to wrap my head around this. "What does that mean?"

"It means that if I graduate high school early, I can enroll at Clemson for spring semester, which is what the coaches want me to do. They think it will help me start as a freshman if I'm there for spring practice."

I let the silence settle over us as I wait for some kind of reaction from Lucy. It's better than when I talked about this with Mom. She cried for two days before realizing what this could do for my football career. That, even though it's sudden, it's the best decision for my future.

"When would you leave?"

I let out a sigh. "The day after Christmas."

"That's in two weeks."

"Yeah," I say as we fall silent again. I know I need to be a man and bring up the topic of she and I, but how do I do it? I don't want to do it. If I had my way, I'd be taking her with me. I can barely navigate the waters of high school and Laurel Heights before it becomes too much for me to process. I need her with me, even though I know I can't have her.

"I'm guessing our date tomorrow night is off?"

"I'm so sorry." The words barely scratch the surface of their meaning. "I wanted this so bad. I wanted us. I just . . . wonder how it will work with me being in South Carolina and you being here."

She sits up and pulls out of my hold and turns around to face me. I wish she would have stayed where she was. Then I wouldn't have to look at her as she fights back tears.

"It wouldn't," she says, reaching for my hands, which I willingly give her. "Maybe if we had been together longer, maybe we could make it work. But long distance is hard. And especially when you're going to college and starting football right away. You'll be busy with football and classes and just being in college. You don't need me here holding you back."

"Holding me back?" I shake my head in denial. "Lucy, you will never hold me back. From the moment I met you when I thought you were a dream, you have made me a better person. This might be the end of us now, but it's not the end forever."

"What's that supposed to mean?"

I shrug, bringing her back into my arms. "I don't know. All I know is that our story isn't done yet. It can't be. There are too many things we still have to do."

"You want things for us?" she asks.

"Hell yes. For one, I want to take you to prom."

"Prom is in April. You'll still be in classes."

Shit, I didn't think of that. "Nope. I'll make it home. I promise. Plus, there's more. Like, I want to meet your parents. I want Uncle Nick to give me the sit down about being respectful while dating his niece."

This makes her smile. "Those all sound great, Bryce, but—"

"No buts," I say before giving her a quick kiss. "I know we can't do long distance, but I also know that I'm not ready to say goodbye to you. I know that sounds selfish, but it's the truth."

She looks up at me, tears filling in her eyes. "I'm not either."

Who knew three words, well, *those* three words could fill me with such hope for the future?

"Listen," I say, turning her so I'm looking directly into the brown eyes I'm going to miss every day I'm away from her. "You're my Lulu, and I know that this might seem insane, but I love you. The thought of leaving you kills me. When I was asked to come to Clemson early, you were the first one I thought of because I didn't want to hurt you."

"You're doing what you have to do, and I'm proud of you for doing this."

She settles back into my arms, and we sit in silence for who knows how long. I know I still have two weeks before I go, but it's going to be so busy that I doubt I'll have time to come up for air. This is it. This is our last night, and I'm determined to take every second of it I can.

"I'm going to miss you," I say before placing a kiss on top of her head. "I'm going to miss you so fucking much."

"I'm going to miss you too," she admits. "But you know you can still call me. We might not be together, but that doesn't mean I'm not your friend. I'll always be there for you, Bryce."

I take her face in my hands and crash my mouth to hers. If I don't, I will start crying. That is how much I hate this, and the only thing that will make me hate it less is her lips against mine.

I'm not sure why I never thought to do this before, but I memorize her taste. The feel of her lips. The way her tongue feels as it dances with mine. I memorize a lifetime of moments in a handful of minutes.

God I'm going to miss her.

I'm going to miss her. So damn much.

"I'll be here. Always," she says after breaking the kiss. "There's no one else. Only you. I love you, Bryce. Now, go be amazing."

THERE ARE things I always miss about Laurel Heights, and one of them is Heights Park. The running trail here is perfect. Just enough shade to block the sun. It's paved so I can let my mind go and not worry about things like twisting an ankle on debris.

I have enough to worry about.

Granted, it's better than it was a few weeks ago when I arrived back in town, and it's a hell of a lot better than it was during the months leading up to my return.

I'm still not back where I want to be, but I know that's going to take time.

Dean has me on weekly calls with a sports therapist, and though I was against it at the beginning, I will admit that some things he's said have made sense.

Today's discussion was about pressure. I'm a professional quarterback. My job is literally done in one of the most pressure-packed situations there can be. Then he talked to me about a different kind of pressure—the kind I face off the field.

In the past, it was about trying to win a state title for an entire town and making my college decision. Today's pressure is more about the expectation to live up to being the most talked about rookie in pro football history and not letting down my teammates, my fans, or my sponsors.

Admittedly, I've never been good at that kind of pressure because I always wanted to please everyone. Malcom tells me that likely stems from wanting my father's approval, which is simultaneously something I need to work through as well as never want to talk about, ever. Nevertheless, the pressure of pleasing everyone became overwhelming, and somewhere along the line, I decided that Lucy was the only one who could help me navigate it. With one little pro-con list, she became my fixer. My go-to when anything in my life felt out of balance.

Then I found out she was engaged, and it was as if someone snapped the supports to my safety net and I was in a freefall. Of course, I was going to crash and burn because I hadn't ever learned to handle that stress myself.

Malcolm asked me today what I did when I felt overwhelmed, and I didn't have an answer for him because I couldn't say, "I call Lucy." He asked if I had hobbies to take my mind off the game. When I said no, he asked if I went to the movies or even took a drive out of the city to decompress.

The answer to all of it was no. I'm a football player who has only ever focused on football. I don't have a life outside of the game.

That was when he suggested I take up running because the physical exertion would help clear my mind so I could focus on the important things. So, here I am, letting the trail take me wherever it may and trying not to stare at the woman in front of me.

That part wasn't suggested by him, but if he were here, he'd understand why I can't take my eyes off her. She's wearing shorts that are glued to her ass. Her petite frame has curves in all the right places, and the brown hair on top of her head gives me all sorts of ideas.

If I hadn't known better, I would have thought it was Lucy. That's probably my mind playing tricks on me. I might not be as familiar with her ass as I'd like to be, but I know my girl, and Lucy hates running. Or walking. Or really any form of physical activity.

I know those things about her, but the longer I look at her like a creeper, the more convinced I become that it's Lulu. There is no one else in this town whose body makes me react like mine is right now.

"Lucy?" I call out as I lengthen my strides, hoping to meet hers. It doesn't take me long to get within a step of her, but she must still not hear me.

"Lucy!" I yell a little louder, putting my hand on her shoulder.

That apparently is the wrong move because, before I know it, her arms are flailing, she's yelling "Danger!" at the top of her lungs as she tries to locate something to subdue me with.

"Lucy! It's me!" I say, grabbing her shoulders. "I'm sorry. I didn't mean to scare you."

"Well, you did!" she yells, shoving away my touch before taking out her earbuds. "You can't just come up on someone in a park and touch them, Bryce."

"I'm sorry, I wasn't thinking. I just saw you, and . . . well, I was surprised to see you."

"What do you mean you were surprised to see me?" she says as she tries to catch her breath. "It's Laurel Heights. Based on the population of the town, and the activities that you and I both like to do, the probability stands high that we are going to run into each other at least four times a week, maybe more depending on the weekly circumstances and event schedule."

"Are you mad at me? I mean, I know I'm probably not your favorite person right now, but I thought after our talk in the locker room last week that we were getting to a better space."

"No, I'm not mad at you—actually, I am. You scared me, and I was just getting into my run."

I send her a questioning look. "You hate running. In fact, I was surprised to see you walking."

"I've changed," she says, starting to speed up. "A lot has changed, Bryce. Like now I'm a runner. See, I'm running."

She takes off, and it takes all I have not to start laughing on the spot. Her version of "running" is more of a fast walk, almost hobble, with a strange arm swing. I don't really know how to describe it, but I'm pretty sure if her gym teacher/football coach uncle saw this, he'd disown her on the spot.

The faster she goes, the more awkward she looks. Somehow her legs are coming out from the sides instead of going back and forth, and her arms have taken on more of a windmill motion.

It's adorable.

Fuck, I still have it bad. I probably always will.

I follow her, picking up my pace to catch up with her. Though, that doesn't take long considering her strides have her running almost in circles. I'm nearly next to her when she turns her head to look at me, which is a horrible decision on her part. It's like her brain doesn't tell her feet to stop, and before she knows it, she's about to tumble to the ground. I quickly reach for her, breaking her fall.

"A runner, huh?" I ask, a hint of teasing in my voice as I help her up.

"Fine, I don't run," she says, smoothing out her shorts. "I do walk, though. Slowly. Sometimes. Usually alone. What are you doing here?"

"It's a public park, is it not?" I ask, doing my best not to stare at the sweat dripping down her face. "I needed a run, and I hate running on the treadmill. Figured I could get in a few miles and enjoy the weather before the temperatures drop."

"That's understandable I guess," she says. "The days of running outside are numbered where you will be able to run outside ... especially ... without..."

I crack a smile because I just realize that Lucy is staring at my chest.

My naked, covered-in-sweat-from-this-abnormally-hot-day chest.

Interesting.

"Without what, Lulu?"

"Without your ..."

"Come on now, use your words."

She shakes her head. "Without your shirt. See. Shirt. Easy word."

I smile, happy to know that I still have an effect on her because she sure as hell still has an effect on me.

How can she not? She's perfect. From her big brown eyes that always pull me in, to the curve of her hips, to her smile that makes me feel like I'm worthy of whatever she's willing to give, she's absolutely perfect.

"Do you have time to sit and talk, or do you have more walking to do?"

She looks toward the end of the trail, then to her watch, and then back to me. "I can stay for a few minutes. I have ... I have somewhere I need to be tonight."

We walk a few more steps until we find a bench.

"Hot date?"

I might say the words with nonchalance, but they taste like poison on my tongue. Still, I give myself a point for effort just because I am being nice and asking about Pizza Boy.

Malcolm will be so proud.

"No—I mean, yes."

"Having a hard time putting words together today? Do you need me to put on a shirt so you can concentrate?"

She playfully smacks my shoulder. "No. And I wasn't staring at your chest."

"Sure, you weren't."

"Whatever. For your information, I am meeting Luciano tonight."

Okay. This is it. This is when I show that I'm supportive. That I'm a friend and not a jealous ex who wants to ring Pizza Boy's neck for being able to touch and kiss and hold the only woman who has ever meant anything to me.

"That's nice. Going over wedding stuff? When is the big day, by the way?"

Instead of answering, Lucy starts coughing.

Like, I-think-she-might-break-a-lung coughing.

"Are you okay?" I ask, patting her back, wishing I had some water to give her. "Why are you coughing so much recently? You did this the other day too. What's wrong? Are you sick? Do you need a doctor?"

I'm mentally going through the doctors in Laurel Heights I can call when I feel her hand on top of my palm. Her coughing is dying down, but she still looks worn out, as if that coughing fit just sucked the energy right out of her.

"I don't need a doctor," she says, taking one last breath in and out. "I just get these coughing fits from time to time. It's nothing to worry about. I haven't had one in a while, and I didn't bring any cough drops with me."

Cough drops...

Those are what she was buying that day I ran into her at the convenience store. At least, I think that was what she dropped on the floor. I was too busy staring at her to really take notice of anything else.

"If you're not okay, you can tell me. I know things have been weird between us, and I say this as a friend, you kind of look like you haven't slept in a week."

"That's a really nice way of telling me I look like shit."

I scramble to backpedal, but then she smiles. God, I've missed her smiles.

"I didn't mean it like that, but as someone who has been through the ringer lately, I kind of know what it looks like when something is weighing heavy on you. And you, Lulu, look like you're carrying the weight of the world on your shoulders."

She lets out a sigh before turning to me. Her eyes are . . . sad. Torn. Heavy.

"Talk to me, Lulu. I might have messed things up with us more times than I can count, but that doesn't erase our history. We can talk to each other about anything. So, talk to me. What can I do to help?"

She lets out a humorless laugh. "Isn't this backward? Aren't you the one who's supposed to be coming to me for advice?"

"Consider this my first repayment on years of old debt."

"You're lucky I didn't charge interest."

"I've always been lucky when it comes to you," I say, reaching for her hand. "Now, talk to me, and if you tell me nothing is wrong, I'll call bullshit. In case no one has told you, I'm kind of the king of bullshit and am in recovery."

I almost pull my hand back, thinking it was too much, but she hasn't moved yet, so I'm not going to disturb the waters.

"How do you know when you're happy?"

I look at her, utterly unable to answer that question.

"What?"

"How do you know if you're happy? Like, what if you think you are but you aren't but you really have never been happy so you aren't sure what it actually should be like?" Her voice cracks at the end, and it almost destroys me.

I still don't have a clue how to answer her, but for years,

this woman did all she could to take the pressure off me, so I have to try. It's my turn to give back.

"I think you're happy when the littlest stuff doesn't get you down. When you sit down at the end of the day, and you can smile. That when you look at everything and everyone you have around you, you realize you have everything you need and are wholly content."

She pulls her bottom lip between her teeth and watches a squirrel run across the running track.

"Do you remember the other day when you said that if I was happy, then you were happy for me?" she asks.

I nod. How could I ever forget that day?

"I don't know if I am."

This takes me by surprise. God, there are so many things I could ask her, but I have a feeling it will be best if I just play it simple.

"You aren't?"

She shakes her head. "I don't think so."

"Maybe a pro-con list will help."

She laughs and rewards me with her smile. "A pro-con list is what got me in this situation in the first place."

"Maybe it's time for another?"

She looks at me, then down at our adjoined hands, then back to me again. "Yeah, maybe it is."

PRO: Parents love him.

Con: You don't love him and you know it's the easy way out.

Pro: You can get pizza whenever you want.

Con: You haven't had sex with him.

Pro: He puts you first.

Con: He's not Bryce.

I throw my notebook into the air and scream into my pillow. This is the fourth time I've tried to come up with a new pro-con list, and when one of the higher pros is pizza, then something isn't adding up.

It's clear. My heart, my lists, and my lungs have been telling me the same thing for weeks—I need to call off the wedding.

How do you tell someone who you do love as a friend but not a lover that you can't marry them? Am I going to crush him? Does he know I've been having doubts? I honestly have no idea which way this is going to go. Some people wear their hearts on their sleeve. Luciano wears his under four layers of wool sweaters.

All I know is that I can't go another day feeling like this any more than I can leave him to stand outside my front door any longer.

"You can do this. This is the right decision. This will be the best for both of you in the end. Be confident. Be strong."

I take a few deep breaths to try to center myself, grab the doorknob, and twist it before I chicken out.

"*Amore*," he says as I open the door. "How are you tonight?" He leans down and kisses me on the forehead. This is normal, any day of the week Luciano. Me, on the other hand? My palms are sweating, my heart is racing, and I kind of want to vomit.

"I'm fine." My voice comes out about three octaves above what it normally is. So much for being strong and confident. "Can we talk for a minute?"

"Of course." If Luciano is thrown by why my voice is switching between octaves or why I'm visibly jittery, he doesn't show it. Instead, he takes a seat on my couch like this is just a normal night.

It's now or never.

I can do this.

I'll never have to buy cough drops again.

"Thanks for coming over tonight," I say, taking a seat next to him as I wipe my sweaty hands on my jeans.

"When your future wife says come over, you come over. Look at us, just a few weeks away, and I already have the concept of happy wife, happy life down."

God, I wish I could read this man. He doesn't seem curious or stumped about why he's here. The lame joke he just made is the same one he'd make any other day of the week. He seems so normal when I'm so twisted in knots.

"Actually, that's what I wanted to talk to you about."

That's good, Lucy. Rip the Band-Aid off.

"The wedding?"

"Yeah, the wedding. I don't really know how to say this,

but . . . okay, here it goes. I love you, Luciano. However, I . . . I'm not *in* love with you—not like that. So, I don't think we should get married."

Silence falls over the room, and I actually have to think back over what I said to make sure I spoke aloud and not just in my own tangled mess of a mind.

He hasn't blinked.

He hasn't taken a breath.

He's frozen. Oh God, is he devastated? Paralyzed from shock? I'm going to need him to say something soon because I have no idea what to do right now.

"Luciano, I'm so sorry," I say as I default to panic mode. "I know this probably seems sudden, and I know how much this is going to screw up, but I—"

His thunderous laughter stops my words.

I didn't even know he could laugh like that. Normally, his laughter is pleasant and almost choreographed. This one? It's like he just heard the world's funniest joke for the first time.

"Are you okay?"

It takes him a second to catch his breath, and he has to wipe tears away from his eyes before he responds.

"Do you know how long I've wanted to call this off but couldn't figure out how to do it? And then, here you are, just *BOOM*! Oh my God, this is such a relief."

Wait, what?

I'm so confused.

"Okay, back it up," I say, still trying to figure out what the hell is going on. "Not that I'm trying to win the award for who called the wedding off, but . . . I had no idea you felt that way."

"Well, then I'm a better actor than I thought I was," he says. "Why do you think I've never kissed you or tried to have sex with you? I was dreading our wedding night, but now we don't need to worry about it! We're not going to get married!"

He sounds almost giddy about that, and I feel like I should be offended . . . or offended that I'm not offended?

"Dreading? Am I that revolting?" I mean, I'm not mad he's happy, but I'm starting to feel a little self-conscious over here.

"No, no!" he says, inching closer to me and taking my hand. The last time he touched my hand was a few weeks ago at the restaurant, which I thought was monumental. This time feels more natural and sentimental then that one could have ever hoped to be. "You are beautiful. I have always thought that about you. Quarterback boy wasn't wrong to be jealous of me back in the day."

"Then why were you dreading the wedding night?"

"Because—" His voice cracks for the first time since we began this conversation and he has to clear his throat. "Because I'm in love with someone else."

My eyes grow wide. Damn, I thought it was going to be big, but I wasn't expecting that. "Who? I mean, not that it's any of my business. I'm just . . . I calculated fifty different ways this conversation was going to go, and I did not see it happening like this."

He chuckles and stands to head into my kitchen. "Would you like some wine, Lucia? I feel like we could both use a glass."

"Oh God, yes please," I say, hoping he brings back the whole bottle I can't help but notice when he comes back into the room, he seems more relaxed. More natural. It's like the stick he's had up his butt for months has been removed.

"So, let's recap," I suggest as I accept one of the two glasses and he sets the bottle on the coffee table. "I don't want to get married. Neither do you. Neither of us love each other in that way, and you are in love with someone else."

He smiles before he takes a sip of his wine. "Something like that."

"Okay, I'm going to need the whole story because I feel like your story is so much better than mine."

He takes another sip of his wine and puts his glass down. "Her name is Celine. I met her during my internship in Italy."

"Wow. Okay. How long after you got there did you meet her?"

He nods. "We met on the first day and were inseparable for the entire year. I fell in love with her from the start. She's beautiful and smart and an amazing cook and . . ."

"And what? You can't leave me on a cliffhanger!"

"And she's French."

My jaw drops. Luciano's parents might have been born in America, but just like their ancestors, they view anyone from France as an enemy.

It has something to do with the wine.

"So, what happened? Did you two break up in Italy?"

He shrugs. "I wanted to bring her back with me. She had never been to America and was so excited. When I told my parents, they flipped out. I believe my father's words were, 'You can leave Frenchie where you found her or you can kiss the expansion location goodbye.'"

"Are you kidding me? That expansion was your idea. You were transforming the menu! And they threatened to cut you out of it because they didn't like a girl based on an age-old stereotype?"

"I know. It sounds ridiculous, which I told them. In no way did I think they were serious. So, I came back from Italy and brought Celine with me. Only they were serious, and Dad signed over the franchise rights to some corporate schmuck from Chicago. I was devastated. I've worked for years on that. That was . . . Celine and I had dreams. We were going to take Tripoli's and make it ours."

"Oh my gosh, Luciano, I'm so sorry. I can't believe your parents would do that."

"Neither could I. It was infuriating. I had my bags packed and was ready to tell them goodbye for the last time, but then Celine left. She wrote me a note, saying how much she loved me but that she wouldn't be the reason my dreams couldn't come true. She went back to France so I could get the franchise back."

Holy shit. I've never met this woman, but I love her already. I'm also now very invested in this story.

"So, why did you ask me out if you were still in love with Celine?"

He laughs. "Would you believe it was because you were there?"

Now it's my turn to laugh. "Yes, because that's actually why I said yes."

"When Celine left, I didn't want to tell them it was so I could get the restaurants back. They would have thought it was some sort of grand plan, which it would have been. I figured that, to prove we were truly broken up, I needed to start dating. What better person than the girl they've wanted me to be with since birth?"

"I get it. I needed to get over Bryce. We . . . well, it had been a whirlwind few days with us that did not end well. When you asked me, it felt like the universe telling me that I made the right decision to move on from him, so I said yes. I must admit, going out with you got my mom off my back about why I didn't date. When she found out it was you, I think I made her year."

We just stare at each other for a second, and for the first time in a year and a half, I don't feel awkward or that I have to force something that's not there.

I definitely don't feel like I'm going to cough.

"I didn't mean for all of this to happen," he says. "I thought that, if I asked you out a few times, it would get them off my back."

"And I thought if I went out with you, then I'd slowly start moving on with my life. Then you proposed, and I didn't know what to do. So, I said yes."

"I really need to apologize for that," he says, shaking his head like he can't believe what's going on. "I never meant to propose to you. Dating was one thing. But marriage? It was never supposed to go that far. Then one day, I came home and my parents were waiting for me, ring in hand. They told me that they reserved the restaurant that night and invited all of our family and friends so everyone could be there when I proposed to you."

This is news to me. "They did what?"

"Yes. That is the true story of our engagement. News flash: my parents are nuts," he says, finishing off his wine. "I really think they were worried I wasn't serious about you. It was like we were both playing this epic game of chicken."

I can't wait to tell Brenna and Megan everything.

"So, let's add all of this up," I say, needing to get my analytical mind around all of this craziness. "You not loving me and being in love with Celine, plus me not loving you and only dating you in a futile attempt to get over Bryce, plus our crazy parents putting unwanted pressure on us equals an engagement neither of us wanted and a marriage we were both dreading?"

"Ding, ding. We have a winner."

I can't help but laugh, and soon Luciano joins me. I mean, what else can we do? This has to be, by far, the most messed-up situation in the world.

Luciano pours us each another glass as our laughter dies down. "What do we do now?"

"We start canceling stuff?" I ask.

"I'll cancel the food."

I nod. "I'll take care of the cake and the flowers. What about the honeymoon?"

"You take it," he says. "The next time I go away, it will be to bring back the woman I am supposed to marry."

This makes me smile. "I can't wait to meet her."

He squeezes my hand. "And I hope that football boy treats you the way you deserve."

This takes me by surprise. "Who says I'm going to be with Bryce?"

"Oh, Lucia. It was only a matter of time before he came back for you. I see the way he looks at you. That man is insanely in love with you, and you might not want to admit it, but your feelings for him have not gone away."

I can't make eye contact with him because if I do I have to admit he's right. Love has never been a problem for me and Bryce.

It's everything else.

"We do have one small problem," Luciano says.

I raise an eyebrow. "Besides figuring out how to get deposits refunded?"

"Worse. We have to tell our parents."

CHAPTER 20
BRYCE

"BRYCE? IS THAT YOU?"

The sound of Lucy's voice makes me jump a little from the seat on the back of my tailgate. So much so that I almost drop the iPad I'm holding.

"Lucy? What are you doing here?"

I came to Lake Laurel to get some peace and quiet—I love my mother but she will talk my ear off if I let her—and I had homework to do for Malcolm.

I slide over to make space for her, and like she's been doing it every day for her entire life, she settles in next to me. "When I need to get away from things or if I'm having a bad day, I come out here. What about you? What brings you out here?"

I put the iPad down and angle myself so I can look at her. "My therapist gave me a quiz to take. I thought maybe if I came out here, it would help me focus a bit instead of being at my mom's."

"Oh," she says, her eyes going wide. "I don't want to interrupt. I'll let you go then."

She begins to get off my truck, but I quickly put a hand on her forearm. "No. Don't go. Stay."

"Are you sure?"

"Of course, I am." I grab a blanket from the pile I have sitting behind me, glad I thought to bring them, and offer it to her.

"Thanks," she says, taking the blanket from me and wrapping it around her shoulders. "So, what is this quiz on. I hope it's not math because I'm going to guess your trigonometry skills have not improved in seven years."

"I didn't know you took up comedy in your spare time." I give her shoulder a little shove with mine, loving the easiness of this conversation. "No, it's about different situations that could cause stress. I'm supposed choose how I would react. We're working on . . . well, we're just working on stuff."

The smile she gives me resembles one she gave after the state title game. It was a smile of pride.

"I'm glad you're talking to someone. I really hope it helps you."

"Thanks," I say as I start rocking back and forth, all of a sudden uncomfortable having this conversation be all about me and my problems. "What part of wanting to get away from life brought you out here?"

She looks away for a few seconds, and it gives me a chance to really look at her. Have I ever really studied her profile and the beautiful lines of her face? Her hair is up on top of her head, which gives me a perfect view of her long neck. If this were seven years ago, my mouth would be on it in a heartbeat.

When she turns back to look at me, the look of pride she had just a minute ago is gone. She doesn't look tired or stressed like she did the other day. She also doesn't look sad like she did when I watched her through the window at her wedding shower. No, right now she looks like everything is finally okay, almost peaceful even.

"Luciano and I called off the wedding."

I'm doing my best not to crack a smile, but it is damn hard.

Is it appropriate to stand and start cheering? I wonder if she'd be mad if I did a backflip. I've never tried, but it doesn't look that hard. Or maybe I can hire the high school marching band to do an impromptu parade tomorrow? That's probably too big.

"You can wipe the smile off your face," she says.

"What smile?" I say, giving up and letting it stretch wide.

"That one," she says around her laughter. "How do you know that I'm not crying on the inside?"

"Because I know you, Lulu," I say, leaning back on my hands with my legs stretched over the tailgate. "If you were really upset, you'd be at home, eating your weight in mint chocolate chip ice cream and watching those movies I hate."

"I did that *once*," she says. "And don't you dare speak ill of *Twilight*."

"She should have ended up with the wolf guy."

This makes her laugh. "I'm not sad. I meant what I said the other day, I wasn't happy, and the closer the wedding got, the worse the anxiety got. He wasn't what I wanted."

"Yeah? And what is?"

I know the question is a risky one, but I have to know because every muscle in my body is aching to touch her. I know I'm supposed to be working on myself and learning to live my life without her, but if she opens that door, there is no way I won't step through it.

"I want to say you . . ."

"I feel there is a *but* coming."

She nods, reaching for my hand, which I gladly give her. "I've never stopped loving you. As much as I've tried, as much as I thought that moving on would be the way to somehow erase my feelings for you, I never stopped."

"Neither did I. I know I fucked up, broke promises, and let you down more than I deserve to be forgiven for, but you have to know that everything I did, every decision I made, you were always on my mind."

"There's a difference between being on your mind and being in your life, Bryce. For years, I lived on empty promises and pipe dreams. I'm not going to deny that I love you, and I believe when you say that you love me, but . . . there is a reason there was never an us. If you tell me, right now, that it's our time, and something ends up becoming more important than us, I won't survive. Not again."

"It is our time," I say too quickly.

She grabs my hand, putting it between both of hers. "I know you think it is, but stop and think. How would this work? And not just right now but also in the long-run. How do you have someone in your life during the season? How do you have someone as a part of your daily life?"

I do as she asks, and really think about it. The problem is that, every time I pictured us together, it was effortless. We were just together and happy and nothing else mattered. Logistics never came into consideration. I just wanted to love her and for her to love me back. For us to be together. To be the team I always thought of us as.

"I know that's not a question you can answer quickly, and you do too," she says, taking a breath. "So, I want you to think about it until I get back in two weeks."

"What? You're leaving?" I say, probably a little too loudly.

"Luciano is friends with a chef at a resort in St. Thomas. It is where we were going to honeymoon, and since that isn't happening anymore, he made a call and got me a room there instead. I had some extra money laying around now that I don't have to pay for flowers or caterers, so I booked myself a ticket. I need to get out of town and think some things through. I want you to do the same."

"But, Lu—"

"No," she says, pressing a finger to my lips. "We love each other. That's not the hard part. That has *never* been our struggle. What we need to figure out is what we want, and you need to figure out where and how I fit into your life."

I let her words settle in. I believe her when she says that if I screw up again, that's it. I'll have squandered my final chance with her, which is the absolute last thing I want to do.

I refuse to do that, so I'll take the time she's telling me to take, and really think about how this would work.

"You know, sometimes I hate how smart you are," I say, pulling her a little closer.

"You're lucky I didn't give you a breakdown of the statistics of long-distance relationships."

"I love it when you get all math geek on me."

"I'll remember that for when I get back from my non-honeymoon at Indigo Royal Resort."

"Or I could go with you and you can give me all the statistics you want? I'm a very good learner, and I haven't had someone give me a breakdown of probabilities and statistics in a very long time. I think it would be good for me to go so you can teach me all of that while you're wearing a bikini."

She smacks my chest playfully before cuddling against me. "As much as I would love to do that, you know we need to do this by ourselves."

"I hate it when you're right," I say. "Though, I would like you to send me daily updates. If pictures are included, I won't be upset, but I require one math fact from you a day."

"Deal."

We fall into a comfortable silence as the water gently ripples in front of us. Soon, her head falls on my shoulder, and instead of moving it, she moves in closer to me.

This. This is what I want. I want her next to me, in my life, and if she wants me to figure out how it's going to happen, then damn it I'll do it.

"So, what do you plan to do on this non-honeymoon?"

She shrugs, but her head doesn't move from my shoulder. "What any girl on the cusp of a breakup and possibly getting back together with her high-school sweetheart would do. Drink a copious number of daiquiris and make pro-con lists about the future."

"That's my girl," I say, kissing her temple. "Nothing gets me going quite like a pro-con list."

"Don't mock the lists."

"I would never."

She turns to face me. "Two weeks. We take that time to figure this out because I might not be marrying Luciano, but I'm not going to settle. I don't care how in love with you I am, I'm not going to be—"

I don't know what she was about to say, but I refuse to hear it.

This is the present, and in the present, I'm going to kiss this girl and make sure she knows how crazy I am about her. That I'm going to move mountains to make sure this works.

I'm definitely not going to let her go away for two weeks without the taste of me on her lips.

Our mouths connect, and for the first time in God knows how long, I feel like I'm home. Her lips are soft and warm and fall into a perfect rhythm with mine.

I feel like I'm more alive than I have ever been. That's what she does to me. Always has, always will.

I also know this. I don't care what I need to do or what needs to happen: Lucy is going to be in my life.

I know what life is like without her, and it almost killed me. If I let this chance go without doing everything I could to be with her, then I deserve to be miserable.

No more waiting. No more excuses. It's our time.

CHAPTER 21
LUCY

"LUCIA MARIE VALENTI, you get your ass out here right now and tell me to my face that the rumor making its way around town isn't true!"

Brenna's voice makes me physically jump out of bed. I put my hand over my heart, making sure it's still there and not somewhere beating outside of my body.

Did I not lock the door? I really thought I did. Then did she pick the lock? I mean, I wouldn't put it past Brenna to do something like that.

"Good morning to you too, Brenna," I say, sitting back down on my bed as my best friend comes into my room.

"Don't good morning me," she says as she aggressively takes a seat at the bottom of my bed. "How can you call off your engagement and not tell me *immediately?*"

"I meant to. I promise. Things just didn't go as planned."

"How do they not go as planned? Oh no. Did Luciano cry? I like the guy and all, but I can see him being a crier."

I shake my head. "No. He laughed."

Breanna's jaw drops open. "I'm confused. Start from the beginning. Leave nothing out."

"Fine, but at least let me get up and make coffee. You might not drink it, but some of us need it to function."

"Can you imagine me on caffeine? The world can't handle that."

I laugh as we make our way to my kitchen where I begin to brew a cup and fill her in on everything from last night.

I tell her about his trip to Italy, why he asked me out in the first place, and how all of this snowballed into something neither of us could stop.

"That doesn't seem so bad," she says as we take a seat at my kitchen counter. "Seems like you two did what was right for both of you."

"We did. Then we told our parents that the wedding was off."

That was our biggest mistake, but at least we did it together.

Pro: We only had to say it once.

Con: Double the Italian outrage.

Dishes were thrown. Voices were raised. There was swearing in both Italian and English. More than once, I heard the phrase "French hussie."

When it was over, I felt like I got ran over by a truck. I needed calm, so I went to the lake. Bryce being there felt like kismet.

I have no idea when I got home. All I know is that I slept better last night than I had in months. Whether it was because the stress of the wedding was gone or because I could still feel Bryce's arms around me and his lips on mine, I'm not sure.

"Damn," Brenna says, her mouth hanging open as I wrap up the events of the night. "That's a lot to unpack. Also, I feel oddly invested in the Celine-Luciano romance."

"Right?" I say, getting up to pour myself another cup. "Is it bad that I'm glad he is in love with someone else?"

"Absolutely not. You guys love each other like family, not like husband and wife. Him loving her helps you know that the decision you made was the right one. Now he can be happy with her, and you and my brother can *finally* be together. Oh my God, we're going to be sisters!"

"Calm down," I say, taking a seat back at the table. "We're a long way from another wedding."

"Semantics. But at least you two are back together now, right?"

"Not exactly."

"What do you mean not exactly? You talked last night. You kissed, which is gross but I'm willing to pretend he's not my brother for you and the sake of our friendship. You both are clearly in love with each other. What else do you need?"

When she says it like that, it all seems so simple when it's anything but.

"We have a lot to figure out," I say. "He might be seeing a therapist now, but he still has a lot of issues to work through. That doesn't happen overnight. Also, I need to make sure what we have isn't something I've built up in my head for seven years. I need to make sure this is the real deal before I uproot my life to Nashville. There's a lot to figure out."

"You're right," Brenna says. "So, what are you going to do?"

She follows me as I stand and head back to my bedroom. "First, I'm going to call all of the vendors and see what kind of refund I can get back on my deposits."

"I wonder if I can get money back on my bridesmaid dress."

"Sorry about that."

"No worries. I'll add it to my growing collection. What about after that??"

"After, I'm going to go on my honeymoon. Alone."

"Why would you do that? And why wouldn't you take me?"

"Can you get two weeks off work in the first two months into the school year with zero notice?"

"No," she grumbles, plopping onto my bed. "But why go alone?"

"Why not? I won't be able to do anything for a while around here without someone asking me what happened. Maybe if I go away for a few weeks, some other scandal will pop up and take over as the biggest news in Laurel Heights."

"If it doesn't, I'll start a rumor about Moriah Marks. Chances are it will be true."

"You're a good friend."

"Damn right I am. Why don't you take Bryce? It would give you two time to reconnect without our nosy, prying eyes looking at you."

"Did he tell you to ask me that?"

"What? No. Why would you ask me that?"

"Because he was trying to convince me last night that I shouldn't go alone."

Saying no to that was harder than I thought because two weeks alone with Bryce at a romantic resort sounds like a dream come true. Beaches. Candlelit dinners. Couples' massages.

Bryce shirtless for most of that time.

Sometimes I really hate being responsible.

"No, we need this time to figure things out. Alone," I say, walking to my closet to get my suitcase. "If we're together, we won't do our due diligence of making sure this is what we want. For so many years, we've been living off teenage dreams and promises. We need to be adults about this. We need time to really figure out if we can do this."

"You're making him make a pro-con list, aren't you?"

I fling the suitcase onto my bed. "Damn right I am. Now

hand me my cell phone. I have overpriced flowers to cancel and a plane ticket to change."

TODAY IS THE DAY.

Today is the day that the rest of my life begins.

Sure, there's a chance that, at some point over the past two weeks, Lucy has decided that it's too much of a risk and we shouldn't be together. Maybe one of the ten lists she made said this wasn't a good idea.

I might love the woman, but if that fucking list exists, I'm setting it on fire.

I know they are part of her process, and to love her is to love her lists, but I don't need a piece of paper to know that I want to be with her. To know that I love her with all my heart.

The clock on my dashboard reads nine in the morning, which I'm hoping isn't too early to ask the woman you've been in love with for seven years to give this a shot. Hell, she's lucky I wasn't waiting on her doorstep when she got back from St. Thomas last night and that I waited until now instead of knocking on her door at five AM when I woke up.

I reach over to the passenger seat to grab the donut and cup of coffee I bought for her this morning, and with one last deep breath, I make my way to her doorstep.

Here goes nothing.

More like, here goes everything.

I knock on her door and look around at the outside of her house as I wait for her to answer. It's white with light-blue shutters and yellow flowers blooming in the garden. Her flowers are perfectly trimmed and planted. The paint is perfect without a chip to be found.

It's the most Lucy house I've ever seen.

I hate that I'm only just now seeing it. I also hate that I had to ask Brenna for her address.

After I left for college, things didn't go the way I thought they would. I thought I'd have the chance to come home more. I thought I'd have the chance to call or text her more often.

Instead, I went silent for months until I needed something, until I needed my Lulu to help me calm the chaos in my head.

Like the angel she is, she always answered.

Like the bastard I am, I took it and ran.

Well, no more. That shit ends right now.

"Bryce?"

Lucy opens her door a few inches, and I almost drop my coffee.

If this is Lucy first thing in the morning, I never want to go another morning without seeing her.

Her hair is in a messy nest on the top of her head. She's wearing pajamas that should not be sexy but are making my mouth water, her face is free of makeup, and if I didn't know any better, I would think the glasses she has on are the same ones she wore in high school.

"Hey, Lulu," I say, holding out the donuts and coffee. "Welcome back."

"What is this?" Her voice is that perfect mix of sleepy and sexy.

"I figured you'd need breakfast."

"So, you came over to my house at nine in the morning, the

day after I get back from my vacation, with coffee and donuts because you were worried about my need for nutrients?"

"Um . . . yes?" Though, I'm not sure if that's the right answer. This is what happens because I went my entire life without seriously dating. I've never had to think about this stuff before.

Just when I'm about to apologize for overstepping, a smile forms on Lucy's lips. "You're my hero. I didn't remember that I had no groceries until I woke up this morning and realized I was out of coffee. Come in, but fair warning, I'm not sharing any donuts."

I follow her back to her kitchen, and I can't help but smile —and not just because the sleep shorts she's wearing give me just a tease of her amazing ass.

I'm smiling because I'm here. It's finally time. The off-season is finally here. I can feel it.

She sets the coffee and donuts on the table, and I grab her hand and spin her around, bringing her flush to me as my lips find hers.

"Bryce," she says, inching herself away. "I told you we needed to talk about everything once I got back."

"I know," I say without letting go of her. "And I thought. I love you. I'm ready. Now, can we kiss some more?"

She raises an eyebrow. "Anything else? What did you put on your pro-con list? We need to compare."

"I didn't make one."

Her eyes grow wide. "You didn't make one?"

I'd be scared right now if her exasperation didn't make me laugh. "Nope. I don't need a list. Pro, I love you and have always loved you. Cons, None. There."

She pushes away from me. "We need to be serious about this. I gave you one job over the past two weeks, and you didn't even do it."

I laugh because I can't wait for this to be the argument for the rest of our lives. "I didn't need one."

"Yes, you do."

"No, I don't. I guarantee that, anything you wrote down on the con side, I have an answer or a solution for."

"You have never been that decisive about anything in your life."

She has me there.

"I am about this," I say, reasserting myself. "Try me."

She raises an eyebrow. "Fine. One of my cons is that I would eventually need to move to Nashville."

"Are you willing to do that?"

She shrugs. "It would be scary. I'd hate not knowing anyone but you and Cole, especially if you're on the road for long periods of time."

She's right. During the season I'll be on the road a ton, and where does that leave her? Alone in a new city?

"All right, how about this," I say, looping my arms around her waist to bring her closer to me. "You don't move right away. I won't be going back to Nashville until the spring. That gives us four months here to figure out what you're comfortable with. It will also give you a chance to meet some people out there before you make your decision."

"That's smart, though we do need to come back to it eventually," she says. "When did you become good at making decisions? You're the king of indecision. That therapist must be really good."

"That was then. This is now," I say, kissing her temple. "Apparently I just needed to make the easiest decision of my life."

This makes her smile. "Fine, but there are more cons."

"And what would those be, Lulu?"

She fights an eyeroll. "What if we sleep on the same side of the bed? What if you're a horrible slob and I can't handle it? What if the other football girlfriends or wives don't like me? Will my relationship change with Brenna?"

"Do you have this list?" I ask, realizing exactly what I need to do.

"I do," she says, walking over to her purse and pulling out multiple sheets of paper.

"Can I see it?"

She hesitates for a second before handing it over. "Sure, but I'm not done with the cons—"

I rip it in half.

"What did you do!" she screams, trying to grab the two halves from me but I am holding them well out of her reach.

"I'm getting you out of your head," I say, throwing them in the air so they scatter across her kitchen.

"Bryce!"

I grab her hands and pull her back into me. "What were your pros?"

"What?"

"I asked, what were your pros? You had valid concerns, and I'm sure very spot-on cons, but what were your pros?"

For a second or two, she lets her fingers play with the fabric of my shirt, her eyes focused on the task.

"That I love you."

I take two fingers and lift her chin up. "What was that?"

"That I love you."

"That's a pretty big pro."

"But is it enough?" she asks, her voice unsure and hesitant. "What if, after all these years, we aren't a good fit? What if love isn't enough?"

I sit down and bring her with me so she's on my lap, which she doesn't fight. "Want to know why I ripped up your list?"

"Because you like driving me crazy?"

I laugh. "Besides that."

"Because you hate making lists?"

"While that might be true, that's not why." I bring her in a little tighter and hope that she hears everything I'm about to say. "I ripped it up because there are some things you can't pro-con. There are things in this world that don't have a predetermined answer and can't be solved by a formula. Sometimes, you just have to see where things go. I don't know how this is going to work. We might drive each other insane or never fight. All I know is that, if we go another day without trying this, then we'll never know, and that seems like the worst con of all."

She looks at me, and for a second, I'm not sure what to think because her eyes aren't giving anything away.

In fact, I'm getting the vibe that she thinks I'm an idiot.

"You really think we're never going to fight?"

I laugh. "That's what you took from that?"

"Well, that . . . and you're right."

"I'm sorry, what? I didn't quite hear you."

Now I get an eyeroll. "You're right. We'll never know until we try. I'm just scared."

"Oh, Lulu," I say, holding her a little tighter. "You don't think I'm scared? I'm terrified. I'm scared I'm not good enough for you. I'm scared that I'll fuck all of this up. I'm scared of what Coach Roberts and your parents and Brenna will do if I fuck this up. Hell, I'm scared of Cole because I know he likes you better than me. Do you want to know what scares me more than all of those combined?"

"What's that?"

"I'm scared of going my entire life and not knowing what it was like to be with you, not to know what it feels like to be yours and for you to be mine. So, what do you say? Want to be scared with me?"

Her answer is to wrap her arms around my neck and tug me closer. The second our lips touch, I feel all of the doubts she has, and all the fears I have, melt away.

And just like that, I know that this is going to be worth it.

It's finally our time.

And I'm not going to fuck it up.

CHAPTER 23
LUCY

IF MY FIRST date with Bryce Donald would have been seven years ago, I might not have been able to handle it. In fact, I *know* I couldn't have handled it because I'm twenty-four years old and can barely handle it.

The touches. The looks. The electricity. It's almost too much to handle.

And to think I was going to marry someone who I didn't feel any of this with.

It started when he picked me up. When I opened the door to find him standing there holding a bouquet of fall wildflowers, wearing tailored black pants and a white button-up shirt with the sleeves rolled to his elbows, my legs almost gave out.

Then there was the hour drive to Cincinnati in which he insisted on holding my hand the whole way. Every so often his thumb would brush back and forth over my knuckles and I know that's not supposed to be anything more than a simple touch, but I felt it in every cell of my body.

Now I'm sitting across from him at a candlelit table at one of the most exclusive restaurants in Cincinnati. The wine is perfect, the meal is mouthwatering, and the view of the river is exquisite.

None of that compares to him.

"You snuck into a bar?" he says in between laughter. "Let me guess, my sister had something to do with it."

"She's the yin to my yang," I say with a little shrug. "We were twenty. Brenna knew one of the bouncers, so she got me in. I was so nervous the whole night I didn't drink and spent the whole time trying to calculate how many ounces of liquor the bar would go through in an entire night. I sat at the bar with my phone calculator open, writing equations on cocktail napkins."

"Now that's the mathlete I know," Bryce says, a warm smile coming over his face as he reaches for my hand. "Who would have thought that you lived the crazier college life than I did?"

Now this takes me by surprise. "No way. You were at Clemson. I've seen pictures of the parties and the sorority girls. No way you didn't have a little fun."

He lets out a breath and takes a sip of his water. "I went to a few parties my freshman year. They were fun, but football was a lot more than I expected. So was school."

"I remember," I say, hoping that talk of college doesn't lead us down a touchy road of past memories.

"I realized that if I wanted to go pro, then I had to stay focused. I think I maybe went to five parties the whole time I was in college, and that was because my teammates dragged me to them. No, I saved my partying for adulthood when I thought I was untouchable."

The silence becomes thick as his words hang in the air.

"I'm so sorry," I say. "I just didn't know how—"

"It's in the past," he says, bringing my hand to his lips. "The past is what it is. It happened. We learn from it. But now? Now I'm only focused on the future."

I smile because that's exactly what I needed to hear.

"Speaking of the future," he says as he stands. "This night is not over yet."

"Really?" I ask, standing as he pulls my chair out. "And what does that have to do with the future?"

"Because," he says, wrapping his arm around my waist to bring me in for a quick kiss. "Tonight is the first night of our future. Come on, I have somewhere I've always wanted to take you."

———

"Heights Park? This is where you couldn't wait to take me?"

He laughs as he puts the truck in park. "What do you mean? You don't like it?"

"I mean . . ."

It's not that I don't like it. Being anywhere with Bryce is better than being most places, but I guess I just thought that maybe we'd take a romantic walk on the riverfront or catch a show.

Not go to the high-school make-out spot back in our hometown.

"I know I was talking about the future," he says as he opens my door a few seconds later and helps me out of the truck. "But before we move on to the future, there are some things in the past I need to make up for. This date is one of the biggest."

He takes my hand and walks me to a spot under a big tree, and I have to blink a few times to make sure my eyes aren't deceiving me.

Laid out is a blanket surrounded by candles. I'm pretty sure if I look close enough, I see a box of cannoli from Tripoli's and two bottles of what look like root beer chilling in a bucket.

In the middle of the blanket is Bryce's old jacket.

"How did you do all of this?" I ask, stunned as I take a few steps closer.

"Turns out my sister isn't that big of a pain in the ass after all." He picks up his jacket and holds it up for me to put on. "And when I told her what I had always planned for our first date, well, let's just say there was no stopping her."

I take another look around, and everything screams seventeen-year-old Bryce and Lucy.

"This is perfect," I say, taking a seat on the blanket. "I can't believe you did all of this. I'm also trying to decide how I feel that you wanted to bring me to the Laurel Heights make out spot on our first date."

Bryce couldn't wipe the wicked smile off his face if he tried. Though, I bet he doesn't want to. "Let's just say that teenage Bryce was very ready to make out with you."

I laugh as Bryce takes a seat behind me, immediately bringing me in between his legs so my back is to this front.

"Lucy, I know I've said it before, and I'm pretty sure I'll be saying it for the rest of our lives, but I'm sorry. I'm so sorry. We've wasted so much time because I was an idiot—"

"Don't apologize." I smile and trap his face between my palms.

"Yeah, but—"

"No buts. We can't change the past. We can only learn from it and move on and work for the things we want."

He lets out a sigh as he weaves his fingers through mine. "How do you do it?"

"Do what?"

"Always know the thing to say to get me out of my head?"

I shrug. "I guess that's my superpower."

"One of many," he says, bringing me the few inches onto his lap where I immediately wrap my arms around his neck.

"I have others?"

"You do." Then he places the softest kiss on my neck.

Sweet baby Jesus.

I hadn't known I could feel a kiss on my neck all the way in my pinkie toe.

"You, my Lulu, have the power to drive me crazy. Do you know how hard it was to keep my hands to myself tonight? That dress just about killed me."

"It did?"

"It did," he says, placing another kiss on my neck, this time just a bit lower. "I'm powerless when it comes to you. Don't you know that by now?"

It could be the moonlight, the candles, his words, or all of the above, but I have never felt a need like this before in my entire life. If I don't kiss him in the next two seconds, I might explode.

I bring his lips to mine and as soon as we connect, a fire rages through my entire body. A fire I never want to put out.

His lips are perfect—soft but demanding. I turn so I can straddle him, and I'm pretty sure I hear the faint sound of my dress ripping. I don't care. I need to be closer to him. I need to be as close as possible.

Kissing him is all-consuming in every part of my body, and I'm pretty sure we are both close to combusting.

My hands slide up the back of his head, my nails grazing his scalp as I urge him closer to me. He must read my mind because his hands trail down my sides and then cup my ass, lifting me slightly so I'm as flush against him as possible. Where he has placed me makes it impossible to ignore his hardness beneath me.

"Lucy," he says, his lips trailing to my neck. "We need to slow down."

"We do?" I ask as I shift away slightly. "Why? Did I—"

"Absolutely not," he says, bringing me in for another kiss.

"You are perfect. God, you are perfect in every way. I would kiss you all night if you let me."

"Then what?" I ask, hating how insecure I sound.

"I have waited years for you. For *this*," he says as he brushes a lock of my hair back and tucks it behind my ear. "I don't want it to be rushed in a park. I don't want it to be in the heat of the moment. I want it to be perfect."

God, this man. Every time I saw him cast as the newest bad boy of football or saw a picture of him with his arms draped around multiple women, I couldn't bear to look at it. I knew that wasn't him.

I refused to entertain the idea that I was wrong and the Bryce I fell in love with was the imposter.

I'm glad I dug my heels in because this is the real Bryce. The caring man. The man who remembers inconsequential conversations from years ago and what my favorite dessert is. He's the man who gives me butterflies just from a look across the room and a touch of the hand.

The man I'm in love with.

CHAPTER 24
BRYCE

I MIGHT HAVE BEEN GONE for a year, but Laurel Heights hasn't changed a bit and neither has this view at the lake.

There is still construction downtown, which has been going on since I started high school. The same old men were talking in the coffee shop when I walked past the other day—no doubt talking about football after their weekly trip to the bank. The only difference was not seeing Lucy's big brown eyes and smile when my mom, Brenna, and I walked into Tripoli's on Christmas Eve. The whole night, I had to see fucking Pizza Boy with a smug grin.

I still hate him, so at least that's the same.

Even hours after dinner was over, I couldn't stop thinking about how much I missed Lucy. I tried my best to stay in touch with her when I was gone, but I really never realized how much football and classes would take over my life. I've never been great at school, so when I wasn't at practice or in classes, I was studying to make sure I was keeping my grades up. It was truly a whirlwind. One minute it was spring semester, which rolled into summer classes, and next thing I knew, it was time for training camp and I'd missed my chance to come home and visit.

"Bryce?"

Lucy's voice pulls me from my thoughts, and I hurry and jump off the bed of my truck.

The second my eyes land on her, it's as if my whole world slams to a stop. I can't believe how much she's changed in subtle ways and my eyes race to note every difference.

She's impossibly more beautiful than I remember, and she isn't wearing glasses, which I strangely miss even if it means I can see her doe eyes all that much better. The curve of her hips are more pronounced, and I have to fight the urge to hold on to them. And her curves up top? When did that happen?

Snap out of it, man. I need to stop acting like a horny teenager.

Except, I still am, I guess. Sometimes college makes me forget that because I may still be a teenager but I have all adult consequences and responsibilities.

"Hey," I say quickly, realizing I've been standing and staring at her. "How are you?"

I hold open my arms for a hug and then immediately put them down.

What's the protocol for how I greet my technical ex-girl-friend who I'm only exes with because I couldn't pack her in a bag and take her to college with me is fuzzy. Oh, and I shouldn't forget that she should hate me for breaking all sorts of promises I made her.

"If you're trying to figure out if you're allowed to hug me, the answer is yes," Lucy says, reading my mind. "You were making the face you used to make when you couldn't figure out an equation."

I let out an uncomfortable laugh as I take the final few steps to her and pull her into my arms. As soon as her head rests against my chest, the stress of the last year lifts into the crisp December air.

"God, I've missed you," I say, squeezing her a little tighter. "Thank you for meeting me."

"Of course," she says, lifting her head to look at me. "I figured it was important considering—"

Considering I haven't talked to her in months. That is what she leaves unsaid. In fact, the last time we spoke was when I texted her to let her know that I couldn't make it home for prom. That was eight months ago.

"I'm sorry," I say, leading her back to my truck and helping her up on the tailgate. "I've been so bad at calling or texting. I just . . . well, the last year has been . . . hard."

Hard doesn't even begin to scratch the surface. Over-whelming. Intense. Those are much better.

"I'm actually surprised you're home. Aren't you going to a bowl game?"

"We leave the day after Christmas. Coaches made everyone go home for the holidays before reporting back."

"Well, that's nice," she says. "I'm sure your mom liked that."

She was thrilled I was home and cried when she found out it was only for two days, but that isn't what I want to talk to her about.

"Lucy—"

"How is—"

We laugh, but it sounds weird. Forced. Not us.

God, I hate this. When did this become how Lucy and I are around each other? Oh, right. When I went off to college and dropped off the planet.

"You're probably wondering why I texted you tonight," I say, rubbing my hands together. Why I thought coming to the lake in December was a good idea is beyond me.

"Honestly? I did," she says. "After six months of silence, I figured I no longer warranted texts or calls."

"I'm sorry. I'm so sorry. It's just . . . college is nothing like I expected."

She lifts an eyebrow. "What do you mean? I thought you were ready for nonstop football."

"I thought I was," I say, leaning back on my hands. "It's so much more than that, though. It's film, then practice, then classes, then more practice, then study tables. It's nonstop. All day, every day, and for what? For me to barely pass classes and ride the bench while a guy I know I'm better than takes the starting position? It's just—it's too much. I'm barely holding on. That was why I never called or texted you. I was embarrassed that nothing was going the way I wanted it to, and . . . and I didn't know how to hide the fact that I'm barely staying above water. So, I just disappeared."

I don't mean to admit all of that, but at the same time, it feels good to finally say everything aloud.

"Bryce, that's nothing to be ashamed of. College is hard for a lot of people, when you add in a demanding sport, it's probably impossible. Your first year is done, so now you have a better handle on everything for next year."

"If there is a next year."

The lake is already eerily quiet. But now? I could hear a pin drop.

"What are you saying, Bryce?"

I take a deep breath because if I say this aloud, then it's out there in the universe. I haven't told anyone these thoughts, not even to Cole, who is the only person who has an inkling of how unhappy I am.

"I'm thinking about transferring." The admission tastes bitter on my tongue and I swallow hard.

"Transferring?" she repeats, clearly stunned. "Bryce, are you sure?"

I shrug. "Maybe? All I know is that I can't sit the bench again next year. And my classes? I know I've never been a great student, but I struggled this year. Bad. I passed, but it wasn't easy. Maybe I should have stayed home and gone somewhere in-state. Maybe a smaller college? I don't know, but if this semester is a preview of my next three years, I'm not going to make it."

I'm scared to look at Lucy because I know how that must have sounded. Pathetic. Embarrassing. Like a failure. That's why I'm startled when I feel her hand rest on top of mine. When I look to her, I don't see someone who is ashamed of me.

I see someone who believes in me.

"Bryce, if it wasn't hard, everyone would do it," she says, bringing our hands together on her lap. "But now I know why you called me."

"You do?"

"I do. It's because you needed to make a pro-con list and you know I'm the best at them."

She smiles, and I can't help but do the same.

"That must have been it," I say, turning to face her. "Too bad we don't have any paper."

"You think this is my first rodeo? We don't need paper. Now, let's talk this out."

For the next hour, that's what we do. Only we move the conversation to the inside of my truck because it's Christmas Eve and cold as fuck outside.

After our hands unthawed, a list has been made and it's clear I'll stay at Clemson.

"You know that's not actually why I texted you," I say.

"It wasn't for my masterful list making?"

I laugh. "Shockingly no. It was just a bonus."

"Then, why? I mean, I'm glad you did, but I figured you needed my help."

I reach over and move a stray hair back behind her ear. I can't stop staring at her. This new Lucy with no glasses and full lips is . . . it's too much.

"I messaged you," I say, placing a kiss on her cheek. One she doesn't pull away from, "because I miss you. Because you get me. Because you're the only one I can talk about what's going on in my head without judgment. You're my best friend, Lulu—no, you're more than that. You're everything to me, and I'm so sorry I didn't call, or text. I'm so sorry."

I feel her hand on my cheek, and I know I'm going to regret being this selfish, but I don't care.

I need to kiss her. I need it more than I need to take my next breath.

"Bryce," she whispers, and that snaps the last of my resolve.

I take my hands and cup her cheeks, bringing her to me. The second our lips touch, I know I'm not wrong. The warmth and electricity I feel every time I'm with Lucy courses through my body.

She wraps her arms around my neck, and I pull her over the console so she's straddling me in the driver's seat. I sure as hell didn't mean for this to happen when I called her earlier, but I can't lie and say I'm mad about it.

It's Lucy. In my arms. On my lap. Kissing me like her life depends on it.

I let go of her hands and trail my palms down her body. I feel the curve of her breasts, and it takes all the willpower I have left not to cup them. I wonder what they would be like in my hands.

Or in my mouth.

"Bryce." She moans my name, and fuck, I am as hard as I've

ever been. I'm not a virgin—that ship sailed sophomore year of high school—but I feel like I am.

Wait, what am I doing? As much as I enjoy kissing Lucy—I really need to figure out how I can smuggle her back to college with me—this isn't right. We're in my beat-up old truck at the lake. We haven't seen each other in months.

I'm being a selfish bastard, that's what I am doing.

"Lucy," I say, pulling away from her lips, which I immediately regret. "Wait."

"What?" she asks. "Is everything okay?"

"No—I mean yes. I mean . . . shit." I'm clearly fucking this up. "I don't want it to be like this."

"What do you mean?"

I adjust her so she's looking right at me, even though that makes me want to kiss her all over again.

"If we keep going, I know where it's going to go, and you deserve more than a quicky in my truck. I want to give you so much more. Romance and candles and the whole nine yards."

"Bryce, I don't need—"

"Yes, you do, and I'm going to give it to you. Some day."

"Bryce. Don't say things you don't mean."

"Don't mean? Lucy Valenti, I'm crazy about you. I know I have a weird way of showing it, but I love you, and I promise I'm going to do better. I'm going to call you every week, text you every chance I get, ask you how your days were. You're going to tell me about school and life, and I'm going to complain about classes. And then, guess what?"

"What?" she says, a hint of a smile coming through.

"Next off-season? It's ours."

"LUCY! I'M HOME!"

I roll my eyes as I wipe my hands on the dish towel in the kitchen.

"Are you ever going to get tired of that?" I ask as Bryce comes into the kitchen, dropping the bag of groceries I asked him to pick up on his way over.

He wraps his arms around my waist and places a kiss on my cheek, one that might seem tame but warms me from head to toe. "Nope. Never."

I might joke with him about the lame throwback to *I Love Lucy*, but it's the favorite part of my day because it always leads to this. Just a few minutes of quiet time for us as our individual days melt into our nights together.

He trains during the day while I'm at work, and he has his appointments with Malcolm twice a week. Sometimes, we cook together, and other times, we get takeout. It's so . . . normal.

I love it.

"How was your day?" he asks. "Anything . . . interesting happen?"

The man might be the best quarterback in pro football, but he's a horrible actor.

"Nope. Pretty normal" I say, going back to chopping the peppers. "People wanted money. I gave them money. Megan complained about being pregnant. Same old, same old."

I'm glad I'm facing away from him because I'm having trouble keeping the smile off my face. I know he's trying to egg me on about the ginormous flower arrangement he had sent to the bank today. It was so big that when Megan brought it into my office, I couldn't see her face. The bouquet is a beautiful red and white rose arrangement that screams Christmas. It also makes my budget-loving heart pound a little harder wondering what it had to cost him.

While the arrangement was gorgeous, it was the card that came with it that sent my emotions into overdrive.

I'm sorry it took me this long to send you flowers.
Love you most, Bryce.

I wanted to text him and thank him right away, but as soon as I picked up my phone, we got busy and stayed that way until I locked the doors at five.

"So, you didn't get anything special at work?" he asks, spinning me around so I can't hide behind the peppers anymore. "Nothing at all?"

I shrug as I loop my hands around his neck. "Not that I can think of. Oh wait! I did get something! It was this little bouquet of flowers. I think one of my clients sent it to me."

"I'll show you little . . ."

Bryce scoops me up and sits me on the counter, bringing our lips together as our laughter fades. I knew what it was like to kiss Bryce when we were teenagers, but kissing him now is a whole new experience. Maybe it's because we're adults and we aren't afraid to hold back. Or maybe because it means something more. I'm not sure, but every time I kiss the man, every time I feel his lips on mine, it makes me feel like I am the most loved and cherished woman in the entire world.

"If we don't stop, we aren't going to eat dinner," I say, though I don't make an attempt to stop him from kissing my neck.

"I don't need to eat," he says before his lips suck on my neck as his hands begin searching underneath my sweater. "Well, food that is."

"Yes, you do," I say. Despite the fact that he has spent every night here since we decided to give this a go, we haven't slept together yet. We're trying to wait and not rush into it. That's becoming easier said than done.

It sounded like a good idea at the time. I guess I didn't factor in that Bryce could make me see stars with just his mouth.

"Fine," he grumbles, placing one more kiss on my lips. "In all seriousness, did you like the flowers?"

I return the kiss and jump off the counter. "I loved them, but they were too much."

"Nonsense," he says as he begins to put away the groceries. "When you told me you had never gotten flowers from anyone, it was basically a challenge."

"You could have just got me a regular bouquet."

He laughs into the refrigerator. "Again, nonsense. You will learn, Lulu, I don't do things halfway. It's all or nothing, baby."

I scoop the carrots into the salad bowl and place it onto the kitchen table as Bryce follows behind, setting out our preferred dressings.

"So, where did we leave off last night?" Bryce asks as he pours us both waters as I put down the lasagna.

"Fears and phobias," I say, sounding more like a category

on *Jeopardy* than dinner conversation. "You were telling me about your very real, and very paralyzing fear of spiders."

"Yeah, let's move on from that one," he says, taking a huge bite of my lasagna. "Oh! I know. Guilty pleasures. We all have them. What is the one that gets my girl going?"

I laugh at the way he says it, his eyebrows wagging up and down like he's about to pull a juicy secret from me.

"Well, you know at night when you see me playing with my phone and I say I'm playing solitaire? I'm really browsing real estate apps and looking up extravagant houses that I'll never be able to afford."

"Really? That's your thing?"

"Definitely. You should see some of these houses. I'm talking about ones that sell for millions and millions of dollars. They are fascinating to look at, but who needs a house with six bathrooms? Then there are the ones that listed for like, two million, and then you look inside and it's like the worst version of a freaky, real-life dollhouse."

"Have you looked at any in Tennessee?" Bryce asks, trying to sound nonchalant. "I've heard there are some pretty nice ones down there."

"I haven't, but maybe I will," I say, feeling the blush creep across my cheeks. I don't know why the thought of looking up extravagant homes in Tennessee makes me nervous, but it does. Maybe because that means I'm thinking about a future with Bryce, which still makes me feel all sorts of ways. "Now, what about you. What's the one guilty pleasure the gossip sites would love to know about Bryce Donald."

He lets out a breath and puts his fork down. "I'm not sure if you're ready for this."

Oh, now I'm intrigued. "Lay it on me, Donald. Tell me that secret love you have."

"I need to preface this by saying it's not just me. It's most of my team, even Cole. It started as something to do together, and it has . . . well, it has grown legs none of us could have predicted."

"Are you going to make me guess, or are you building anticipation? Because if it's the latter, it's working."

"I'm trying to figure out how to tell you so you don't look at me differently."

"That is now out the door. Spill it."

"Fine," he says, picking up his glass and taking a healthy sip of water. "Most of the guys and I on the team are a part of Bachelor and Bachelorette nation. We are in fantasy leagues for them. We never miss an episode. Our Tuesday meetings can't begin until we've done episode recaps, and we send each other articles updating each other on past contestants. I'm actually glad we brought this up because the new season starts next week, so guess what your Monday nights now include."

My jaw drops a little more with each word that comes out of his mouth. Of all the things he could have told me, that was the absolute last thing I thought would be said.

"Come on. Give me shit. I know you want to," he says, digging back into his lasagna.

I don't. Instead, I stand and walk to the other side of the table, where I situate myself on his lap.

"I think that is both hilarious and amazing. I can't wait to watch with you."

This earns me a quick kiss. "Remember that when I go crazy on the hometown dates."

"I'll try to remember that. Now, if I'm going to be watching the show with you, I need you to do something for me."

"Anything, Lulu."

"You say that now . . ."

"Oh, come on. What could it be? Want me to buy you a ridiculous house in Tennessee? You got it. Want a bigger flower arrangement each day of the week? No problem. Hell, I'll even let you tutor me for old time's sakes. There is nothing you can ask me that I would say no to."

I glance down before letting out a breath. "I'd like you to come to Christmas Eve dinner with me at my parents' house."

His eyes go wide, realization setting in about what I'm asking him to do. This isn't a normal meet the parents. This will be the first family get together since I called off the wedding.

My parents and I have spoken, but it hasn't exactly been warm or loving conversations. They didn't come out and say it, but I know they think I called off the wedding for Bryce. When I remind them that neither Luciano nor I loved each other, they ignore it.

But it's Christmas, and Christmas is meant to be spent with those you love.

"My answer does not change. I will absolutely be there," he says right before placing a kiss on my nose. "Though, I might need a bit of encouragement beforehand. You know, something to pump me up."

I wrap my arms around his neck and pull his lips into mine a little more forcefully than I usually do. I'd say this takes him by surprise by the sudden bulge I feel underneath me. Though I wouldn't say he's complaining about it considering his hands are now digging into my hips in the best way.

"Like that?" I say, placing one more kiss on his upper lip.

He swallows hard, readjusting me on his lap. "Something like that."

"So will you come with me?"

He plants one more kiss into my neck as he quickly sweeps me up into his arms. "I'm still not sure," he says, carrying me away from the dining room. "I think I need more convincing."

"BREATHE," Lucy says as we walk up to her parents' door, and I slightly adjust the bag full of gifts we brought. "They are going to love you. Plus, Uncle Nick is here as a buffer."

I relax a little as Lucy kisses my cheek.

I wanted this, right? When we were younger, this was one of the things I couldn't wait to do. Except then I was a dumb teenager hoping her parents would like me enough that they would let me take her out to a movie. Now I'm the guy she started dating days after calling off her wedding to the man they might have loved more than Lucy.

Her words, not mine.

It doesn't help that it's Christmas Eve because, why not meet your girlfriend's parents on a major holiday?

"Are you sure this is a good idea?" I ask, unable to hide the nervousness from my voice. "I don't want to ruin Christmas. I can meet them on December twenty-seventh. That sounds like a great day."

"Stop," Lucy says as she puts her hands on my cheeks. "Get out of your head. It's game time, Donald. You ready?"

Her attempt to sound like one of my coaches makes me smile. "You hyping me up?"

"Hell yeah I am," she says, putting our foreheads together. "Let's do this."

I lean down and give her a quick kiss. "You're really cute when you do this."

She smiles. "I'll remember that for the future."

I kiss her again, but as soon as our lips touch, I hear the sound of her front door opening.

"Are you going to stand there and make out with my daughter or are you going to come in so we can get this night started?"

I jump away from Lucy and clear my throat. "Hello, sir. Nice to meet you. I'm Bryce Don—"

"I know who you are. You cost me money in the season opener last year. Now get in here so I can start eating the appetizers."

He walks away, and I'm left stunned as I follow Lucy into the house.

"See, that went well," Lucy says, taking off her coat. After a second, I set the bag on the floor and pull my own jacket off.

"How in the world did that go well?"

"He let you in, didn't he?"

I blink a few times. "Was there another option?"

Lucy just shrugs. "Honestly, I have no idea. This is all new to me, and I'm just hoping we make it out of here tonight with minimal tears and bloodshed."

I pick up the bag and as soon as I do, I feel a cold blast of air hit my back.

"Lucia?"

You have got to be fucking kidding me.

Pizza Boy is standing in the open doorway, wearing a fucking Christmas sweater. Why does that not surprise me?

"Luciano," Lucy says, clearly as confused to see him as I am. "What are you doing here? And is this . . ."

My gaze shifts to the blonde to his left.

"Lucia, meet Celine," Pizza Boy says, his eyes never leaving Celine, who is wearing a matching sweater.

I don't care how much I love Lucy, I will never, ever, wear matching sweaters.

Oh, who am I kidding? If she asked me to dress up as a reindeer I would.

"It is nice to meet you, Lucia," Celine says, her French accent thick as she and Lucy shake hands.

"You too." She turns to Luciano. "I thought this year our parents were doing Christmas Eve apart?"

"I thought so too," Luciano says, taking off his coat before helping Celine out of hers. "But yesterday Mama messaged me to come here instead."

"Oh God," Lucy says, her face turning whiter by the second. "Our parents are unbelievable. They knew I was bringing Bryce, and your parents knew Celine would be here. Whatever they're up to, it's nothing good."

"Sounds about right," Luciano says. I guess I can refer to him as that now that I know the French girl exists. "What's the plan?"

Lucy looks to me, to Luciano, and then back to me. "We stick to our guns. No matter what emotional blackmail they try to use, we are with the people we want to be with and we are happy."

"Sounds good to me," Luciano says as he extends his hand for me. "And, Bryce, I know we've never seen eye to eye, but for tonight, can we leave the past in the past?"

I don't offer mine back right away because years of jealousy is hard to drop in a second or two. Yes, I can admit I was jealous that he got to be around Lucy and that he knew her longer than I did. In my mind, it meant that he knew her *better*, even if that wasn't the case. When I found out they were engaged? I'd never had murderous thoughts before, but I was certain I wanted to kill him.

Now I know where Lucy and I stand and can appreciate that they needed each other for different reasons over the course of their dating and engagement. It probably doesn't hurt that he looks at Celine the way I look at Lucy. I might not want to go golfing with the guy, but I can at least make it through the next few hours with him.

"Sounds good to me," I say, extending my hand. "Now, let's go see what we are in for."

———

I wasn't ready.

Though in my defense, even if I'd had years to prepare and a cheat sheet, I wouldn't have been prepared.

This dinner, is by far, the most uncomfortable thing I've ever been a part of, and I once had to take pictures with a very handsy female senior citizen group who were lifelong Fury fans.

There have been subtle digs at Celine and me. Apparently, I'm a dumb, manwhore jock, and she's unable to understand their inside jokes because she's French. I don't know how Luciano kept his cool with that. I almost punched a wall, and she's not even my girlfriend. It's one thing for them to say shit about me—I deserve it, but making fun of this woman because of her nationality? There are names for that.

Then there was the not-so-sly remark about how this was supposed to be their first Christmas as a united family.

Now we're seated around the table, and the passive-aggressive comments are through the roof.

"How have workouts been going?" Coach Roberts asks, doing his best to try to break up the awkwardness. "Thanks for letting a few of my players come in and lift with you. It's good for them to see what it's going to be like at the next level."

"Anytime. They're cool kids," I say. "But I should be thanking you for letting me use the facilities. It's really been a help."

"I mean, you paid for it. It's the least I could do."

"What did you pay for?" Mrs. Valenti interrupts.

"Mom, he and Cole upgraded the high school football team's weight facility," Lucy says, reaching for my hand under the table, which I gladly give to her. "You knew that. Uncle Nick couldn't stop talking about it for months."

"Oh, I must have forgotten," she says nonchalantly as she sips her wine. "But do you remember when Luciano donated new jerseys to the little league team and gave them a pizza party after their season? How nice was that?"

"Mrs. Valenti, our family has done that every year since I was a kid. That's nothing special."

"Oh, shush now," Mrs. Valenti says. "Don't downplay your efforts in the community. And when did you start calling me Mrs. Valenti? It's Anne Marie. Or Mom. You know that."

I clench my jaw as I listen to her talk to Luciano, and for once, the rage isn't toward him. I've never met Lucy's parents before, but it doesn't take a rocket scientist to see that it doesn't matter who I am or what I mean to Lucy. I'm not Luciano. That's all that matters. Her dad, on the other hand? He hasn't said a word since he opened the door for us. Maybe if I pay him back what he lost on our game last year it will get me into his good graces.

"Celine, how are you liking Laurel Heights?" Lucy completely ignores her mom's comment as she turns to Celine with a smile. "Have you made it down to Cincinnati yet? The restaurants down there are amazing."

"I love it here," she says. "Actually, we stayed in Cincinnati a few days when—"

"Lucy, how is the bank?" Mrs. Tripoli asks. "You must be really busy with it being the holidays."

Lucy's eyes show nothing but shock as she stares at Mrs. Tripoli. "They are, but I was asking Celine a question—"

"So, Bryce, when are you going back to Nashville?" Mrs. Valenti asks.

Apparently, we're not going to let Celine talk tonight.

"Sometime in April. I have some things to take care of before optional camp starts. Celine, what were you saying about Cincinnati?"

"That's too bad," Mrs. Valenti says, not giving Celine a chance to talk. "I'm sorry you and Lucy will only have a few months together."

Excuse me?

"Mom, just because Bryce has to go back to Nashville, it doesn't mean we are going to quit seeing each other."

She starts laughing under her breath. "What are you going to do? Move with him? Be a football player's girlfriend? Ha! Quit acting foolish, dear."

"He's a good kid, Anne Marie," Coach Roberts says in my defense. "You don't need to treat him like a drug dealer."

Mrs. Valenti waves off her brother. "He's a manwhore and not good enough for my daughter. I saw the tabloids last year. Despicable."

If that is the only objections about me, then it would be easy enough to clear the air. Only, it isn't. It's just a convenient excuse.

"Ma'am, I know what you saw last year, and I'm not proud of what I did," I say, my words as apologetic as I can make them. "But please know that I would never cheat on Lucy. I love her, and I'd never want to hurt her."

Mrs. Valenti looks directly at Lucy. "You know, if you and Luciano would just get back together, you wouldn't have to consider moving or worry about what he's doing on the road. You'd be here. Where you want to be."

"Mrs. Valenti, we are not going to be getting married," Luciano chimes in. "We don't love each other like that."

"Oh, stop, Luciano," Mrs. Tripoli says. "You and Lucy belong together, and the quicker you both get over"—she waves dismissively—"whatever these are, then you two can get back together and the wedding will go on as planned."

Lucy stands and screams, "There. Is. No. Wedding!"

I didn't even know her voice could get that loud. "There is no wedding, and I refuse to sit here and listen to you bad mouth the man I love and a woman who is perfectly wonderful and is clearly in love with Luciano."

"You don't love him. You love Luciano. He loves you. You can't fake what you two had."

"Oh my God! Were you that blind?" Lucy yells. "The man could barely stand to touch me in public. The kiss at the engagement party? That was the first time we kissed. Ever. For God's sake, we never even slept together!"

Did she just say what I think she just said?

"Wipe that smile off your face," Coach Roberts whispers to me. "Though, thanks for providing the most entertaining meal in family history."

"Well, I think that waiting is romantic," Mrs. Tripoli says. "You both were waiting for the wedding day."

"No, Mama," Luciano says, reaching for Celine's hand. "I was in love with Celine, and I couldn't bring myself to do it. Plus, Lucy is like my sister. It was . . . well, the thought of it was kind of gross. I was dreading the wedding night as much as I was dreading the marriage."

"Speaking of the wedding day," Lucy chimes back in. "Did

no one notice that every time it was brought up, I went into coughing fits? No way you missed that, Mom. I went through two bags of cough drops at the shower."

"You were just caught up in the excitement of the wedding," Mrs. Valenti says as she chugs the rest of her wine. "Once Bryce goes back to Nashville and Celine goes back to France, we can all sit down and get this all back on track."

"Are you not listening to anything we are saying? We aren't in love. We aren't getting married. I love Bryce, and I'm eventually moving to Nashville."

"Shush. You have no clue what you're talking about."

"No, you two are the ones who don't know what you're talking about. You know the only reason Luciano and I didn't call the wedding off sooner? Because of you all. We each felt this immense pressure not to let all of you down. Then, when we both come to you, asking you to let the people we truly love into your lives, all you can do is bad mouth them because they don't fit in to the story you started writing when we were kids. Well, I'm not going to sit here a minute more and listen to this. Merry Christmas."

Lucy moves her chair back to exit the dining room, and I am two steps behind her. As I pass him, I make eye contact with Coach Roberts, who gives me a subtle head nod.

At least one person in her family likes me.

I catch up to Lucy at the door, where she is frantically trying to get our coats out of the closet. I put my hands on her shoulders, hoping to calm her down.

"Hey," I say, my words finally breaking her trance, "breathe for me."

She does, but I can still feel the tension and anger radiating from her as I turn her toward me.

"What you said in there was amazing. You are amazing. I

didn't know I could love you any more than I already did." I press a kiss to her forehead.

"For once, I agree with Bryce," Luciano says as he comes into the foyer, hand-in-hand with Celine. "You said everything I wanted to but couldn't. Just like always, you're the brave one. Thank you, Lucia. I owe you."

Lucy seems to relax a bit, despite the background noise of yelling in the dining room. "You don't owe me anything. I meant what I said. I'm just sorry the night went like it did."

"Is this not traditional American Christmas?"

We all look at Celine and immediately start laughing. We're so loud we actually drown out the yelling coming from the other room.

"Well, we really didn't eat," Luciano says, checking his watch.

Lucy furrows her brow. "What are you thinking?"

Luciano reaches for Celine's coat and holds it open for her. "I can't believe I'm saying this, but would the two of you like to come back to the restaurant? Maybe a double date of sorts?"

I look at Lucy, who is giving me a pleading look.

My first Christmas with Lucy is going to be spent with the man I've hated most of my life, who is also her ex-fiancé.

It's a damn Christmas miracle.

"Fine, but only if we can get a supreme," I say. "And don't hold back on the breadsticks."

Luciano laughs. "I would never. Though, this will be the first time I've made you a pizza without spitting in it."

My eyes grow wide. "What did you say?"

"I'm kidding. I swear, but your face was priceless. That was the only Christmas gift I needed."

"DID THIS WHOLE NIGHT REALLY HAPPEN?"

"Depends. Did I really volunteer to help move Celine in with Luciano?"

I laugh as I take off my coat. "You did, and then I offered to help them decorate."

I have no clue what to call tonight. A disaster? A break-through? A fight twenty-five years in the making? Honestly, I'll go with all of the above.

About an hour after the epic fight at my parents' house, Uncle Nick messaged Bryce to tell him he was leaving because he couldn't take it anymore and they were out of wine.

Then there was dinner at the restaurant with Luciano and Celine, which was actually pretty great. We all got along, laughed, and told stories. Luciano and Bryce tried to decide who won every fight they had ever been in. The night ended with hugs and handshakes. Bryce even invited Luciano to be a part of next year's Bachelor fantasy league.

I feel like I'm living in a jacked-up version of some Christmas movie where you're in an alternate reality but you don't realize it until you wake up.

"Please tell me tomorrow isn't going to be as eventful," I say as I ungracefully plop onto my couch.

"Unless the Grinch steals the presents and tree from my mom's or Brenna doesn't get her yearly wine subscription, tomorrow will be much less eventful," Bryce says as he sits next to me and then tucks me against his side. "And I bought Brenna her wine."

"I still can't believe my parents treated you like that," I say, laying my head on his shoulder.

"Your dad wasn't so bad."

I sigh. "He and Mr. Tripoli learned long ago not to get involved with any scheme involving my mother and Guiliana. This one, though? This might have taken the cake."

Bryce kisses the top of my head as the weight of the night comes down on me.

"I'm so sorry." I've probably said it a hundred times tonight, but it doesn't seem like enough.

"Don't be," he says, running his fingers up and down my arm. "Plus, the night wasn't a total wash. I learned some interesting tidbits tonight."

"Like what?"

"I seem to remember you telling everyone at your parents' house that you and Luciano never slept together."

I freeze for a second. Crap. I completely forgot that I admitted that.

"Did I say that?"

"You kind of yelled it, but yes," he says, picking me up so I'm now straddling his lap. "Was it true? Or was that just something you said to get your mom off your back?"

I look down, not really wanting to have this conversation, but his finger under my chin tilts my face back up.

"You can tell me anything, you know that right?" he asks.

"If you aren't comfortable talking about it, then that's fine too."

"It's fine." I clear my throat before saying, "No, Luciano and I never slept together. In fact, I can count on one hand how many times he kissed me. The wedding night would have been interesting, to say the least. The man could barely hold my hand."

When he laughs, I wish I hadn't admitted any of that to him.

"Don't laugh." I try to shift off his lap, but his hands clamp on to my hips and hold me in place.

"I'm sorry, I can't help it," he says. "I'm just thinking back to all those times that I was jealous as hell of him. And all he was doing was playing pretend."

"That's actually kind of what we were both doing. It was a relief when I found out we were in it for the wrong reasons."

Bryce's laughter dies down, and he gives me a quick kiss. "How could you want to marry someone you've barely kissed, Lulu?"

"We should go to bed," I say before trying to slid off his lap again. "We have a long day tomorrow and it's late."

"Whoa, wait there." All signs of levity have melted away, and his brow pinches with concern as he catches my eyes. "Did I say something wrong?"

I tip my head to the ceiling and try to find the words I want to say—no, that I *need* to say.

"You really want to know how I could marry someone I didn't love?"

"I do."

I let out a breath. "Because I didn't think I could marry the man I actually loved. I said yes to the first man who asked me because I thought the man I wanted was never going to."

I can see the moment my admission hits him where it hurts, and I hate it, but I couldn't lie to him.

"Lucy, I'm so sorry. I know it's not enough, but—"

I shake my head. "It's in the past, Bryce. We're here now. No use dwelling on it."

I try to stand, but once again, Bryce keeps his hold on me. "You got to talk, now it's my turn."

"You don't need to say anything."

"But I do. I did you wrong for so many years. I made stupid promises that I wanted to keep, I just didn't know how. Since I've been home, I really see that. I've also come to realize that it doesn't have to be one or the other, that I should be able to have both. It was stupid of me to think I had to wait for one to be ready before I could invite in the other."

"Life doesn't work like that."

"I know that now. I don't know why you have given me another chance because we both know that I don't deserve it or you. I never have. But please know that I am never, ever going to let you down again. This? You and me? It's forever, Lulu. Now, that I have you, I'm never letting you go."

For years, I have heard versions of this speech. For years, I've heard words like "forever" and "love" and have latched on to them like a lifeline.

In this moment, there is something different. It could be what we've been through or that the emotions and adrenaline of the day have caught up to me, but this time? This time, I believe him.

This is it. This is happening.

Our off-season is finally here.

"Bryce . . ." I say seconds before my lips press into his. He claims me as fiercely as I claim him, and the second our tongues meet, I feel a surge of heat that I've only ever felt one other time in my life.

His hands travel up my back and quickly make their way to the sides of my breasts. Before I know it, he's cupping each, and if my mouth weren't so busy memorizing the feel of his, I'd be crying out for more.

His fingers find my nipples through my shirt, and with a gentle tug of each, my core clenches and begins throbbing for more.

My hands find the hem of my shirt, but before I can pull it up, Bryce's hands are there, doing it for me. I barely have time to notice the chill of the air on my skin before he's unclasping my bra and tossing that to wherever my shirt landed. Then his mouth is trailing down my neck and chest before it closes over one of my peaked nipples.

Oh sweet baby Jesus . . .

His tongue circles my nipple before he closes his lips around it. I can't help but stare at the act as my hips begin to writhe in his lap.

"Bryce." I moan as he changes his focus to the other side. "More. Please. I need more."

"More of this?" he asks before his tongue starts doing something I hadn't known tongues could do. "Or maybe this?"

"Ah!" I scream when he gently bites my nipple and his hand cups my center through my pants. He might not be making direct contact, but the pressure is enough to set my body on fire.

"Take me to bed, Bryce. Now."

Our eyes lock, and I see nothing but fire in his as I'm sure mine are burning for him.

"Are you sure?" he asks. "Because this is it, Lulu. Once I have you, I'm never going to let you go."

"Promise?"

His smile turns devious as he stands, and I hook my ankles

around his back. Then he's kissing me again while he ascends the stairs and strides into my bedroom.

"I love you," he says, laying me on my bed. "I love you so fucking much."

I want to say the words back to him. They are on the tip of my tongue. However, I'm currently rendered speechless as I watch Bryce strip in front of me.

I've seen him shirtless. That is enough to stop traffic. But as my eyes travel down as his pants slide down his muscular legs, I can't help but stare at his very hard, very well-endowed, penis.

I hurry up and do about fifteen calculations in my head. In none of those does the math work out that his dick is going to fit inside me.

And I don't mess up math.

"Hey," he says, climbing onto the bed with me. "I don't want to see your thinking face right now."

"My thinking face? I don't have a thinking face."

He laughs and places a kiss on my nose. "You do. And it's adorable. Now, whatever has you doing math in that head of yours, I want it to go away. Just lay back and relax. All I want you to do tonight is feel."

I try to do as Bryce says as he kneels in front of me, slowly sliding my leggings down.

"You are so beautiful," he whispers, kissing his way up my leg before placing a gentle kiss on my center. "Are you relaxed yet?"

I close my eyes, doing my best to melt into the feeling of being touched by Bryce. His lips are softly kissing my stomach as he slides off my panties. When they are off, his fingertips slowly trace back up my legs, his feather-light touch leaving goose bumps in its wake. When he lands at my pussy, his fingers begin to circle in my wetness.

"Fuck, Lulu. You're ready for me, aren't you?"

"Please, Bryce," I beg, but I can't help it. Between his touch, his lips, and his words, I'm a mess of emotions.

"Shhh. No more talking," he says. "Close your eyes and feel."

I do as he says, not knowing what to expect next. I want to peek because the anticipation is killing me. Then I feel his mouth on my breast, his tongue circling my hardened nipple again, and it takes all I have not to moan and embarrass myself. Then his warm palm blazes a path down my side, over my hip, and then to my center before he slides a finger into my core.

"Mmmm." I hum, my back arching and my hips raising as I silently beg for more. His free hand cups my breast, giving him more to suck on as his finger works in and out of me. I don't know which one to concentrate on. His mouth is warm, and each time he nips my skin, it sends a throb of heat straight to my clit. The finger he's sinking into me is making my toes curl, and when he adds a second one, it steals the breath from my lungs.

"Oh!" I whimper as Bryce hits the spot inside me that sends sparks dancing along every nerve in my body.

"That's it, Lulu. You're so close. I can feel how close you are." Bryce's finger continues to work inside me, but his lips have made their way to my mouth. I grab his face and pull his lips against mine, needing to drink in the taste of him as much as I need something to hold on to. God, I feel like I'm about to explode all over this room.

I want to beg him to stop in one breath and demand he keep going with the next because he's making me feel too much all at once. I'm not sure I can handle it. Then his lips swallow all the needy noises that fall from me as his thumb presses against my clit.

My entire body starts to vibrate, and the only thing I can focus on is the press of his fingers inside me and the slow circles of his thumb on me before I'm exploding for him.

He brings me down slowly from my orgasm, and when he releases his fingers, I immediately miss the feeling of him inside me. I want to scream for him to get back here and to keep doing whatever it is that he was doing.

Because that was really freaking good.

I open my eyes, feeling slightly drunk, and before I know it, Bryce is back on the bed, sheathing his thick cock.

Please math be wrong. Please math be wrong.

"I love you, Lucy," he says, slowly kissing me as he lines himself with my center. "I have loved you for so long."

"I love you," I say back, wrapping my arms around his neck as he slowly pushes into me.

I tense, expecting it to hurt, and he pauses, tucking his face against the crook of my neck. There is a slight tremor in his shoulders, as if it's taking everything inside him to hold still so he doesn't hurt me.

"I got you, Lulu. I got you," he says as he presses open-mouthed kisses up the column of my neck. "I've got you."

Slowly, I relax around him, but it isn't until I rock my hips a fraction, inviting him to push deeper, that he relents. His arms snake under my body so his hands can hold on to my shoulders and tuck me against him. The man is everywhere around me and inside me, and it's so much more perfect than I thought it would be.

That is, until he starts to move. The way he withdraws from me is close to torture, and when he sinks back in, I'm so full it's almost as if I can't breathe. His lips are relentless as they taste my skin. His words are sweet nothings that become a litany of praise as his hips move.

"God, Lucy." He moans into my neck. "You feel so good. Too good."

"You feel—" Whatever I was going to say is stolen from my thoughts when he seats himself deep inside me and rolls his hips.

I thought it felt good when his fingers were doing the work. But now? Feeling his cock inside me? It's better than anything I can think of.

"Bryce!" I rock my hips up to meet his. My eyes close so I have no choice but to only feel everything he's doing to me. "Bryce, don't stop."

He's going to make me come again, and I chase the high like an addict. I didn't know before tonight that orgasms like that even existed, and now, I get two of them? My mind wants to figure out that probability, but then he leans back, flips me, over, and pushes back into me so I couldn't do basic math if I tried.

When he pulls my hips back against his thrusts, it's almost too much, and my arms collapse, dropping my chest against the mattress. His pace falters, and he lets out a low groan of appreciation.

"Do you know how hot you look right now?" he asks as one of his palms burns a line along the length of my spin, coaxing me to arch my hips higher before reclaiming its grasp on my hip. "So beautiful, LuLu."

Holy fuck, I want to hold out longer, but the feeling of this position is too good to ignore. So, when my body clamps around him and my vision narrows down to the flood of plea-sure rioting through my blood, I let myself fall into it.

"So perfect," is the last thing I register before he stills, his release pulsing into me as his grip on my hips turns bruising. I'm too blissed out to care, though.

The math was wrong. Thank God the math was wrong.

Soon we collapse on the bed, Bryce just to the side of me as we try to catch our breath. I almost think we fall asleep until I feel the bed move as Bryce gets up to dispose of the condom.

For years, I wondered what this would be like. I've had fantasy after fantasy, each and every one a little different from the one before it.

Never once did I imagine it would be like that simply because I had no idea sex like that even existed.

"YOU OKAY?" Lucy asks, squeezing my hand. "You know you don't have to do this today?"

"No, I do," I say as I try to force my feet to move forward. "It's been too long."

I'm standing staring at the Nashville Fury facility, paralyzed by the fear of what I'm about to do.

Apologize.

I haven't been here since I was put on the injured list three months ago. The last time I was here, I told off my coaches and said a bunch of stuff I'll never be able to take back.

The fact that Coach McAvoy and Coach Davis are even willing to talk to me today is some sort of New Year's miracle in and of itself. I wouldn't talk to me if the situations were reversed.

"I'm right here," Lucy says. "I'll be right beside you for as long as you want me in the room. You've worked hard, Bryce. They have to know that or else they wouldn't have agreed to meet you."

They did agree to meet with me. However, to make sure we didn't stir up a story that didn't need to be reported yet, they are meeting me at six in the morning on New Year's Eve. Also known as the butt crack of dawn on a day the reporters all have better things to be talking about.

"All right, let's go." I say, taking one last deep breath as I walk into the facility hand-in-hand with Lucy.

I didn't expect anything to change in three months, yet, it feels almost foreign to me. The murals of Fury teams of the past are still on the walls. Pictures of great plays and memories are still in the same places, and at the end of the hall, there's the newest addition to the mural—Cole lifting me up in celebration after we made it to the playoffs our rookie year.

We could have done it again this year had my head not been so far up my own ass.

I fucked it all up because I acted like a spoiled brat who didn't get his way.

"Bryce," Coach McAvoy says as we turn the corner to the locker rooms and his office.

"Coach." I extend a hand, which he accepts. Just that act alone relaxes me slightly.

"Good to see you," he says. "And this must be her?"

Lucy's cheeks turn red as I bring her a little closer to me. I almost forgot how much I loved that blush. "Yes, sir. Lucy Valenti, Coach Hunter McAvoy."

"It's nice to meet you, Lucy," he says. "Come on back. We are all waiting for you."

All? Who else is here besides him and Davis?

Turns out that the answer is everyone. It's a full house when we enter Coach McAvoy's office. Sitting on the corner of his desk is his fiancée Sadie, a sports reporter who used to cover the Fury. That is until her and Coach McAvoy started dating. Now she's a national reporter with *US Daily,* who is kicking ass and taking names.

Coach Davis is sitting on a chair, but he hasn't made eye

contact with me yet. He's too busy holding who I'm guessing is his daughter, as his fiancée, Bethany, looks on.

Leaning against the wall, wearing a shit-eating grin, is Cole.

"What are you doing here?" I ask as I give him a hug.

"Coach told me you reached out and asked me if I could come in. I debated, then he said Lucy was coming and she's really who I wanted to see."

"It's good to see you too, Cole" she says, stepping to him so he can give her a kiss on the cheek.

"Well let's get started," Coach McAvoy says, sitting down. "How you doing, Bryce?"

I begin to answer, but the sound of a wail cuts me off.

Damn Davis's kid has a pair of lungs.

"She's hungry," Bethany says. "I'll take her so you guys can talk."

"Lucy and I will come!" Sadie says as she jumps off the desk.

"You don't have to," Bethany says, giving Sadie a questioning look.

"Apparently, you missed the part of the plan where the only reason we came at this ungodly hour was so we could meet the woman who made this man act like a fool. No offense, Bryce. You boys have fun. Come on, Lucy. I want to know how you pulled his head out of his ass."

Lucy looks slightly horrified and confused as Sadie leads her out of the office.

I just give her my best reassuring smile because she's in good hands. Sadie might be a little over the top, but she's good people. She and Bethany are exactly the kind of women I can see Lucy becoming friends with.

"Does she have a filter?" Davis asks Hunter as Sadie shuts the door.

"Never has, and I hope she never will," Hunter says with a smile. "Now, where were we?"

All eyes in the office shift back to me. The only thing that is missing is one of those old-time interrogation lamps. My throat goes dry, and everything I'd planned to say somehow disappeared the second Lucy walked out of the office.

"I swear I knew what I was going to say when I woke up this morning," I say, trying to figure out the best place to start.

"How about we help," Hunter says, sitting back in his chair. "How are you doing? And if the word *fine* comes out of your mouth, this meeting is done."

I crack a smile. "I'm . . . better. Well, getting there. As Malcolm likes to tell me, I'm a work in progress. He's done a lot to help me identify my triggers and is helping me find healthy ways to deal with my issues. We're starting to focus on my return to football, and how I need to take on little bits at a time so I'm not overwhelmed and shut down."

"And the drinking?" Davis asks. Just like him to cut to the chase.

"Besides one lapse in judgement three months ago, I haven't had a drop. It's just easier to stay away from it."

"So, you're sober?" Davis reiterates.

"I guess I am," I say, though I've never thought about it like that. The transition to being sober wasn't one I made consciously. I just knew that, when I was drunk, I made bad choices. I almost ruined my career as well as the two best relationships in my life.

I needed those back, and to make sure that happened, I needed to stop making bad decisions.

"Well, you look good," Hunter says. "Working out? Doing drills?"

I nod. "Every day. Doing as much as I can without a

receiver. It will be nice to get back into the routine with the guys."

A silence falls in the room.

Shit . . . did I overstep? I assumed the injured tag meant I was free to come back when next season started. Did I assume wrong? Am I not going to be back in Nashville next year?

"You know it's not going to be as easy as you walking back into the locker room and saying you're back, right?" Hunter says. "You alienated a lot of your teammates before you left."

I look at Cole, who raises an eyebrow as if to say I should have expected this. I never thought coming back was going to be easy, but I guess I underestimated how hard it was going to be.

I was an asshole to everyone. Cole tried his best to defend me and defuse situations, but I know that only went so far. When I think about how I treated Dexter, I want to throw up. I was horrible to him, and the kid did nothing wrong. He's also not a kid. He's a year younger than I am, and I treated him like shit on my shoe.

"Seems like I'm going to have a lot of steak dinners to buy," I say, trying to make a joke.

"The words 'I'm sorry' will also go a long way."

I meet Davis's eyes. Out of all the people I treated horribly over the past year, he's the one I need to be apologizing to the most. He was the one who noticed before anyone that I was falling down the slope. He tried on more than one occasion to pick me up, but I wasn't having it.

"They will," I say as I move to stand in front of him. "And you need to be the first one in this room that I say that to. I'm sorry, Coach. I'm sorry I acted like an idiot. I'm sorry I didn't take your help when you offered. And . . . I am so sorry for the things I said on that last day here. That was one of the worst things I've ever done in my life, and I'm ashamed thinking about it. Please know that's not who I am, and if you and Coach McAvoy will allow me, I promise you I'll be the best damn quarterback you ever coach."

I have no idea what's about to happen. Is it too little, too late?

"I don't want that. We don't want that," he says, motioning to Hunter as my stomach drops to my feet.

"No," Hunter says, standing and walking around his desk. "We know you're a good quarterback. We wouldn't have drafted you if we weren't. What we want is for you to be the best man you can be for your teammates, your family, yourself, and that girl out there who clearly loves you."

I look over my shoulder and see Lucy holding Davis's baby. She looks up and meets my gaze, gifting me a smile that could melt an iceberg.

"It's not going to be easy," Hunter says, bringing my attention back to him. "There are going to be questions. You're going to have to do a media tour. You're going to have to mend a lot of bridges with your teammates. Are you ready for all of that?"

I look at Cole, who gives me a nod. It's one that screams that he's had my back since we were little and that isn't going to change anytime soon.

"I am," I say. "Let's get to work."

"IT'S SO LOUD!" I yell as Bryce and I try to move through the groups of people packing the sidewalks on Broadway.

"It's Nashville, Lulu!" Bryce says as we break free so we can cross the street. "Come on, we're almost there."

I grip Bryce's hand a little tighter as we walk another block to the restaurant where we're meeting Cole. Bryce told me that Nashville on New Year's got a little crazy, but I had no idea this is what he meant.

I also didn't realize how many people I would see not-so-discreetly taking pictures of us. Then there were the two girls who didn't know the meaning of the word discreet as they pushed me out of the way to take a selfie with him.

Is this going to be my life if I move here?

We enter the dimly lit restaurant, and Cole's voice stops me from going down that rabbit hole. "Bryce! Lucy!"

"Hey, man," Bryce says, dropping my hand so he can man-hug Cole. The two slap each other's back a few times, and I can't help but get a little choked up at the sight.

These two have been best friends for so long, and I'm really glad that Cole has been there for Bryce when he needed someone.

"Hey, Lucy," Cole says, leaning in to give me a kiss on the cheek. "Even though I know you've been here for a few days, let me officially welcome you to Nashville."

"Thanks," I say as the hostess takes us to our table at the back of the restaurant. I don't know if it is on purpose, but I'm thankful for the semblance of privacy.

"Has the news broke that Bryce Donald is back in town? Or did the meeting stay quiet?" Cole asks as we take our seats.

"Not that I've seen," Bryce says. "Though, judging by the pictures I know were taken tonight on our way down here, I'm sure the news will get out soon enough."

"Better you than me," Cole says as the waitress places waters on our table and takes our drink orders. "So, how is Laurel Heights?"

"Same as usual," Bryce says. "Except now I've replaced you as my best friend."

"With who?"

"Luciano."

Cole nearly spits out his water. "I'm sorry, are we talking about the man Lucy almost married?"

"One and the same. Oh, and he wants in on our fantasy league next year. The man knows his stuff."

I look over the menu as Bryce and Cole catch up on the events of the last week. Normally, Cole would have been home for Christmas, but his family decided to spend the holiday in Florida this year with his sister and her family.

If my family had done that, maybe we would still be speaking.

I figured we would need a few days to calm down after what I'm dubbing as The Laurel Heights Christmas Massacre. Then they somehow found out I was coming to Nashville, and my mom lost it. I'm not going to let that stop me from having a good time, checking out the city, and maybe taking a drive through Franklin to see the houses I bookmarked on Zillow.

"What do you think of Nashville, Lucy?" Cole asks after the waitress drops off our drinks and takes our orders.

"It's something," I say, not wanting to lie, but not knowing the exact words I want to use. "It's busier than I thought it would be."

"Maybe New Year's wasn't the best time to bring you down here," Bryce says, reaching for my hand under the table. "It usually isn't this packed."

"The country music festival would have been worse. Oh, and most weekends, which are bachelorette party central."

"If the Rockers make the playoffs. Then the city becomes hockey crazy."

"I can't wait until we make the championship game," Cole says. "This place is going to be nuts."

My eyes bug out a little more with each event they name. While I'd love nothing more than to be here for a championship parade for the Fury, I could do without the other random, loud weekends.

I didn't realize until I got here that I'm a small-town girl at heart. The people and the crowds are okay in small doses—like, maybe once a year.

"I'm glad we could do this," Bryce says. "I hope I didn't take you away from a hot date."

Cole laughs under his breath. "Why in the world would you think I had a date?"

"Oh, come on. It's New Year's. You're a good-looking, single guy. Why wouldn't you have a date?"

"Aw, you think I'm good-looking."

"Of course, I do," Bryce says. All I can do is shake my head. These two are like an old married couple. "Plus, when Lucy moves here, I'm sure she'll want a friend to hang out with when we're on the road or in training camp hell."

"Oh no," I say, shaking my head in disagreement. "Do not bring me into this. I'm sure Cole is very capable of finding a date whenever he wants one."

"Thank you, Lucy," Cole says. "Plus, I'd never take a girl out on a first date on New Year's Eve. That's way too much pressure."

"Brenna is on a first date as we speak."

"What? With who?" Bryce asks.

"Not sure. She met him online." I shrug. "I asked if she wanted to come so I had someone to hang out with when you were meeting with the coaches, but she already had plans made. Plus, I think it's romantic. If it goes well, she can say she started her year by finding love."

"Excuse me," Cole says, standing so quickly that he almost runs into the waiter bringing our food.

"What's that about?" More specifically, why did Cole's face drain of color when I said Brenna was on a date.

Interesting.

"No clue," Bryce says, leaning over and silently asking for a kiss, which of course I give to him.

"Oh my gosh, Bryce Donald!"

Our kiss is interrupted, and the second our lips release, Bryce goes from my Bryce to football player Bryce.

I haven't seen this version of him in person since high school, and I don't miss it. Correction, I didn't miss the women throwing themselves at him.

"Hi," he says to two blondes, who apparently aren't fans of skirts that cover more than a bare minimum of skin. "Nice to meet you."

"Oh, we met last summer at Tootsies," the girl on the left says, inching her way closer to him. "Don't you remember?"

Bryce's face goes white for a second, and I know exactly what he's thinking.

He's trying to remember if he slept with them or not, and considering it isn't going back to its natural color, I'm going to guess the answer is yes.

Breathe, Lucy. You knew this was a possibility. It's just happening sooner than you thought.

"Can't say I do," he says, bringing me closer to him. "Now, if you ladies can excuse me, I'd like to get back to dinner with my girlfriend."

Their gazes immediately snap to me, and I think they honestly didn't realize I was here.

Bitches.

"Oh, we didn't think this was . . . a thing," the one on the right says.

"Ladies, I don't want to be rude, but I'd really like to go back to having dinner with my girlfriend."

"Oh, come on, Brycie, just one picture for old time's sake?"

"He said no," I say. Or did I yell? I'm not sure but I probably yelled it. There are far too many people staring over at us for me to have just said it.

"Excuse me? What did you say?"

I square my shoulders because, apparently, this girl woke up today and chose violence. "I said, he said no. So, move it along and take her with you. Find another jock to chase."

I don't know where this sudden burst of confidence is coming from. It's like Brenna is sending me her don't-fuck-with-me vibes all the way from Ohio.

"You heard her, ladies," Bryce says, and the smile on his face stretches from ear to ear. "Have a good night."

With a huff, an eyeroll, and a turned heel, the two cleat chasers stomp off. Before they are even five steps away, Bryce's mouth is on mine in a kiss that is not appropriate for public.

"We need to go," he says as he breaks away, grabbing his wallet and throwing a few hundred-dollar bills onto the table.

"What?" I ask, still dazed from the kiss that almost knocked me off my chair.

"That was the hottest thing I have ever seen, and if we're not back at my place in ten minutes, I'm going to fuck you in the street and I don't care who is watching."

Well then.

"NOW THIS IS part of Nashville I can handle."

I chuckle as Lucy situates herself between my legs and rests her head against my bare chest. We're relaxed on one of the chase loungers on the patio of my penthouse apartment, watching the sky light up with New Year's Eve fireworks.

There are a few perks of signing the biggest rookie contract in league history. One of them is being able to afford this penthouse with a spectacular view that overlooks the whole city.

It also has enough privacy that Lucy and I can be out here naked under a blanket after having the most intense sex of my life.

Watching her tell off those groupies was a shot of pure adrenaline straight to my dick. We weren't even inside five seconds before I had her stripped and was eating her pussy against the door of my penthouse. I really meant to take her to bed because I needed to be inside her more than I needed to breathe, but we only made it to the living room.

"I can't believe you have this view," Lucy says.

"I know," I say, lifting the blanket to get another look at her spectacular tits.

"I meant of the city," she says before playfully slapping my hand. "How do you live here? Maybe I've been in a small town too long, but there were . . . just so many people."

"I know," I say, kissing the top of her head. "This may be about as crazy as it gets, but it's still a pretty busy city."

"I guess I'll have to get used to it." There is a lilt of sadness in her tone that I can't ignore.

"You know we don't have to live in the city," I say. "Those big ol' houses that we drove by earlier? We can get one of those. Or we can build you one."

She turns her head to look up at me. "But won't it be hard for you to get to the facility during the season?"

"There are things called cars. And, you might not realize this, but I make a lot of money and can afford one," I say, situating her so she's now sitting across my lap, which is probably how I avoided an eyeroll for my smartass comment. "I know the city isn't for you. All night, I could tell how uncomfortable you were. I want you to be happy here. Though, I'll admit, living downtown was fun for me these last couple of years."

"Sure, it was," she says with an exaggerated eye roll. That one I couldn't hide from.

"It *was*. That's not who I am anymore. There are plenty of really nice areas that aren't a bad drive in and out of the city. You never know, we could move in next door to some famous country stars. If that doesn't work, then I bet I could talk Cole into moving in next to us. Then whenever he meets his future wife, you two can become best friends and we can raise our kids together. Despite what he said earlier."

By the time I'm done, I'm sitting up straight and I'm pretty sure my voice hit an octave I'm not used to hitting. I can't help it. The thought of planning my future with Lucy gets me all sorts of excited. It's like I'm a kid seeing Santa a week before Christmas and I'm rushing to tell him everything on my list.

"You have it all planned out, don't you?"

"I do. It doesn't hurt that Cole and I have had this plan since our freshman year to either marry sisters or best friends and live next door to each other so we could grow old together."

"Speaking of Cole, have you heard from him since he took off?"

"Yeah, he's fine," I say. "He said something came up."

"On New Year's Eve? He seemed pretty upset when I brought up Brenna. Is that why he left?"

"To go to Ohio and chase her down? Absolutely not," I say. "She's a little sister to him. That's Bro Code 101. Thou shalt not think another bro's sister is hot."

"Still, something seemed off," she says, but I really have no interest in talking about Cole. I'd much rather be kissing her, so that's what I do. I lower my mouth to hers and kiss her as if there is nothing else in the world but us and this moment.

"What was that for?" she asks as I slowly pull away.

"Because I wanted to."

She giggles as I lean forward to claim her lips again, and quickly, that laughter turns into moans. Moans that go straight to my cock.

I could kiss this woman forever. What am I going to do when I'm on the road and I can't wake up next to her? Or steal a kiss just because I can? It's going to be miserable, which is why I need to make sure I don't waste a second that we are together.

In such a short amount of time, I've become addicted to her. Yes, I've wanted her for years, but I never let myself have her. Now I know what she tastes and feels like. I crave her when she's not around. Her kisses, her body, her laugh, her everything.

As I kiss her under the open sky, fireworks glowing above

us, I know for a fact it's only her. It's only ever been her. It will only ever be her. She's it for me.

I'm going to marry this girl.

Our mouths separate, and she slowly starts placing kisses along my jawline before she's trailing them down my neck. Then to my chest as her body slides down the front of mine.

"What are you doing, Lulu?"

She moves a little farther down, placing one last kiss on the tip of my cock. "You had your fun earlier. Now it's my turn."

Then Lucy's mouth is taking me all in, which is not an easy feat. Her hand is working me in conjunction, and holy hell, this is the best thing I have ever felt in my life. And not just because my girl knows what she's doing but because she's the one doing it. It's my Lulu, and watching her take me in and out of her hot mouth? Hearing her little moans as I slowly thrust up and down? It might be the best thing I have ever seen in my life.

"Jesus, Lucy." I moan as I fist my hands at my sides so I don't sink them into her hair. "Baby that feels so good."

When I bump the back of her throat, my restraint almost snaps, but when she hums her pleasure and I feel the vibration in my balls, I can't take it anymore.

"Come here." I pick her up and shift her so she's straddling me.

"I didn't want to stop."

"Tough," I say before dipping my head and closing my lips around her nipple. I've learned if there is one thing that gets my girl going, it's this.

And I make sure to do it every damn time.

She arches her back, giving me all the access I want. I switch to the other one, flicking my tongue across her nipple.

"Bryce," she moans as she slides herself over my hard cock. "I need you."

"I got you, Lulu."

Just as I'm about to line myself up with her, I stop and groan in frustration.

"Hold on," I say, lifting her off my lap. "Do not move a muscle."

"Wait," she says grabbing my arm and pulling me back down. "Are you . . . are we safe?" I pause and raise an eyebrow, silently asking her for clarification. "I'm on the pill, and I know you've—" She presses her lips together to stop whatever she was going to say.

I sit back down and press a kiss to her lips, hopefully chasing those thoughts right out of her head.

"I've always been safe," I say. Even in my drunkest hook ups, I always remembered to wrap up. "And I got tested at the start of camp because the team required it. I'm safe. I'm clean. But are you sure?"

She nods and kisses me again. "I trust you."

I didn't know those three words could have such an effect on me, but they do. It's like she just gave me a gift I didn't know I wanted.

Without breaking the kiss, Lucy pushes me back and then shifts to straddle my lap again. The second she lowers her hot, wet center onto me, I swear to God I see stars.

Being with Lucy is a dream. This? With nothing between us? This is something that there are no words to describe.

"Fuck." I hiss the word through gritted teeth as I sit up and smash her chest against mine. "Fuck you feel so good."

My tone is deep as I take her hips in my hands, guiding her up and down as she rides my cock. I lay back, wanting to see every moment of this. I need to capture the beauty that is Lucy as she braces herself on my chest as she rides me. She is so uninhibited, so free. She rarely lets herself go like this, but when she does, it's a beautiful sight to watch.

"Yes," she cries as she grips my shoulders for balance. "More, Bryce. I need more."

That is a request I can fulfill. With her tight against me, I shift us so her back is pressed to the lounger. She's gasping for breath, and her whole body arches in pleasure as I force her thighs wide before moving her legs to rest against my shoulders.

Almost desperately, she reaches for me, for something to hold on to, and I groan in encouragement as her nails bite into my hips.

"More," she begs, and I kiss away her plea as I give her everything.

"Ahhh!"

Her orgasm is too much for me to handle, and I thrust so deeply into her that I hope I stamp myself onto her soul as I explode. Never in my life have I climaxed so hard that it made me dizzy, but I'm pretty sure I black out for a second. Holy shit. . . I want that again.

I don't have the words.

My brain is broken.

As I scoop her into my arms, kissing every part of her I can, all I know is that I'm never letting her go.

Yup. I'm marrying this girl.

"BRYCE."

I hear Lucy's sleepy, sexy voice as she gently tries to wake me up, but I don't open my eyes. Instead, I just reach for her, bringing her warm body closer to me.

"Bryce, you need to wake up. Your alarm is going off."

I blink my eyes open, wondering why it didn't wake me up.

Actually, I do know why I didn't hear my phone: It's all the way across the room in the pocket of my jeans. Last night Lucy yanked them off me and tossed them after we got back from our double date with Celine and Luciano, and I had better things to think about other than my cell phone.

Have I said before how much I love this woman?

Unwillingly, I let Lucy go and roll out of her bed, stumble across the room, find my phone, and then silence the alarm. Instead of staying up and getting dressed, I climb back into bed with her, quickly bringing her back into my arms. It's March in Ohio, which means the mornings are still cold. What better place to be than in bed with a naked, soft, and usually horny in the mornings Lucy?

"What are you doing?" She might be asking me the question, but that doesn't stop her from burrowing her head into my shoulder and hiking her leg over my hip.

"I'm going to take the day off," I say, kissing the top of her head.

"Can you do that?"

"I've been working out or running drills or watching film every day for five months. I think I can take a little break and have a lazy Sunday morning with my girl."

I don't tell her that today's lazy Sunday is brought to us courtesy of Malcolm. While he said that he's proud of me and the strides I've made, he doesn't want me to burn out before I'm even back.

I'm not going to argue with him about getting to spend more time in bed with Lucy.

"So, what do you want to do today?" I ask. "Options are to stay naked all day, go grocery shopping, or start to pack your things for Nashville. I, for one, am a big fan of options one and three."

My hands move across her soft skin before she shifts off me and rests her hand under her head.

"Actually, we need to talk about Nashville."

"That wasn't an option," I say, leaning in for a kiss, which I'm denied.

"Bryce, we need to figure some things out, and we don't really have a whole lot of time left to do it."

She's right. I know she is.

"Fine," I say, sitting up against her headboard, "but we're talking naked."

She rolls her eyes and pulls the sheet up to cover herself. Guess that means no morning sex. "Fine. But you can't look, you won't concentrate."

She knows me so well.

"First things first," she begins, and even though she doesn't have a list in front of her, she might as well. "Time frame."

"I have to go back at the end of April," I say. "Everyone thinks it's best that I get in early and meet with the public relations department about how we're going to handle my coming back. Then there is rookie camp in May, which I'd like to be there for, then training camp at the end of July."

"Megan's baby is due in the second week of May," she says. "And she'll be on maternity leave through July. I promised the bank that I would get them through that before I left."

"I can come home in early July," I offer. "That will at least break it up a little before I report back for training camp."

"You can?"

"I don't see why not," I say, reaching for her hands and linking our fingers together. "July is everyone's last chance at freedom. All of the coaches and players are with their families. Plus, after the media tour, I'll be ready for a few days with you."

I thought that would make her happy. Hell, just the thought of coming back and getting to see her makes me happy. Only, she doesn't look as happy about it as I am.

"Lucy? Talk to me. What's the matter?"

She looks away, quickly catching a rogue tear that has fallen from her eye. "I want to believe you. I want exactly what you just said. This is balance. This is us talking and planning together to make sure you do what you need on the field while making sure I'm still part of your life. It just . . . it seems too good to be true. All I can think—"

Nope. I know what she's about to say. She's going to bring up the last seven years, but I need her to know this time is different.

"I know I can't erase the past no matter how much I want to. But I promise you, Lucy Valenti, I will do everything I can to come back in July. I want this more than I want my next breath. Now that I know what it's like to wake up every day with you in my arms, there is no way I'll give it up. I can't do this life without you. I love you, Lucy. So, trust me—trust us to make this work, okay?"

That stray tear that escaped a second ago is nothing compared to the tears falling from her beautiful eyes right now. I'd be worried if she weren't also smiling and biting her bottom lip like she does when she gets overwhelmed.

"That's all I ask is that you come back to me."

"And I will. I'll be back in July for a few weeks before I go to camp."

"I know you'll be busy with training camp that you won't even know what day it is, which I'm prepared for. I'll take that time to move down there so we're settled before the season starts. How does that sound?"

How does it sound? It sounds too good to be true. It sounds like everything I've ever wanted.

I lean in and kiss the corner of her mouth. "Nashville by September?"

She smiles, giving me a little nod. "Nashville by September. We can do this."

We can do this. For the first time in my life, I feel like I have everything I could ever want or need. I have Lucy, I have Mom and Brenna, and my football career is back on track.

This is it. Now, not to screw it up.

"Well, if this conversation is over, then I suggest we get back to what I want to do today," I say, reaching for Lucy and bringing her to my chest.

"Maybe I'm not done," she says.

"Yes, you are," I say before kissing her, and it isn't just any kiss, either. It's one that screams we aren't going anywhere today. "We only have one more month before I leave. I'm not wasting a second."

CHAPTER 32
LUCY

I FEEL as if I've been holding my breath for two days, waiting to see if the other shoe is going to drop.

I don't think anyone would blame me considering my history with Bryce.

Yes, he says all the right things. Yes, his actions match his words, but it's easy to keep his promises when I'm his only focus. It's when he has to split his focus that I worry about. He's always drawn that line between football and the rest of his life, and my gut tells me that changing that habit isn't going to be quite as easy as he seems to think.

We hadn't spent a night apart in four months until two nights ago. The first night made sense since he was exhausted after helping his mom relandscape the yard for spring and crashed at her house.

Last night, though, I didn't so much as get a call telling me that he wasn't coming over. No good-night text or quick message to let me know he'd talk to me in the morning.

Nothing.

When I finally got ahold of him today, he blamed it on the fact that I had to tutor this morning and he didn't want to wake up that early. It's never stopped him before, but I didn't press.

I've been trying not to let these thoughts stir in my brain, but when I'm not busy, it's all I can think about. More specifically that it's two weeks until he leaves for Nashville, and something happened in the last few days that made him realize this.

And now he's starting to pull away.

"Have you had a chance to sign the loan approval papers yet?" Megan asks, which causes me to jump out of my seat.

"Shit! You scared me!"

"Sorry," she says, waddling her way over to my desk. The woman is thirty weeks pregnant and looks like she could pop at any time. "I knocked so I thought you heard me."

"You're fine. I'm just . . . let me grab those for you." I scramble to find the papers that are stacked somewhere on my desk.

"Everything okay?" Megan asks, taking a seat in one of the chairs in front of my desk. "I'm getting vibes of pre-Bryce Lucy, and I don't see rainbows coming out of your butt. What's going on? Oh shit, do you need cough drops?"

Ugh, it's really annoying that Megan's bullshit meter has only grown during her pregnancy and she's even less cautious about calling me on my own shit.

"It's Bryce," I say. "He's been acting strange the past few days, and I don't really think it's a coincidence that it's getting closer to when he has to go back to Nashville. I'm . . . I'm just worried he's starting to pull away."

I tell her about the past few days, hoping that she'll pull me out of this spiral of paranoid thoughts and tell me I'm overreacting.

"That is weird," she says. "I don't blame you for freaking out."

"Really? No, 'Don't worry, Lucy, everything is going to be fine?'"

"Do you want me to lie to you? I mean I can if you want."

"No," I say, sliding down farther into my chair. "I know I need to talk to him, but he won't answer my texts."

"Have you tried to call him? Or Brenna? Maybe she knows."

"I did," I say. "She was acting weird too, which doesn't make any sense. Unless she knows something that I don't. Oh God! What if he's going to break up with me, and she knows but doesn't want to be the one who lets it slip?"

Now I'm panicking for a whole other reason. Is that what's about to happen? Has he realized that push is coming to shove, and he can't balance football with what it takes to make a relationship work? Is he going to end it before he leaves for Nashville?

"Okay, you need to calm down," Megan says. "Do my breathing exercises with me. I feel like they could help."

"I don't need to do Lamaze," I snap. "I need to talk to him. I need to nip this in the bud before I have a panic attack."

"We don't need that," Megan says, slowly pushing herself up from the chair. "How about you take an early lunch. Try to find him and hash this out so you can quit having your mind go in all sorts of directions. Take all the time you need."

"Really?" I ask, a little confused as to why she'd volunteer that option. "It's your lunchbreak, and the last time you missed lunch, you almost attacked a customer because you were hangry."

"I'll be fine," she says, waving me off. "Plus, I have a feeling you won't have to go far."

I have no idea what she's talking about, but I grab my purse out of my desk drawer and I all but sprint out of my office. I'm not even two steps out when I'm stopped in my tracks.

There are balloons everywhere, and there are bouquets of flowers on almost every surface.

"What in the world . . ."

My eyes don't know where to look, but as I scan the room, I realize I missed the five people standing in front of me, each holding a piece of posterboard with a letter on it.

Brenna is holding a P.

Luciano is holding an R.

Celine is holding an O.

Cole is holding the M.

Then there is Bryce, who is holding a question mark and wearing the biggest grin I have ever seen.

"What is this?" I ask as I fight back tears.

Bryce lowers his sign and comes to me, taking each of my hands in his. "Apparently, this is how guys these days ask girls to prom. It's called a Promposal—or, at least, that's what my workout buddies tell me. The balloons were their idea."

"The flowers were mine," Luciano chimes in proudly.

I can't help but laugh. Also, somewhere deep inside me, seventeen-year-old Lucy is freaking out.

"Seven years ago, I had to break my first promise to you. I promised you that I would take you to prom. I wanted nothing more than to see you in a beautiful dress, put on a tuxedo, and dance with you all night. Now, I know it won't be the same and we will be going as chaperones because apparently twenty-four is too old to go to prom, but Lucy Valenti, will you go to prom with me?"

"Yes," I say between laughter and tears. "Yes, I will go to prom with you."

Cheers erupt as Bryce scoops me in his arms, stealing a kiss in the middle of the bank lobby.

"Is this why you've been acting strange?" I ask.

"Yeah," he says as he puts me down. "I was scared I was going to slip. I figured it would be safer if I stayed away."

"I thought you were breaking up with me!" I yell, gently slapping his chest. "And you!" I yell, pointing at Megan, "Were you in on this?"

"Of course, I was," she says as she blows the imaginary dust off her nails. "I was the distraction so they could get this all ready. If you weren't in a talkative mood, I was going to force you to talk about baby names."

Everyone congratulates us before making their way out of the bank. Bryce is the only one who hangs back, and he moved to lean a shoulder against the threshold to my office.

I walk over to him and snake my hands around his waist.

"I love you," I say, going up on my toes for a kiss. "But next time you plan a big surprise, please don't pull away. I honestly thought you were going to break up with me."

"I'm sorry," he says before he flashes me his best pouty lip. "I promise I'll make it up to you."

"You better." I steal another kiss. "Now, I have another ten minutes for my lunch break. Want to—"

Bryce picks me up, cutting off my words, and slams the door to my office closed behind us.

PROM NIGHT seven years ago might have been one of the worst nights of my life. Maybe only second to the night I found out Lucy was getting married.

I found out that day she was at prom with Luciano—a fact I had to pry from Brenna. I laid in my bed all night, frustrated as all hell that he was the one who got to dance with her. That she was in his arms and not mine. All I could picture was his smug smile taunting me that he was with her and I wasn't.

Funny how life works out sometimes.

I laugh as I think about that as I hold Lucy close to me and we dance to some slow song I've never heard. I didn't think I was old until I heard what kids listened to these days.

"What's so funny," she asks without looking up. She keeps her cheek on my chest, exactly where it belongs.

"I was thinking back to prom night and how I wanted nothing more than to murder Luciano because he was here with you and I wasn't."

"That was funny?"

"Not back then. Though, it is funny now that Luciano is the one insisting on throwing my going away party."

"I always told you he was a good guy," she says as she looks up at me.

"Yeah, yeah," I say, leaning down to give her a kiss. Before I can make it too illicit, a hand on my shoulder is pulling me back.

"Hey! None of that!" Coach Roberts says "I didn't set this all up so you two could make out all night. You're supposed to be chaperones."

"Relax, Uncle Nick," Lucy says, "At least we're not as bad as those two over there. Would you like to break that up or have us do it?"

He glances to where Lucy is pointing, and sure enough, two kids are . . . holy hell, are they going at it.

"Son of a bitch," Coach Roberts says before stalking toward the teenage couple. "Stop that now! There will be no nookie on my watch!"

We both laugh and exit the dance floor when the song ends.

"Have I told you tonight that you look beautiful," I say as we head back to our table in the back of the gymnasium.

"Only about twenty times," Lucy says, wrapping her arms around my bicep. "And if I haven't told you, you look incredible."

"Have I told you tonight that I love you?"

"Not tonight."

I take her hand off my arm and spin her around so she stops in front of me. God, she's beautiful in her pale-pink dress that hugs every single curve on her body. It has one strap that goes over her shoulder, which leaves the other one completely bare. I've kissed that spot every chance I've gotten tonight. As soon as she stepped out of her house when I came to pick her up, all I could think about was taking that dress off her tonight.

Slowly. Methodically. Maybe with my teeth.

Then again, she looks good in an oversized T-shirt and a pair of my boxers. No, Lucy's true beauty comes from within. Her soul and her spirit make her the most beautiful woman in this world. It's in the way she sees the good in everyone, how she believes in people when they don't deserve that kind of faith.

She has seen that in me from the first time we met. To her, I was never the dumb jock or the kid who could only throw a football. I was always Bryce. I could live for a million years and not be able to return that kind of love.

But damn I'm going to try.

"Well then, I need to tell you for the first of many times tonight. I love you so damn much, Lucy Valenti."

She takes each of my lapels in her hands and pulls me to her. One more kiss won't hurt.

"I love you too, and thank you for all of this. This is . . . it's more than I ever dreamed of."

"Do you ever think about this night?" I ask, unsure of where the question came from, but I keep going with it. "If I had been able to come home. Do you ever wonder what would have happened?"

She fidgets with my lapels. "I'd be a liar if I said I didn't."

"And?"

Her big brown eyes fill with a twinge of sadness, and I cup her face between my palms.

"Hey, none of that," I say. "If it makes you sad, I don't want to talk about it. I don't even know where the question came from. Forget I said anything."

"No, it's fine," she says, taking a deep breath. "It's just . . . I had the stupid fantasy that every stereotypical girl has about prom night, and I figured that we would . . . that it would have been the first time for us. Silly, right?"

Her admission is a punch to my gut. Because it's the exact fantasy I had.

"Not silly at all. If it makes you feel better, I had the same one."

This gets me a smile. "You did?"

"I was so mad that I wasn't there. All I could think about was you and me dancing. The way you'd feel in my arms. I pictured us slow dancing and then sneaking off to the library and kissing you in the spot where we met. And then, if I was lucky enough . . ."

The way her body shivers in my hold tells me she knows exactly what would have happened that night.

"You know"—she runs her hands up and down my jacket lapels—"we could make one of those things happen tonight."

I look down at her, a little confused. "And what is that?"

She presses onto her toes and leans in close enough to whisper, "I have a key to the library. They gave it to me when I agreed to tut—"

I grab her hand, snag her purse from our table, and all but sprint with her out of the gym.

"Bryce!" Lucy laughs, trying to keep up with me in her heels.

Heels that I'm going to need her to leave on all night.

I take a look around to make sure no one followed us as Lucy frantically tries to open the door. Luckily, the coast looks clear.

We're really the worst chaperones ever.

"There," she says, turning the lock.

I guide her inside, turning back to immediately lock the door as well as the deadbolt.

Then I'm pulling her out of view of the door and kissing her like I've wanted to all night. Judging by the way she's kissing me back, she has wanted this as much as I have.

Our mouths are hurried and sloppy. Our hands are trying to be in every spot possible. She begins to undo my shirt, but a sliver of the light from the hallway distracts me.

"Not here," I say, breaking our lips as I pull her toward the back of the library. "Go to our table."

Somehow, even with no lights on, we find ourselves exactly where we met all those years ago. The place I first fell in love with her. I still remember that first day she walked up to me. Those big brown eyes penetrating my soul. Her no-nonsense demeanor throwing me for a loop, and her beauty taking my breath away.

"Come here," I say.

I bring her to me, and as soon as our lips connect, the rush from earlier fades away. This kiss isn't frantic like before. It's not messy or chaotic.

No, this one is tender. Loving. We both know the significance of where we are, both figuratively and literally. This is seven years of emotion pouring through our mouths.

"I love you," I whisper, my lips trailing down her neck and over her exposed shoulder. "I love you so damn much."

"I love you too," she says, arching her back as my lips trail to the top of her tits.

Her hand begins to slide down the front of my suit, stroking my aching cock from outside of my pants.

"You better watch it. I've been hard for you all night."

"Oh really?" she says, stroking it more. "Well then, we should probably take care of that."

Lucy undoes the button to my pants and quickly lowers the zipper, giving herself room to reach down through my boxers and take me in her hand.

"Who knew Lulu was such a bad girl," I tease, letting my fingers trail over her hips before I start to work her skirt up.

Only then do I realize that my girl has been hiding something from me all night. "Are you not wearing panties?"

"Can't have lines, now can I?"

I didn't know my cock could get any harder, but it has. I lift her up and place her on the table before I kneel in front of her.

"I've wanted to do this all night," I say, lifting both of her legs over my shoulders and diving into her sweet and wet pussy.

She moans as soon as my tongue makes contact with her. Honestly, the sounds she makes when I do this are enough to make me lose it. I almost have a couple times. There is nothing quite like having the girl of my dreams sinking her fingers into my hair and forcing my mouth against her harder.

It's the hottest thing I've ever seen.

I slide two fingers into her center, working them around like I know she likes it.

"Yes," she moans as I begin flicking her clit with my tongue as my fingers hit the spot inside her that makes her crazy. Soon, she's squeezing around me and my fingers are coated with her juices.

"Oh my God," she says between breaths. "Bryce . . . that was . . ."

"Shhh," I say, bringing her lips to mine so she can taste herself. "We're not done yet."

I shove my slacks and boxer briefs down just enough to free myself and spread her legs as wide as they'll go. As I slide into her, I swallow her moan and smile against her mouth.

"Fuck, Lucy," I say, slowly beginning to work in and out of her. "You feel too good."

"Harder, Bryce," she says, reaching to grab on to each of my biceps. "I need to come again."

The thought of getting caught is real, and it's only making

everything that much hotter. Not to mention her heels digging into my ass as I thrust into her.

"I love you," I say as I pull out, force her to her feet, and then bend her over the table. In her heels, she's just at the right height for me.

When I push back into her, the whole table shakes. I'd be worried that I'm being too rough, but she doesn't seem to care at all. If I listen close enough, I swear I can hear her begging me for more with each pant of breath she releases. Pleasure saturates her features as her body grips me and she loses herself to the orgasm.

I'm a goner. I spill into her as she also comes down from her own orgasm. How we both don't fall to the ground in a puddle I'm not sure.

"That was . . ." she says, her voice hoarse.

"Yeah," I say, placing a kiss on her back as I slowly pull out of her and tuck myself back into my pants. "If I would have known you had a key for here earlier, we would have done this a long time ago."

This earns me a laugh as she stands and begins fixing her dress.

Her hair is mussed. Her makeup is smeared. Her dress is wrinkled.

She has never looked more beautiful.

"Come here," I say, pulling her to me so I can kiss her long and deep.

"What was that for?" she asks when I finally release her lips.

"I'm trying to remember . . . I think I did, but I wanted to make sure . . . have I told you tonight I love you?"

Her laugh hits me in all the right spots. "Only a few times."

I lean back on the table, keeping her in my arms.

"You know"—I turn a little and pat the table—"this is the spot where I fell in love with you."

Her eyes grow wide at my statement. "You did? When?"

"The day you asked if I was Bryce Donald."

Her eyebrows go up so high it's comical. "The first time you met me? Bryce, you didn't even know me. I was the new girl in town who spouted off math stats to anyone who would listen."

"Yeah, you were." I can't help but smile at the memory. "I knew from the first moment I laid eyes on you that you were different. I didn't know it was love then. I was a teenager and stupid and thought the only thing that mattered was football. Yet, from the moment you walked into my life with your big brown eyes and your huge heart and random math facts, you've made me a better man. You've made me want to be a better man, even though I didn't always show that. You changed my life that day, and I've loved you ever since."

Her eyes soften as her hands travel up to cup my cheeks. Usually when she does this, she's bringing me in for a kiss. But this time all she does is let her thumb slowly stroke back and forth. Like she's memorizing my face. I should know. It's what my hands do every time they touch her body.

"Do you want to know the moment I knew I loved you?"

I lean forward so our foreheads are touching. "When was that?"

"The first time you called me Lulu."

I chuckle softly before kissing her forehead. I stay there a little longer than I intend to. It helps me push back the stray tear that's trying to come out.

"I knew you loved it."

"I only loved it because it came from you."

I tip her chin up and lean in, bringing our lips together for the hundredth time tonight.

"I'm going to miss you so fucking much."

My voice cracks, and she runs her hands through my hair, trying to soothe me. "I'm going to miss you too, but it's only a few months. We're different now then we were then. We love each other and have thought this through. We've got this. You and me. September will be here before we know it."

Her words are strong. Confident.

She believes in us. She believes in our love.

She believes in me.

I guess I only have one thing to do: make sure I'm worthy of it.

CHAPTER 34
LUCY

APRIL, SENIOR YEAR, COLLEGE

"HEY, LULU."

This isn't the first time I've been to Lake Laurel since high school. In fact, I come here pretty regularly. It's been the place where I can get out of my head. Today, is a beautiful spring day so I decided to take advantage of the warm April weather and study for my finals where I can smell spring grass instead of the inside of a pizza parlor.

In all the times I've been here, I've spent my fair share of time thinking of Bryce since this is kind of our spot. I've replayed dozens of conversations we've had here, and even imagined dozens more we might have in this spot. However, not once in any of my daydreams did I hear his voice quite so clearly.

So, imagine my shock when I turn and find Bryce Donald standing there in all his future-pro football player glory.

"Bryce?" I blink a few times because I'm still not sure if my mind is playing tricks on me.

"Yup. It's me," he says, his smile piercing through my

senses as he takes a few steps toward where I've laid out a blanket on the grass. "It's been a long time."

I want to tell him exactly how long it has been—three years, three months, and twenty-nine days. Not that I was counting. The last time I saw him was the Christmas Eve when he was thinking about transferring. We sat at this lake. We talked about his future and football and caught up on life.

He kissed me like I've never been kissed before.

"Yup. A long time," I mutter. "What are you doing here? Why aren't you in Cincinnati for the draft?"

The fact that the draft just happened to be in Cincinnati this year, which is just about an hour away from our town, has only added to the frenzy that has taken over Laurel Heights. Busses are shipping people down to watch Bryce and Cole get drafted. Others who can't make it have set up a watch party at the high school gym. This is a big deal for our town. Two guys from Laurel Heights about to make their dreams come true playing professional football? This is the stuff movies are made of.

Uncle Nick has been over the moon for the past few weeks because the media has been talking up Bryce as the eventual top draft pick. It looks like Nashville is going to draft him. Cole is projected to go in the second round, and that's only because he was injured last year. They even say there's a slight chance he could also be drafted by the Fury.

"I've given every interview I possibly can," Bryce says as he takes a seat next to me on my blanket. "I just . . . I needed to get away for a minute. It has been insane the past few months. So, I got in my truck and started driving. Somehow, I ended up here."

"It always has been a good spot to think."

"Yes, it has."

For long minutes, the only sounds around us are the gentle

ripples of the lake and a few birds flying back and forth between the trees. I keep sneaking glances at him, though. In the one-thousand two-hundred and fifteen days since I saw him, he's changed so much. His muscles are more defined than I remember. I keep thinking his shirt is about to rip if it gets any tighter. His hair, which he's always kept short, is longer than I've ever seen it.

"What are you staring at, Lulu?" he asks, that smile that does me in every time forming on his mouth.

"You, I guess." No sense in hiding it. "I can't believe you're here."

He turns to look at me. At least his eyes haven't changed. I always thought they could see through my soul, which is what they seem to be doing right now.

"Honestly, neither can I," he says, letting out a breath. "Tomorrow, I'm going to be the number-one draft pick. Before I drove up here, I gave my agent the nod to finalize a contract that is worth more money than I'll ever spend in my life. Nashville promised me they were going to do what they could to also draft Cole. It's more than I ever could have asked for."

"But?"

"How did you know there's a but?"

I let out a chuckle. "I might not have talked to you in three years, but that doesn't mean I can't tell what's going through your mind."

It's his turn to laugh. "You always got me. When no one else understood, you did."

"Quit stalling. Tell me what's wrong."

He shifts his eyes away from me to the ground.

"What if I fail?"

Years ago, we sat in almost this exact spot and had the same conversation. It was the only time I heard Bryce Donald unsure of himself.

"What if you don't?"

He shrugs. "I'm about to set a new rookie contract record. I already have four endorsement deals. After I'm introduced to the media tomorrow, I'm scheduled to do a photo shoot with the PR department for the campaign they are going to run with my face plastered on it. I'm going to be across billboards all over the city."

"Sounds exciting." I don't know if I mean that, but it feels like the right thing to say.

"It's not exciting; it's terrifying. What if I don't produce? What if I can't hang? What if it's like freshman year of college when I didn't get the starting position? What if this team invests all this money and time into me, and I can't do it? What if I fail, Lucy?"

"Again . . . what if you don't?"

"I know you're trying to make me feel better, but there is a very good chance—"

I turn to face him more, cupping both of his cheeks to turn his head and make sure he hears this loud and clear.

"Bryce Donald, don't you dare start talking about chances because I will come back to you with statistics and probabilities that will make your head spin. I don't care if we don't talk for another ten years, you don't take that away from me."

He starts laughing, which is good to hear. He gets like this before every big decision and moment in his life, which is probably why I haven't heard from him in three years. He hasn't had a decision to make. When it comes to pressure on the field, the man is a pro. Off the field? When there are so many people riding on his success or failure? It paralyzes him.

"Now, as I was saying," I continue, "what if you get to Nashville and this is the best group of guys you've ever played with? What if your coaches are great? What if you don't fail?

What if you take the league by storm and be the Bryce I know you can be?"

I really don't expect him to answer me, but I really don't expect him to say what he does next either.

"I miss you."

I'm pretty sure I stop breathing, unsure if I'm shocked, angry, or confused by that statement.

He misses me? While I love hearing those words, how dare he drop that now after all this time.

"Bryce, don't say things like that."

"But I mean them," he says, turning toward me and taking my hands in his. "I miss you. I have missed you. Not talking to you these past three years? I hated it. I felt like a part of me was missing."

"Then why didn't you call? And don't blame it on football."

"I don't know," he says. "Because I'm a guy, and I'm an idiot? What would I have said? 'Hey, Lulu. Sorry I haven't called and that I broke all my promises to you. Can we chat?'"

"That would have been a decent start."

"I never knew what to say, so I didn't say anything at all." He pauses to take a breath, and I'm glad he did. It's allowing my brain to catch up on what's happening here. "There were so many times I had your number ready to go, but I chickened out."

"Why now, Bryce? Why say all of this now?"

He lets go of my hands, pulling at his hair a bit. "Because I always thought . . . that when tomorrow happened, we'd be together. That you'd be sitting next to me, holding my hand when a team called my name. I'd turn to Mom and give her a hug and then turn to you and kiss the hell out of you before walking on stage to receive my jersey. That was the dream."

"Bryce—"

"I know. It's silly. We were high-school sweethearts what

feels like a million years ago. Hell, we haven't talked in years. All I know is that, when I think of my future, or my perfect partner, or who I want to go on this life's journey with, you're the only face I ever see. So, yeah, I miss you. I miss what we could have had. I miss what we could have been. I just . . . miss you."

"I . . ." Even though my heart knows this is true, I'm scared to say the words. If I do, then they are out there in the universe and I won't be able to take them back. It has been three years, and I'd finally gotten over the fact that Bryce and I were never meant to be.

"What, Lulu? What is it?"

I take a deep breath, mustering all of the courage I can. "I miss you too."

I barely get the words out before Bryce's lips are on mine. At first, I'm too stunned to respond. Never in my wildest dreams did I think this is where today would lead, but here I am, my tongue tangling with his. All the while, my brain is stirring with crazy ideas like a future with the only man who has ever made me feel like I was more than just the smart girl.

Bryce lowers me back to the blanket, one hand on the back of my head while the other guides my lower back. Our lips release, and all I can do is stare up at this man. This man who somehow dug himself a place in my heart when I didn't even know he was doing it. A man who is so much more than people give him credit for. A man who I know I'll love until my dying day.

"Is this real?" he asks, his hands gently pushing back a piece of hair off my forehead. "Because if this is a dream, I don't want to wake up."

I bite my bottom lip because it's all I can do to stop the tears from coming. This. This right here is why I was never able to move on. I tried. Lord knows I did. I tried dating or going to parties and meeting people, but every time I thought a guy had a chance, I would always come back to Bryce. No other guy gives me the million butterflies like Bryce did.

"You need to quit doing that," he says, a wicked grin coming over his face.

"Doing what?"

"Biting that lip like that."

I loop my hands around his neck, gently letting my fingers play with the hair at his nape. "Why is that?"

"Because it makes me want to kiss you again."

"Maybe that's what I wanted you to do."

And he does. God does he kiss me. He kisses me like I'm his. Like this is our first kiss and the promise of a million kisses to come. I never want this to stop.

Unfortunately, his ringing cell phone has other plans.

"Are you going to get that?" I reluctantly ask. I know he should, but I'd rather him not stop doing whatever he is doing to my neck right now.

He lets out a groan before taking his phone out of his pocket. "Yes, Dean?"

I don't know who Dean is, but it must be someone important because he's quickly sitting up, leaving me strangely cold without his body weight on top of me.

"Fine. Yeah, yeah. I'll meet you at the hotel in a few hours."

He ends the call and lets out the most frustrated breath I've ever heard.

"You have to go back, don't you?"

He nods as he brings his knees up, letting his arms hang over them. "That was my agent. Apparently, there are a few things the Fury want to go over before tomorrow. I need to meet with them tonight."

"I understand," I say as I sit up. It doesn't mean the selfish part of me likes it, though.

"Lucy. Will you come with me to Cincinnati?"

How many times had I wished for him to ask me that? Hundreds? Thousands? Each time, I always figured my answer would be a resounding yes, and I hate that I can't have that.

"I can't. I have finals this week."

"Oh," he says, letting his head hang back down. "I just thought maybe . . ."

"What did you think?"

He finally looks back up to me, and the sadness in his eyes reminds me of when we said goodbye before he first went to Clemson. "I thought maybe this was it. That this could be our take two."

"Really?" Even though those were the words I wanted him to say, I honestly didn't think he would. "You'd be willing to have a relationship during the season? Because you're about to go pro, Bryce. This isn't high school anymore. This isn't even college. This is the big leagues. Are you sure, in your heart of hearts, that you're ready for this? For us?"

I wish I didn't have to say all of that. Every cell in my body is screaming at me for giving him this out, but I'd rather him tell me that maybe he isn't ready then promise that he is and get my hopes up again.

I start preparing myself for the speech. The one he gives me every time about things being different if I only give him a few months. That's usually what it is. So, I can't hide the shock on my face when he turns toward me and moves to one knee as he takes my hands in his.

"I know I've always said I can't date during the season. I know I've always felt that I needed to wait for the perfect time, but this is our perfect time. We're starting new chapters of our lives, and I want to do it together. So, even though it can't happen tonight, it's going to happen soon. You're going to nail your finals and graduate. I'm going to go to

Nashville and find us a place to live. Then you're going to come down, and we're going to be together. For real this time."

"And what about during the season?"

"You'll be my biggest cheerleader. The one I come home to every day. My partner in crime. What do you say, Lulu? You in?"

Is he for real? I search his eyes, looking for any hesitation or hint of unsurety, but all I see is love. Love for me. For us. For our future.

"I'm in," I say, a smile so big you can see it a mile away.

Bryce scoops me into his arms, picking me up like I'm a feather and twirling me around. I'm sure if someone were watching us, they would probably think we were crazy, smiling and laughing like we are.

And maybe we are a little crazy. Bryce and I have never computed on paper, but in actuality, we are a perfect formula.

"I hate that I have to go back to Cincinnati," he says, putting me down.

"It's okay," I say. "I'll be watching tomorrow. They're having a huge thing at the gymnasium."

"I'll be thinking of you." He links our fingers together. "And the first second I have to call you, I will."

"I believe you," I say, bringing him into me for one more kiss. "Now, go be amazing."

———

Three days.

It has been three days of unanswered calls and unreturned texts. I thought about sending him a picture of my boobs just to see if that would get a reaction out of him, but I was worried that maybe he didn't have his phone on him. Then I saw a live report on television with a picture of him walking into the Fury facility, phone in hand.

I don't know who he was texting in the footage, but it sure as hell wasn't me.

When he told me he would call me on draft night, I actually didn't expect that. He was the number-one pick. I knew he'd be doing countless interviews, but by Sunday? I figured things would have died down. I figured wrong.

"How stupid am I?" I ask myself as I get in my car to go to the grocery store, slamming the door behind me.

I can't believe I let myself fall for his lies again. Maybe it was because I was seeing him for the first time in so long. Maybe because I was drunk from his kiss and I would have believed anything he said, but it doesn't really matter what the excuse is. I fell for the song and dance yet again.

If he can't do something as simple as return a call or a text, how can I uproot my life and move to Nashville? Graduation is next week, and I have a job lined up at the bank in town. Why would I leave stability behind for a man who can't be bothered to text back something as small as a thumbs-up emoji.

"Ice cream," I say as I pull into the grocery store. "Ice cream will fix it. Ice cream and a supreme pizza."

I call in my order at Tripoli's before making my way in to the grocery store. I sure as heck hope I don't see anyone. Between finals this week and crying each night because of Bryce, I can safely say I look like hell.

I keep my head down as I walk into the store, taking a basket just in case I see anything else along the way. I hurry down the first aisle and take a sharp left, making a beeline for the frozen foods, which is why I don't see the person making a right. The person I promptly run into.

"Ouch!" I say, losing my balance and falling backward onto my ass.

"Are you okay?" Luciano says, and my face blushes scarlet as I accept his hand and let him pull be back to my feet. Of course, he would be the one I run into because, why not?

"I'm fine." It's when I release his hand that I finally look up.

I haven't seen Luciano Tripoli since the day he left for his year-long internship in Italy. I've heard his parents talk about him coming back, but I guess I hadn't realized he was home already.

"Wow, it's good to see you." We both come in for a hug that's part awkward, part friendly. "I didn't know you were back in town."

"Just got in a few days ago."

The silence that settles between us is awkward. Do I say thanks for helping me up or ask how his trip was?

"Well, it was good seeing you," I say because, frankly, I just want to go home, put on my comfy sweats, eat a stupid amount of food, and watch a sappy movie. "Maybe I'll see you around the restaurant."

I start to walk away, but I only get a few steps before I feel Luciano's hand on my elbow.

"Lucia?"

"Yeah?"

"I was wondering . . . well, I was curious . . . I thought that maybe—"

"Luciano? What are you asking me?"

"Will you go to dinner with me?"

I'm taken aback a bit because, wow, that's not what I was expecting.

"Luciano . . ." I'm about to tell him thanks but no thanks. That we'll see each other soon enough at the next dinner party our mothers throw. I'm about to say all of this to him when my cell phone starts vibrating in my back pocket.

I hurry and grab it, knowing that it has to be Bryce finally texting me back.

> Brenna: Finals are done! What are we doing tonight?

It takes all I have not to drop my phone and fall to the floor in tears. That's what I want to do. But I won't. I can't.

It's right there, in the middle of the town grocery story, that I decide that I've wasted enough time and tears on Bryce Donald.

I'm. Done. Waiting.

"You know what? Yes, I will go out with you. How does tomorrow sound?"

"TWENTY-NINE, toss . . . twenty-nine, toss . . . ready . . . set . . . hut!"

I take the snap from my center and roll to the right, all while faking a handoff to the running back. The defense can't touch me, the benefits of being a quarterback during camp, but I still feel the pressure as they come toward me. I look down the field, and exactly where he's supposed to be is Dexter. I reach back, wind up and give my wrist a flick as I throw the ball thirty yards down the field, right into the arms of my wide receiver in the end zone.

It might only be minicamp, but throwing a touchdown never gets old.

"That's how we do it, boys!" Davis yells from the sideline. "Offense, bring it in. Defense, gassers. Go!"

I can't help but smile as we jog over to Davis and Hunter, who are waiting on the sideline.

"Good practice today, guys. Good way to finish this session," Davis begins as we all take a knee around him. "Take the next weekend to rest up. I'll see you next week."

"Bring it in, guys," I say as we all stand and huddle up. "Team on three. One, two, three, team!"

We all start dispersing back to the locker room when I feel a hand slap me on the shoulder pad.

"Looking good out there. How are you feeling?"

"Feeling really good." For the first time in a while, it's not a lie. "It's like riding a bike."

"And the other stuff?" Davis asks, stopping in front of me. "You've had a busy few months. How are you handling it?"

I will give Davis credit. He's really had my back since my return. Apparently, it was his idea to put me on the injured reserve list. I'll never be able to pay him back for the way he's looked out for me. Even when I didn't want him to.

"I'm still getting there, but feeling good," I say as we start walking again. "I'm not going to lie. The press tour was rough. Interview after interview about mental health and what happened last season. How I handled coming back to the team. It was a lot."

"I can imagine. I watched a few of the interviews, though. You did a great job and handled yourself well."

"Thanks," I say even though, somewhere inside me, I don't think I deserve praise for coming back from self-destruction. That's a conversation to have with Malcolm and not Davis for a different day. "I'm not going to lie, admitting to the world that I let down my team, my family, and my fans was hard. But I'm better for it."

"You are. And you look like a decent quarterback too," Cole says as he comes to a stop next to me and Davis. "I forgot you knew how to throw like that."

"Me too. Nice to know I can put some throws in the play-book this year."

"Very funny," I say as Davis is called back over to the field. "I'll talk to you guys later."

Davis makes his way back to the practice field as Cole and I continue walking to the locker room. Cole's locker is right next to mine—it's been that way since high school—and I might be straight as the day is long, but I can't help but stare at Cole as he takes off his pads and shirt.

"How the hell did you get bigger? I didn't think that was physically possible."

Cole laughs as he tosses his pads and helmet into his locker. "I hit the weights a lot this year. Not like I had anything else to do."

"I hoped that, once you were done pulling my ass out of the gutter, you'd get yourself a girlfriend."

"I've told you, I'm not interested," he says.

"Why not?" I ask, taking off my jersey. "I meant what I said at New Year's. When Lucy gets down here, we're going to need double-date partners. Are you really going to make me ask Wes and his wife?"

"Hey now!" Wes, our veteran tight end, calls out. "Just because I've been married longer than you've been shaving doesn't mean the wifey and I aren't fun."

"So, you and your wife would be down for a night of doubles bowling?"

He shakes his head. "Me? Hell yeah. I'll even buy the first pitcher of beer. Cara, though? The day I see her in rented bowling shoes will be a cold day in hell."

"See!" I say, pointing at Wes. "That leaves you, buddy. Do I need to download an app for you? How about that Left for Love app? Hell, I hear that video app, what's it called? ForU? I hear that people are hooking up off that."

Cole mumbles something under his breath that sounds strangely like, "Fuck you." Man, I forgot how fun it was to mess with the big guy.

"What was that? I didn't hear you."

He flashes me a look that would make a normal person piss themselves. But to me? It's just Cole trying to look tough.

"Maybe you were better as a drunk. You didn't talk as much."

"Whatever man," I say, tossing my sweaty jersey at him. "You missed me."

He gives me an eyeroll before he heads to the showers. "I hate that I did."

"Love you too, buddy! See you tonight. It's *Bachelor in Paradise* premiere, so bring your notebooks because we're drafting right after."

I laugh as I hear him continue to grumble toward the shower and I take the moment of privacy to grab my phone out of my locker.

> Lulu: Hey you. Hope you have a great
> practice. I miss you. Counting down the days.

I can't hide the shit-eating grin that comes across my face when reading that. It has been a few days since we've talked, and I'm just glad to see her name on my screen. Sometimes, she'll send me a funny text, and other times, she sends me updates about her day. My favorite text of all time was the pro-con list of sexual positions. That was a fun conversation later that night.

Then there are days like today when I just get one that says "I miss you" and it takes all that's in me not to jump in my truck and drive the five hours back to Laurel Heights just to kiss her.

> Bryce: I miss you too.

I start to get ready to hit the shower when my phone buzzes. All someone would have to do is look at my face to know who it is.

Lulu: How was practice today?

Bryce: Great. We won. Again. Cole is being pissy because he hasn't been laid in a while. How was your day?

I don't get a response right away, and I know that means it was another rough day for her. She's been having a lot of those lately. Megan is officially on maternity leave. She and her parents still aren't talking, and as if that weren't enough, her car stopped working last week and it's going to take at least two weeks to fix.

I offered to get her a new car, but before I'd even finished suggesting it, she was spewing all the reasons why I shouldn't. I knew it was best not to argue.

I'll just get it for her when she moves here.

Lulu: Mrs. Tripoli came into the bank today. That was awkward. I'm pretty sure she called me a bitch in Italian. But I don't want to talk about my day. I want to talk about good things. Tell me everything about practice today.

She deflects a lot. It's as if she doesn't want to bother me with her problems. But what she doesn't know is that I want her to. For years, she has carried the weight of my problems for me. She never asked for it. I just put it on her, and like the true angel she is, she bared it.

Well, now, I want to take some of that from her.

Bryce: Don't deflect. You know you can tell me everything, right? Get your bad day off your chest. I'm here Lucy.

Lulu: Can I call you later? It's just too much to text, and I need to finish closing things up.

> Bryce: Absolutely. I love you.

"How's Lucy?" Cole asks as he comes back to his locker.

"Busy," I say as I start stripping off my sweaty practice gear. "I wish she'd let me do more for her."

"All you can do is be there for her. Make sure she knows that."

I look back at my text messages, hoping she knows I meant every word of what I just wrote.

> Lulu: Love you more.

"She does," I say confidently. "She absolutely does."

"I'M SO SORRY, Lucy, I really thought I had my checkbook."

"It's fine, Mr. Coffman. Take your time."

That might be what I said, but inside, it was more like: *you don't need your fucking check book to take out cash even though you insist you do.*

It's fine. Everything is fine.

I try to make myself take a few deep breaths as my ninety-year-old customer writes a check to cash. I should be happy that I have a few minutes just to breathe, but not going eighty miles per hour also gives me time to think.

And that is the last thing I want.

"Here you go," Mr. Coffman says, handing me a check written to cash for seventy-five dollars. "How is that boyfriend of yours? Hopefully he's going to play better than he did last year."

I try to laugh off the comment because I know he doesn't mean any harm by it. "He does too. Have a good day, Mr. Coffman. See you next Friday."

"Goodbye, dear," he says as he slowly walks out of the bank with the help of a cane. I know I need to make sure he gets to his car safely, but the feeling of my phone vibrating in my pocket makes me want to shove him out the door.

"Come on . . ." I say, bouncing on my heels as my phone continues to ring. Finally, Mr. Coffman is out of the door, and I sprint back to my office, simultaneously swiping right to answer the call.

"Hello," I say, sounding as if I just ran a marathon.

"Are you trying to run again? I didn't think that went well last time."

The tension immediately eases just hearing Bryce's voice. "I'll never make that mistake again."

We both laugh as a comfort washes over me and I sit in my desk chair. "How are you?"

"I was going to ask you the same thing. Been a few days since we've talked."

Four. Four days. "Yeah, I'm sorry about that. Things have just been nuts here."

"Still struggling with Megan on maternity leave?"

I slide a little farther down into my chair, the stress of the day, hell, the week, finally catching up to me. "Yeah, working open to close every day has been rough. But that's not the only bad news."

"Oh no. What happened?"

"Well, a teller quit on me last week. Said she wanted to chase her true passion or some crap like that."

"I know it leaves you in a bind, but I think it's cool that someone wants to chase their dream."

"Her dream is beekeeping, Bryce. Beekeeping."

"Well"—I can hear him taking a big swallow, not knowing how to navigate out of this conversation—"good for her."

"I hope she gets stung."

"No you don't. You're too good of a person for that. You're just stressed."

"I know," I say, which almost comes out like a sigh. "But that's not even the worst part."

"There's more?"

"Unfortunately, yes. I thought Megan would be back from maternity leave in August. Turns out, now it's going to be more like September."

He doesn't say anything, and he doesn't have to. I know what he's thinking. That means I won't get there until October. I haven't even begun to start thinking about packing or anything along those lines. If these were normal circumstances, I could ask my family for help. But they still aren't speaking to me because of the Christmas catastrophe. If I ask them to help me pack my house to move to Nashville, I'll likely get called a football floozie or get flooded with guilt about how I'm not following their wishes.

"Well, I guess this is the time for me to tell you my bad news."

This makes me sit up in my chair. "What? What happened?"

I try to steel myself for whatever bad news is about to come my way.

"I'm not going to be able to get home in July," he says dejectedly.

It takes every fiber of my being not to scream in frustration. Though, if I'm being honest, I should have known. This is how it always happens.

"Here we go again," I say softly I'm not sure I actually said it or just thought it.

"Excuse me? What did you say?"

Well, apparently, I did. No sense in taking it back now. Especially when it's the truth. "I said 'here we go again.' Because I should have known this was going to happen."

"How was I supposed to know the team would want me to

do a second press tour? That wasn't part of the plan they gave me."

"It never is. It's always something that just pops up." I let out a breath because I'm trying to keep my cool, but it's really hard when the world feels like it's crashing down on me. "This is how it always starts, though. First, it's a few missed phone calls, which we've already managed to check that off the list."

"I can't be the only one blamed for the missed phone calls. You've missed your fair share as well."

Oh, he wants to go there? Let's go there. "I'm sorry I fell asleep at seven last night because I was exhausted from work and missed one phone call Bryce. I didn't see that you called until this morning, but I didn't want to wake you up."

"You know you can call me anytime," he says, his voice fighting back anger. "I don't care about getting woken up."

"Ha! Is that so?"

"What's that supposed to mean?"

"It means that when I called you last week at eight in the morning, I was told to call back in an hour. Then later that night when I asked why you were in a mood, you said it was because I woke you up."

"That was because I was out late and grumpy. You caught me on a bad morning."

"You were out?" This is news to me. "Who were you out with?"

"Some teammates. Dexter. A few of the defensive guys. They invited me to a bar, and we got home late. It wasn't a big deal. I was just more tired than usual."

"No big deal? Bryce, were you drinking? I thought you quit. You chose to quit! I thought that was part of your plan?"

"I can have a beer, Lucy," he says, his voice filled with annoyance. "I chose not to for a while, but I'm doing better. I feel that I can have one beer with the guys on occasion. Don't worry. I'm a grown man. I know what I'm doing."

"I know you're a grown man, and if you think you can have a beer here and there, then who am I to stop you?"

"Exactly."

"Then again, I can't even get you to keep a promise about coming home when you were the one insisting you would."

"That's low. You know I can't control what the team wants me to do."

"I know you can't. But that's not the point."

"Then what is? Because I have no idea which way is up in this phone call."

I suck in a frustrated breath. "I'm sorry. I apologize for what I said about not making it home. You can't control what the team wants you to do. Those were words of frustration and stress. I do take those back."

"I understand you're frustrated by it. So am I. But I have to go. After the first press tour went so well, public relations and Dean think it will be good to do a full-scale Bryce-is-back campaign. Morning talk shows, guest spots on *SportsCenter*, the whole nine yards. They have me booked from now until the week before camp starts. They think that if I do this then I won't be hounded by reporters during the season. That we can officially put last year behind us."

I sink back into my chair. It makes sense. I might not like it, but I get it. And I know it's what he needs to do.

"I understand," I say, hoping not to sound as depressed as I feel. "But Bryce, drinking? Going out until all hours?"

"It was just one night Lucy."

"I don't care if it was one night or every night since you've been back. You worked hard and you even admitted that drinking was part of your problem so you cut it out. I just don't want to see you throw away months of hard work just to be with the boys."

"You have nothing to worry about," he says. "It was one night. I know the work I did. I was just tired of sitting at home. Let's not fight, okay?"

"Okay," I say, hoping that everything he is saying is on the level. "Also, I know you have to go back on the road. But that doesn't mean I have to like it."

"You can say you hate it," he says. "Because I do."

"You do?"

"Of course I do. I miss the fuck out of you. I was counting down the days until July. I also hate fighting with you, and I'd rather never do this again."

I smile. "Same. I miss you too. I'm sorry I flew off the handle, it's just . . . I'm scared, Bryce. I'm stressed, and I'm scared, and this is a hell of a lot harder than I thought it would be."

"I know," he says. "But we're almost there, right? Three more months. And your birthday is in August. I'll definitely be home to celebrate that. I can't do this without you. I need you here with me. I know it's hard, but we're almost there."

I look at the calendar, which I just turned to July the other day.

"Three more months."

"Three more months," he repeats. "I love you, Lulu."

"Love you more."

"HI. You've reached the voice mail of Bryce Donald. Leave a mess—"

I toss the phone onto my couch and resist the urge to scream into a pillow. I could recite every word of Bryce's voice mail because I talk to it more than him these days.

"I know that look," Brenna says, walking into my living room with two glasses of wine. "What did my idiot brother do this time?"

Poor Brenna. She has had to take the brunt of my moods these past few months.

I sigh, taking the wine glass from her. "Just another day I get sent to voice mail. Happy birthday to me."

This isn't exactly how I thought I'd be spending my twenty-fifth birthday—fighting the urge to cry into my wine glass because my idiot boyfriend hasn't called. Brenna begged me to go do something, even if it was just to have dinner with her, Luciano, and Celine. Only, it didn't feel right without Bryce here, so I said I wanted a quiet night at home.

I should have taken her up on her offer.

"Maybe he doesn't have his phone on him?" she says, taking a seat next to me. "Or maybe he's in an interview and can't answer. I'm sure he's going to call. You never know, he could be on his way up here to surprise you?"

I just shrug because we could play the guessing game all night and still not know what the heck he is doing.

Most of July was filled with press tours and appearances. I was proud of him when he spoke of his struggles with anxiety and how mental health was just as important as physical health. He admitted to using alcohol to try to cope with it, which only created a bigger problem. Bryce was also doing his best to normalize seeking help in terms of therapy.

The one thing he hasn't done is return most of my calls or messages. After our fight in June, I made sure that I did my part. Even if I worked a ten-hour day, I made sure to call. I sent him a text every morning and every night.

Sometimes, I get to speak to him, but more often than not, my call goes to voice mail or the message goes unreturned for days. I know he's busy, and I know he's back and forth between traveling and Nashville, but he's managed to find time to go to dinner with his teammates and the opening of a new bar on Broadway. At least, according to some of his teammates' Instagram stories.

Ugh . . . I hate sounding this way. I don't want him to be a hermit. I want him to have a life. I want him to bond with his teammates and have a life outside of football. I just want him to miss me as much as I miss him.

I thought maybe today of all days he'd put his football responsibilities and his teammates to the side and be with me on my birthday. Even if he couldn't get here, it would have been nice of him to FaceTime me. Heck, I would have settled for a happy-birthday text.

Anything.

I already know what it's like not to be first on Bryce Donald's list. But this? This is the worst of all.

If I were to make an assumption based off the events of the last month, tonight, and—if I'm honest—the past seven years, I know exactly how this is going to go.

It's football season. Nothing else matters.

Not even me.

Especially not me. I know I should be upset about that. I should be in a full-on rage, but I don't have the energy. I'm just . . . I can't. I'm too deeply disappointed to be angry because on some level, I only have myself to blame.

"When was the last time you talked to him?" Brenna asks.

"Tuesday."

She gives me a small smile. "That's not so bad."

"Of last week. Tuesday of last week."

"What is wrong with him?" she asks, though I think it's rhetorical. "He messaged me last week to ask what color you preferred in jewelry. I just don't understand what is going on with him right now?"

"He's busy . . ."

"Bullshit!" Brenna's voice gets so loud it nearly makes me jump out of my skin. Apparently, the anger I can't feel has been transferred to her. "People can be busy and also make time for the ones they care about. There is always time, especially on their girlfriend's birthday. It's just about wanting to find it."

She's right. I've been making excuses for weeks now.

"Why doesn't he want to use his time on me?" I ask. "How could he say he loves me but then push me aside like this?"

The tears burst out of me like a breaking dam. I've been keeping them in for too long, so I was bound to burst at some point. Brenna hurries toward me and wraps me in her arms. I just cry. These are tears that I've been holding in for weeks now. Oh, who am I kidding? These are tears that have been building since the first time he made me a promise he didn't keep.

Why did I ever think that this time would be any different? Why did I think he'd change? I always thought I was a smart girl, but apparently love has made me stupid.

It's the only explanation.

"I wish I knew what to say," Brenna says. "Except that I hope you know that in no way, shape or form is this your fault. Frankly, I'm ashamed to call him my brother. What is he even doing right now? It's your fucking birthday, and he's making you cry because he's an idiot? Not on my watch. Fuck this shit."

I hear Brenna start clicking through her phone. If there is one thing I can say about Brenna Donald it's that the woman has zero fear. She also gives zero fucks. She's the borderline crazy girl who should be hired by the FBI because she can find something online in five seconds with just the first name of the person's cat. It's kind of impressive.

It's also kind of frightening that she teaches children.

"Oh hell no!" she yells.

"What?" I ask, though I don't look up.

"Who is Dexter?"

"One of his teammates," I say, inching closer to her to see what she's looking at.

"He's hot."

"Focus, Brenna."

"Oh shit. Sorry. Apparently, you and Dexter are birthday buddies. And judging by the pictures, the Fury guys are having *quite* the time at his birthday party."

I take the phone from her and have to blink a few times because, even in my worst thoughts about Bryce, I didn't think this was a possibility.

Bryce and the entire Fury team are at a VIP lounge at some bar. Cole is there, though, it seems as if he'd rather be anywhere else. As for Bryce? He looks quite content holding a glass of something in one hand as a girl takes up residence on his lap.

And not just any girl; it's the girl from New Year's Eve.

What the fuck?

"I . . . who . . . what the . . ." My brain can't form coherent sentences.

"I'm going to kill him. I don't care if he's my blood. I'm going to fucking kill him."

I hear Brenna, but I can't say anything. It's as if I'm stunned silent and the only thing tossing around in my brain is the events of the last few weeks.

Yes, we've had trouble reaching each other, but then there has been the drinking and the partying. Apparently, there has also been the other girls since I'm not in Nashville to keep them off his fucking lap.

"You need to call him. Now," Brenna says, taking the phone from my hand and handing me mine. "He needs to fucking explain himself."

She's right. I need to hear from him what the hell is going on.

It rings and rings. With every ring my imagination runs a little wilder.

Why haven't we talked in more than a week?

Is that woman more than just someone he hooked up with once?

Why isn't Cole stepping in? Isn't he on Team Lucy or is he helping Bryce with this?

"Hi. You've reached the voice mail of Bryce Donald. Leave a mess—"

I hit the red button and launch my phone across the room.

"What do you need?" Brenna asks as the tears start falling again. "Because right now, everything from a shoulder to cry on to committing a felony is on the table. Just let me change my shoes if we're burying a body."

I want to laugh, but I can't make myself.

"I just want to go to sleep. Hopefully, I wake up tomorrow this will all have been a bad dream."

Brenna brings me into a hug again. "I'm sorry you're hurting. I wish there was more I could do."

"Me too."

I'm not sure how long I sit crying on Brenna's shoulder before I pass out, but when I wake up in the middle of the night with a blanket draped around me, there still isn't a response from Bryce.

LAUREL HEIGHTS: ten miles.

"She is going to be so surprised," I say to myself as I press on the gas a little harder. I've cut the five-hour drive from Nashville to Laurel Heights down by a half hour, but I don't care if I get a ticket. I'm making it home for my girl's birthday.

Today is going to be perfect. And that's what we need, a reminder of how perfect we are together. So, despite my still being slightly hungover from last night's festivities and that I'm going to have to explain why I haven't answered her calls the last few days, I know that after today we're going to be back to the old Bryce and Lucy.

These past months have been hell for both of us. We've missed calls, got in arguments, and went days without talking. Most of that is because of me and my insane schedule this summer, but that isn't something that I didn't warn her about. Yes, I've had some fun too. Not the fun I was having when I was trying to forget who Lucy Valenti was, but it was nice to be out and act like a normal twenty-five-year-old. Well, as normal as a bunch of professional football players can act when they have black cards to burn in a city they rule.

Then there was the past week where I was too scared that

I'd give something away about her birthday surprise that I'd dodged her calls.

I pull off the freeway and expertly maneuver my way through the roads of Laurel Heights to Lucy's house. I'm pretty sure I run five stop signs, but again, I don't care.

I take a final breath as I make my way onto Lucy's front porch. If she heard me pull in, she hasn't showed it yet. In fact, I don't hear anything as I step up to knock on the door.

"Brenna?"

I know it's not crazy for Brenna to be over at Lucy's house, but what isn't making any sense is why my sister is looking at me with such hatred. It's like little knives are coming out of her eyes.

"You have a lot of fucking nerve," she says, stepping outside and closing the door behind her. "What the hell are you doing here, Bryce?"

"What do you mean? I'm here to surprise Lucy for her birthday."

I try to step around Brenna, but she moves to block me from the door. "You aren't going in there."

"Excuse me?" What gives her the right to say that I can't go into my girlfriend's house? "I don't know what's up your ass today, but let me in."

"I said no," she says. "Not until you fucking explain yourself."

"Explain what?" I ask, thoroughly confused by this situation. "I'm here to see my girlfriend on her birthday. Does that need an explanation?"

Brenna laughs, only it sounds like how a super villain would laugh. "Her birthday was *yesterday*."

I blink a few times as I let that process. Then I decide that I'm hungover and must have heard her wrong. "What?"

"I said that, her birthday was yesterday, you fucking dumbass."

I think I'm going to vomit.

Oh God, I missed Lucy's birthday.

"I have to see her," I say, trying to push past Brenna. "Lucy!"

"No," she says, blocking me again from going inside. "You don't get to barge in there. It's more than just the missed birthday. You really fucked—"

"Let him in, Brenna," Lucy says softly as she opens the door. As soon as I see her, my heart drops to my feet. Her eyes are puffy as if she's been crying all night. Her nose is red. Her hair is a scattered mess.

God I am such a fucking asshole.

"Lucy," I say, "I'm so sorry."

"We need to talk," she says as she steps to the side to let me in. "Thanks, Brenna. I'll call you later."

"Are you sure? The offer for me to go change my shoes is still on the table."

"I'm good," Lucy says as she gives my sister a hug. Brenna starts walking to her car, which I hadn't noticed when I pulled up.

"Lucy," I say as I step inside. "I'm so sorry. I—"

"No, Bryce. Sit down first. Let me go get dressed. I'll be down in a few."

I nod and do as she says. When I walk into her living room, all I see are pillows, blankets, and used tissues. There are also two empty wine glasses and a half-eaten pizza.

God, she spent her birthday crying and eating pizza on her couch while I was out celebrating with Dexter at a fucking club.

Fuck I am the worst.

Lucy comes back down the stairs in a pair of leggings and

an oversized sweatshirt. "What are you doing here?" she asks as she sits about as far away from me as she can get.

"I was going to surprise you for your birthday, but I am the worst person in the world and got the dates wrong. I honestly thought your birthday was today. I don't know how I fucked it up. I would have been here yesterday had I known, and I am so fucking sorry, Lucy. God I am so sorry. How can I make it up to you?"

"You can start by explaining why another girl was sitting on your lap last night."

I shake my head in confusion. "What?"

"Dexter's party. The girl on your lap. The girl who tried to pick you up on New Year's? She looked comfortable on your lap last night."

I rack my brain, trying to remember back to last night. Dexter got us in to a club that just opened. It started out as just us, but eventually, a bunch of groupies talked their way in.

"Can't remember? Maybe I can jog your memory."

Lucy tosses me her phone, and as soon as I see it, my stomach falls.

There I am, sitting in the VIP area. I'm holding a glass of whiskey—one that just kept getting refilled without my having to ask—and looking at one of the guys with the groupie sitting on my lap.

"Yes, it was her. Yes, she got in to the VIP area. She somehow always does. That picture was taken at the exact moment she sat. It took me a split second to realize what was happening, and when I did, I told her to get off. Call Cole. He'll vouch. He'll tell you that after I told her to leave, she got so mad that she and her friends stormed off. Dex and the rest of the guys got pissed at me for chasing off the women. But I swear, Lucy, nothing happened."

She doesn't say anything right away, and I wish I could hold her, but it's clear that is the last thing she wants from me.

"Please say something," I plead. "You have to believe I didn't cheat on you. I never would."

"I know," she says softly.

"And you have to know that, if I were any good at keeping things straight, I wouldn't have been out with those guys last night. I would have been here. With you."

I start to move closer to her, but she holds her hands up to stop me.

"No, Bryce. You don't get to come in here and spew apologies when I spent the last twenty-four hours crying and wondering why my boyfriend doesn't love me."

"What?" I ask, leaning closer to her, but I stop as she holds her hands up again. "How can you not think I love you?"

"Gee, let me see," she says sarcastically. "We haven't talked in weeks. When we do, it's either a fight or so short it was barely worth it. You never have time for me, but you always seem to find time for your teammates and football. There will always be time for football."

"You know what I had to do this summer. We talked about it. You were okay with it."

She nods. "I was, and I'm proud of you. It took a lot of courage to talk about what you did."

"Then what's the matter? What do you want from me, Lucy?"

"What do I want?" she yells, all but jumping from her seat. "What I want is to have my boyfriend, the man who says he loves me, to put me first for a change. For him not to make me feel like I'm somewhere down the list of things in his life he needs to attend to or that he'll get to eventually. I deserve to be first too sometimes, and I never am with you. I never have been, and I don't think I ever will be. It's football or your team-mates or your public relations responsibilities. Hell, I wasn't even important enough for you to write down the right day for my birthday. I'm never a priority, and damn it, I deserve to be."

"What do you mean you're never a priority?" I say, my voice getting louder as I also stand. "You're the *only* priority!"

"You have a funny way of showing it."

"You are!" I yell, beginning to pace as I pull at my hair. "Everything I do is for you. For us. For our future."

"Forgetting my birthday and getting drunk with your teammates is putting me first?"

"I said I was sorry!"

"What are you sorry for? Because I don't even know if you know." She takes a breath, which I think is to stop herself from crying, but the tears welling in her eyes are threatening to kill me. "We can't talk on the phone because you're either playing football, prepping for an interview, or sleeping because you had to do one of those things. You go out with your teammates at night because you think you need to bond with them, never mind that you said you were done drinking. That has been your life for the past four months. Do you want to know what mine has been? I work and then come home, hoping that maybe my boyfriend will take an hour from his day to see how I am doing. But he never did. I have waited so damn long for you, but I don't think I can do it anymore. It hurts too much. Last night? Last night was the final straw. I'm done. I can't wait anymore."

I blink a few times because she can't have said what she just said.

"Lucy, no." I scramble off the couch and literally fall on my knees in front of her begging. "Let's talk. I'm sorry. For every-thing. What do you want me to do? I'll do anything. I'll quit football. Right now. I'll call the team right now."

I move to grab my cell phone, and Lucy puts her hand on top of mine, lowering it back to my side. "You're not quitting football. I'm not about to be the Yoko Ono of professional football."

"Then what do you want? Because I can't lose you. I can't."

Tears well in her eyes again, only this time a few spill over. "Nothing. You can't do anything. You're football, Bryce. That's what you were meant to do. This? You and I? It just wasn't meant to be."

"Not meant to be!" I yell, as I push down tears of my own. "If there was anything in this world that was meant to be, Lucy, it's us. I have known I've loved you since the first day I met you. This is our time. We are so close."

"And then what happens when I move to Nashville? You go out with the guys after a game and forget to tell me? I have to see pictures of you out with the guys and the cleat chasers of whatever city you're in taking convenient pictures with you? I'll be alone while you're off being King of the Town. At least here I have friends, and maybe one day, I'll have a family again."

"It won't be like that," I say. "I prom—"

"Stop," she says. "Don't say that word. I hate when you say that word because you don't know what it means. You've broken every promise you've ever made me, and I refuse to let you do it again. No more empty promises. No more desperate pleas. I can't do it anymore. I won't do it anymore. This is over."

The finality in her voice is clear, but I refuse to acknowledge it.

"Lucy, please—"

"Don't. Don't make this any harder than it needs to be," she says, standing and walking past me toward the door. "This is for the best."

"For who?" I say as I follow behind her. "Cause it sure as hell isn't what's best for me."

"It will be," she says. Then she pulls the door open while refusing to look at me.

I grab her shoulders and sink down until she's forced to look me in the eyes. I need her to see that this isn't what I want, that I love her, and that I'm willing to put in the work if she's willing to let me. "You don't mean this."

She finally looks at me and shrugs out of my hold. "I do. I deserve to be on someone's priority list. I deserve good morning texts and calls at the end of the night. I deserve a boyfriend who writes down the right day for my birthday. I love you, but you will never be able to give me that. Now, please leave."

I stare at the tears streaming down her cheeks. Tears I caused.

"This isn't over," I say. "It can't be."

"It is," she says, opening the door wider for me. "Goodbye, Bryce."

I take a step out but turn around to take one more look at her. This can't be how it ends.

"I love you, Lucy. Please. Don't do this."

She blinks away her tears, and for a second, I think she might take back everything she just said. I slip my hands into my pockets to keep myself from trying to take her in my arms.

Instead, I wrap my right hand around the small velvet box in my pocket. The one that holds the ring that I was going to give to her today.

I almost blurt out the question that will prove to her that I'm all in. The four words that I've practiced saying to her a thousand different ways. They are on the tip of my tongue, but just when I'm about to let them slip free, she says the four words that make me know that we're done. That I've ruined the best thing to ever happen to me.

"Go be amazing, Bryce."

Then she shuts the door.

SEPTEMBER, ROOKIE YEAR

"WHAT DO you think of a fall wedding?"

"Or maybe winter? Do you remember when we dressed our dolls up as brides and had a Winter Wonderland wedding, Anne Marie? It was just perfect. Lucia, what do you think?"

Out of nowhere, a coughing fit takes over my body, which is weird since I don't feel like I'm getting sick.

"Here, take a drink of water," Mom says, handing me a glass. "Now, what do you think. Fall or winter wedding?"

I drink the water, though it doesn't help the cough. Either way, I have to answer my mother and Mrs. Tripoli or they will just start making decisions on their own. They are having a little bit of a hard time understanding that it's not their wedding.

"Um, fall," I say. "Fall is fine."

"Fall it is then," Mom says as she makes a note in her book. "Fall flowers can be beautiful."

"Pumpkins!" Mrs. Tripoli offers.

My mom smiles. "And the leaves are stunning around here."

"Oh, it will just be wonderful."

"Our babies are getting married! All of our dreams are coming true!"

I get up from my childhood kitchen table and head outside. If I have to listen to them take another trip down memory lane, I might pull my hair out. This is the third wedding "meeting" they have called. It's also the third meeting that has ended with them talking about how they can't believe their babies are getting married.

Not like they haven't been planning this for the better part of twenty years. I'm honestly surprised they let me pick the season. Usually, they ask for my opinion but just go with what they want.

Which is fine. I've never been that girl who had every detail of her wedding planned out.

But if I did, it wouldn't be to who I'm marrying.

"No, don't go down that road," I say to myself. "Bryce isn't coming for you."

Every so often, I let the thought of Bryce go through my head. Then I remember every broken promise he has ever made and remind myself that it's for the best that I've moved on.

My cell phone vibrates in the back pocket of my jeans, and I laugh because Brenna is punctual as always. I told her to call me around this time to get me out of wedding planning. I wonder what crazy "emergency" she's going to come up with to get me out of here.

Last week, she needed help walking her pet octopus.

Except, when I look at the screen, it's not Brenna's name. In fact, it's a name I don't think has ever called my phone.

"Cole?"

"Hey, Lucy, sorry to call you out of the blue."

"It's fine. I'm just surprised. Is everything okay?"

I haven't the faintest idea as to why Cole is calling me, not that I've been paying any attention to what's happening in football. After the draft, it took Bryce nine days to send me a text message, and all it said was, "Hey, Lulu." I never responded to it. I haven't talked to him since that day at the lake.

"I'd be lying if I said yes. He's not good, Lucy. He's in his head. Ever since training camp started, he hasn't been able to throw the ball. He can't focus. I'm pretty sure his dad popped back up. He's just . . . I've never seen him like this."

I sit on the porch and let out a deep breath. "What does that have to do with me?"

He doesn't answer right away, and I hate the way anxiety is twisting inside me.

"I hate asking you this, and you can tell me no and to go to hell, but he needs you. I've tried to talk to him, and he keeps shutting me down, and I'm worried about him. His head is all over the place. It's like he's forgotten how to throw a football. He's been drinking more than usual. I'm worried about him, and I was hoping you'd be willing to talk to him. You're like the Bryce whisperer, so if he'll listen to anyone, it's going to be you."

I pinch the bridge of my nose, wanting to scream at the top of my lungs because no matter what I do, I can't yank myself out of Bryce's orbit. Something is always trying to drag me back in.

"I don't think that would be a good idea," I say.

"Why not? You don't have to come to Nashville. I'll bring him to Cincinnati. Could you meet us there?"

"It's not the distance, Cole. I'm . . . I'm engaged. I've moved on. Plus, I've been fixing him for way too long. He needs to learn to do this without me."

Nothing I said was a lie, and I owe Bryce nothing, but the guilt still wraps around my throat and squeezes.

"Wow, you're engaged," Cole says, though his voice doesn't sound very congratulatory. "Congratulations."

"Thanks. I'm sorry, Cole. I can't do it. The box is finally shut. It needs to stay that way, but I hope Bryce is able to work through whatever he's dealing with."

I'm just about ready to hang up when I hear words that I don't think I'll ever be able to resist.

"He still loves you, Lucy. He might not say it, but I know it. And I know it's really unfair of me to ask this of you, but . . . I hope you change your mind, if only for this last time. He really needs you."

———

"What are we doing here?" Bryce says from the adjoining room. I can't hear what Cole is saying, but I'm guessing he's either lying about why they are in Cincinnati or bracing him for what's in the other room, which is me and Brenna.

Bringing her was my condition to talking to Bryce.

"Am I really doing this?" I ask Brenna as I pace the room. "Maybe this isn't a good idea."

"You're helping a friend. And your best friend's brother," she says. "Now quit pacing before you leave tracks on the carpet."

I sit and clasp my hands together as I try to prepare myself to see him. It's only then that I feel the metal on my hand.

"Shit! My engagement ring," I whisper-yell, not knowing if they can hear me. "What do I do with it?"

As far as I know, Bryce doesn't know I'm engaged. Cole promised he wouldn't say anything, and considering he's in an apparent fragile mental state, it's probably for the best he doesn't know.

"Take it off. Now," Brenna says, holding out her hand as I

slip it off my finger. "I'll hold on to it. The last thing he needs to know is that you got engaged, let alone to Luciano."

She's right. He hates Luciano, and if Cole is to be believed and Bryce still loves me, the last thing I need to do is throw gas on the fire with news of my engagement.

I hear the sound of the adjoining door begin to open and I take one last breath.

This is it. This is the last time. Do it for your friendship. Do it for Brenna. Do it for the first boy you ever loved.

I fight back the tears as Bryce enters the room, confusion etched on his face as he sees Brenna and me sitting on the beds.

"Lulu? Brenna? What are you two doing here?"

I'm frozen, too caught up in the memory of that day at the lake. I still remember what his weight on me felt like. I can still taste his lips as he kissed me, and still feel his hands as they slid over my skin.

I know I'm engaged and that this man is my past, but Bryce Donald will always be the most beautiful man I've ever met.

Then I look at his eyes. I've always loved them. Except now they look . . . blank. I've never seen him look like this, and my heart breaks for him.

"I asked Lucy to come," Cole says, stepping into the room. "Brenna is just an added bonus."

"You know you missed me," she says as she pulls Bryce into a hug and then Cole, who seems to tense when she wraps her arms around him. "Now come on, Campbell. Let's get out of their hair. Know of any good parties around here?"

"Never again," Cole grumbles as they exit the room, leaving Bryce and me alone.

Wonder what that was about?

After a long moment, he's the one to break the silence.

"I'm sorry—"

"No," I say cutting him off. That's not why I'm here, and I can't go down that road. "We don't need to talk about that."

His shoulders slump as he hangs his head. "Did Cole call you here because I'm broken?"

"Something like that," I say as we take a seat on the bed. "I take it professional football isn't going well?"

He laughs, but there is no humor behind it. "I think Brenna could play better than I am."

"Bold statement."

He laughs again, and this time it sounds lighter. "Well, it's true. I have no idea what's wrong with me. It's like I got to the league, and my brain decided that it was going to forget every ounce of football I ever knew."

"Why is that?"

He just shrugs.

"Yes, you do," I say, my voice as gentle as can be. "It's me. You know you don't have to hold back. Talk to me. What's going on in that head of yours?"

A sad smile crosses his beautiful lips. "You don't have to do this, you know? I know how much I screwed up."

I inch a little closer to him, but not close enough where he can reach for me. "That's in the past, so let's focus on how I can help now. Come on. Let's figure this out."

I turn to grab the hotel notepad and pen off the end table.

"A list? We can't pro-con this, Lucy."

"Do you think that's the only kind of list I can make? It's like you don't know me at all."

"Fine." He sighs. "We'll do it your way."

And for the next three hours, Bryce tells me everything. The stress of his schedule. The complexity of the playbook. The pressure of living up to the hype as the top draft pick. The endorsement deals that are almost like a separate job. And yes, the infrequent-but-frequent-enough calls from his dad asking him for money or seeing if Bryce was willing to throw a game.

It's a lot for anyone, but when it comes to Bryce, who has let other people's demands and expectations rule his brain for his entire life, it's overwhelming. No wonder he can't throw a football.

So, we make a priority list. What he needs to focus on first, then second, and then last. Sometimes the lists change. Sometimes his focus shifts. But having a list gives him focus.

"There's one thing missing," he says as I hand him the papers.

"What's that?"

"You're not on here."

I freeze, not knowing how to react or what to say. I've been able to keep his attention off me for this whole conversation, and he seems to be a better Bryce than the one who walked into this room a few hours ago. Still, I know I should tell him about Luciano, but I can't. He'll find out eventually, but today isn't the day.

"That's okay," I say, cleaning up pieces of paper that weren't used. "You have a lot on your plate right now. Those need to be your focus."

"I meant what I said before the draft," he says. "I guess I just got a little ahead of myself. These lists? They're going to help me have the best rookie year ever. And then, I'm coming home and I'm picking you up, and I'm finally taking you on that date."

He leans in to kiss my cheek, and I don't move. It's the last time Bryce's lips are going to touch me, and selfishly, I want it for as long as possible. I know I'm never going to make a priority list for him or ever come before football or his career. I know that. It's why I'm marrying Luciano.

At the beginning, I truly believed Bryce and I would get a

happily ever after, and it took me years to realize that was nothing but a daydream of a naïve little girl.

I never thought it would end like this though. With me being the one to say goodbye.

Only, it's what I have to do. It's what's best for the both of us.

"Goodbye, Bryce," I say, finally stepping away. "Go be amazing."

And with that I turn and walk out of the hotel room.

CHAPTER 40
BRYCE

"COLE! OPEN THE FUCKING DOOR!"

I saw his truck where he normally parks it, so I know he's home.

"Coming!" he yells before he opens the door. "Bryce? What are you doing here? Why aren't you with Lucy?"

His question is valid. He knew I was going home today to see Lucy. He also knew that I planned on popping the question. If everything were to have gone right, I should be in the middle of celebrating with her—hopefully naked—before we went out and screamed to the entire town that we were engaged.

But no, I fucked up. Royally. And I need to fix it.

I just don't know how.

"Because, and for the life of me I can't figure out how I did this, I wrote down the wrong day for her birthday."

His eyes grow wide as he falls into one of his oversized leather loungers. "Oh fuck. So, on her birthday . . ."

"Yup. I was drunk with you, Dexter, and a handful of groupies. As an added bonus, there are pictures all over the internet to show it."

"In my defense, I wasn't drunk and actually didn't want to go. You made me."

"Not the fucking point, man. The point is that, while we were at some fucking club, Lucy was crying herself to sleep and Brenna was figuring out how to kill me and bury my body."

"Fuck. What did she say?"

"She ended it. She said she couldn't do it anymore."

He shakes his head in utter disbelief. "She can't mean that. It's Lucy. How do you know she just doesn't need a few days to cool off?"

I fall into his other oversized chair, the defeat coursing through my body and finally taking over. "She told me to go be amazing. Those were the exact words she told me in Cincinnati. She's done, Cole."

For the next hour, I fill Cole in on everything. It really doesn't take an hour. For most of that time, we just sit in silence. I can't believe twelve hours ago I was on my way to Laurel Heights, thinking that today was going to be one of the best days of my life.

"Does she know about the ring?"

I shake my head. "Honestly, I forgot about it the second Brenna opened the door. I knew something was off. One second, I'm psyching myself up to ask the woman I love to spend the rest of her life with me, and the next, I was trying to figure out which way was up. It all happened so fast."

"What did you do after? Did you drive straight back here?"

I crack my neck, trying to figure out how I want to answer this. "Yeah. Straight back here."

His eyebrow goes straight up. "Really? You did nothing between leaving Lucy's and driving here."

"I stopped for gas and a Gatorade."

"Quit bullshitting me, Bryce. Did you go to the liquor store or a bar? And don't lie to me. We've come too far for you to try to talk your way out of this."

I fall back, letting my head hit the back of the chair. I could lie to him or I could be honest. After everything we've been through, and as much as I've bullshitted him in the past few years, the man deserves my honesty.

"When she first shut the door on me, I was stunned. I don't think I moved for ten minutes. When I finally made it back to my truck, my gut reaction was to drive to the liquor store then drive to the lake and drown myself in the bottle. When I pulled into the liquor store parking though, I cut the engine, and . . ."

"And?"

"I didn't go in."

Just saying those words feels . . . freeing. Like some sort of weight has been lifted. I don't know how else to describe it.

"You didn't go in?"

"No. I just sat there. Hell, I probably sat there longer than I stood on her porch. All I kept thinking about was how my drinking got me into this situation. Everything comes back to my using alcohol to cope with stress. Instead of manning up and figuring out a way to move on with life, I dove into the bottle. That isn't something I want to do again. So, I turned the car around, got back on the highway, and came straight here."

"Wow," Cole says, shaking his head in disbelief. "I'm proud of you. That was a really big moment for you."

"Yeah. A little too late, though."

"Says who?"

I give my head a shake, because clearly, he didn't hear me. "Says me. Lucy's done. You should have seen her. She was devastated, and I don't blame her. This wasn't just some other broken promise that I made to her. I forgot her birthday. I spent a day that I should have been worshiping the ground she walks on with you guys and some cleat chasers. This was the final straw. I could see it in her eyes. The play clock has run out. Game over."

Cole leans forward, putting his elbows on his knees. This is when I know I'm about to get a speech. This is Cole's version of the Dad-lecture pose.

"You say she's done, but do you really believe that?"

I think back to everything that has not only happened today but also over the past seven years. "Yeah. I think so. Who could blame her Cole? I broke every promise I ever made."

"You did. That's true."

"Gee thanks."

"Am I wrong? When was last time you kept a promise you made to her?"

I sit back and think. I think all the way back to that first time I met her in the library. I promised her a date after our championship game. That didn't happen. I promised to come back for her prom. That didn't happen. I promised her I'd come back this summer. I never did. Between all those are a hundred smaller unkept promises.

"I don't know if I ever have."

"Exactly," Cole says, inching a little closer to me. "Actions speak louder than words. She needs you to show her that you're the man she always knew you could be. The guy you could be if you could just get out of your own way. Want to know how I know that?"

Oh man, he's really in Dad mode. "Please, Father Cole, tell me in all your brilliance, why you know I can do it?"

"Because you didn't drink today. Not one soul on this planet would have blamed you for drinking a bottle of whiskey after the love of your life told you it was over, but you didn't. That's your first action. So now, the real question is, what's going to be your second?"

I let his words sink in, and the longer I sit here, the more I realize he's right.

I did something today that the old Bryce could have never done.

Maybe this isn't as over as I thought?

I push myself up from the chair, but in doing so I feel something between the cushion and the arm rest.

"What are these?" I ask, holding up a pair of lace panties, which I guarantee do not belong to my best friend.

Cole jumps up from the couch and rips them from my hand. "Not your concern."

I smirk, a little mad at myself that I didn't throw them in his face. Literally. "I have so many questions."

"None of them I'm going to answer," he says. "Focus. This is about you. What are you going to do to get Lucy back?"

"I'll make you a deal. I get Lucy back, and you tell me who those belong to."

He gives me a healthy eye roll. "Fine. Now, what's the plan?"

I'm not exactly sure yet, but I do know this. It's not going to be quick. It's not going to happen overnight. Cole is right; this isn't about my words. This isn't about empty promises. This is about actions.

"I need to call Sadie. I need a favor."

CHAPTER 41
LUCY

"DO I HAVE TO?"

Brenna shuts off her car and snaps her head at me. "Yes. I love you like a sister, but you have to come back to the world of the living. Plus, opening night of Luciano and Celine's restaurant is something you have to do. You'd never forgive yourself if you miss it. Now, buck up, buttercup. Put on your big girl panties, and let's go."

I scowl at her and contemplate refusing to get out of the car. I haven't worn jeans and a sweater in who knows how long. The only reason I have makeup on is because I had to go to work today, and even then, I only wore it to cover the bags under my eyes.

It's been a rough month since I shut the door on Bryce, and well, the chance of a future with Bryce. I get up, go to work, come home, and lay on the couch. I have eaten my weight in mint chocolate chip ice cream and can't remember the last time I ate a real meal.

Most nights I cry myself to sleep. I always wonder what could have been different. And every night I hurt. I thought by now it would have gone away. I've gone months—hell, even years, without Bryce in my life. It's not like this is foreign territory.

The difference is now I know what it's like to be with him. I know what it's like to fall asleep in his arms. I know what it's like to feel him inside me. I know what it's like to be surrounded by his love.

That's when I cry because I know I'm never going to feel like that ever again.

"You can do this," Brenna says, giving my arm a squeeze. "We'll get dinner. Say our hellos and get out of here. Okay?"

I give myself a mental shake. "Let's do this."

As soon as we open the door, the smells of sauces and herbs attack our senses. This is one way to wake someone up who has been a zombie for the past month.

"Lucia! You made it!" Luciano says before we're more than two steps into the restaurant, and then he's wrapping me in a hug. Funny to think that at this time last year we were still faking it and this hug would not have existed.

"Of course I did," I say, hoping that comes out more enthusiastic than I feel. "It looks great."

Luciano's father held strong that he wasn't going to give him what he needed to franchise. So, Luciano decided to strike out on his own. He realized he didn't need his family to be happy with his career or with who he chose to love. He had been saving money for years because that's the kind of responsible man he is, and between that and what Celine brought to the table, the two of them were able to open their own restaurant—Lucine. It's a romantic Italian restaurant that looks as if it should be in a big city, not little Laurel Heights. The tables are covered with beautiful crème-colored tablecloths and each has a small tea candle floating in a shallow bowl. The music is soft and beautiful. I can already tell it's going to be the perfect date night restaurant.

I push back the tears, not letting myself go down the depression hole as Celine comes up to us. "Lucia, I'm so happy you could make it! Brenna! Good to see you!"

I give her a hug and Brenna does the same as she takes us back to a table. The restaurant isn't full since it's the soft opening for family and friends, which I'm glad for. The last thing I need is someone walking up to me and asking why I'm here and Bryce is in Nashville. Though, I do wish we were in a private dining room. The few that are here I swear are staring at me. At least, I feel like they are.

"Let me get you some wine," Celine says as we take a seat in a comfortable booth. "And whatever you want from the menu just let us know. Tonight, it's our treat."

I start looking at the menu, which makes my stomach turn. Not because of the food itself—it all looks delicious—but because the thought of eating more than a few bites of soup sounds horrible.

"That boy has been playing out of his mind." I hear a man say from the booth behind me. I want to ignore them, but it's hard to when the music is soft and there are only a handful of tables seated around you.

Where is Celine with the wine?

"I know it's only the preseason, but he's looking damn sharp out there," another voice says. "If this is a preview for the season, the Fury will be in the playoffs for sure."

"I'm going to have the calamari!" Brenna yells loud enough to draw everyone's attention, and my eyes go wide with shock. She's at a volume thirteen while everyone else is at a six. "What do you think you're going to have, Lucy?"

"What are you doing?" I whisper-yell.

"I know your no-Bryce-talk rule, but others don't. Since I can't police the entire town to make sure they don't talk about him in your presence, I'll just talk loud enough to drown them out. Now, where was I, oh that's right!" Her voice is getting louder and louder with each word. "The chicken francaise sounds delicious!" By the end, she's full-on screaming, her face is red, and everyone seated around us is staring at her slack-jawed.

I just stare at Brenna, and before I know it, I feel something weird coming from my stomach. I try to hold it in, but I can't, letting the sip of water I just took come out of my nose.

Oh my God. I laughed. I'm laughing. I don't remember the last time I did that.

"There she is," Brenna says in a normal voice and with a sympathetic smile. "I've missed you."

"Is that a smile I'm seeing on our girl's face?" Luciano says as he brings out our wine and a dish of Italian greens with bread. "What did you have to do to coax that out of her?"

"Just be my usual, ridiculous self," Brenna says proudly.

"Well, whatever works. I know Celine said you can have whatever you want tonight, but that's a lie. I'm already making you two something special, so you will eat what I put in front of you."

"That's so nice of you," I say.

"Well, I'm doing it so you aren't mad at me."

I scoff. "Why would I be mad at you?" Only he and Brenna look far too serious for him to be joking. "What did you do?" I ask.

"Your parents are here."

I shoot up from my seat, nearly knocking over the table as I watch my parents walk in to the dining room. When I realize I likely look like a lunatic, I sit back down, but not before my mother sees me and begins walking toward my table.

"Sorry," Luciano says before disappearing back into the kitchen.

"How do you want to play this?" Brenna asks.

"I don't know," I say truthfully. We've been in a standoff since Christmas. From what Uncle Nick told me, she won't talk to me until I come to my senses. I won't budge because she's crazy.

"Lucia. Brenna. How are you tonight?"

I take a healthy sip of wine before making eye contact. "Good. Thanks."

An awkward silence falls over the table. One of those silences that only last for maybe five seconds but feels like five minutes.

"I'm going to go pee!" Brenna says, right back to her yell she was using before. "I mean, I'm going to use the restroom. Why don't you have a seat, Mrs. Valenti?"

"Thank you, Brenna."

Brenna slides out of the booth and doesn't make eye contact with me as she walks away, which is good. If she had, she would have seen me trying to kill her with my stare.

"I'd ask how you've been, but I think I know the answer."

"Really, Mom? This is how you're going to start a conversation after ten months?" I really don't want to cause a scene on Luciano and Celine's big night, but if she keeps this up, I can't promise good behavior. "If you came over to gloat about how things didn't work out with Bryce, please leave. Enjoy your dinner. I don't want to hear it."

She doesn't say anything, nor does she get up. In fact, the only movement she makes is to hang her head.

"How did it get to be like this, Lucia?"

I let out a sigh and take another drink of my water. "You wouldn't accept anything other than me living the life you wanted me to. You made me feel guilty about not doing what you wanted, and when I put my foot down, you refused to return my calls or texts. Your best friend called a very nice woman, who I now consider a friend, a slut to her face and you did nothing to stop her. You refused to accept that I loved a man you didn't approve of. Any of this ringing any bells?"

She raises her head to look at me, and I'm pretty sure her eyes are welling with tears. "Why did she have to be French?"

I chuckle. "You can't help who you fall in love with, Mom."

"And you're sure you're not in love with Luciano? Look around. This here? This could be yours."

"No, it couldn't. Lucine would make no sense if it was the two of us."

"Don't joke," Mom says, though I can see a smile creeping onto her lips.

"In all seriousness, you have to know that the decision that Luciano and I made didn't come lightly. We were both unhappy, and we love each other enough to know that we would never have been happy. Plus, when a man is more affectionate with you after you call off your engagement, that's a pretty good indication that he's not in love with you."

She lets out a big sigh. "I just wanted you two together so badly."

I reach for her hand. "I know, and it would have been a great story. Two best friends have their children fall in love. It's the kind of story you read about in books. But that's not our story. He's with Celine, who is amazing and loves him the way he deserves to be loved. You guys would know that if you got to know her. And as for me . . ."

I trail off because I'm speechless. How do you admit to your mother that even though you followed your heart, it wasn't enough? That love wasn't enough?

"I'm sorry it didn't work out."

I just shrug. "It just wasn't meant to be."

"I don't believe that."

"What?" I ask, clearly confused. "What don't you believe?"

"That it wasn't meant to be." She wipes the stray tear from

her eye and sits up a little taller. "I might have been pushing Luciano on you, but I would have had to be blind not to see how you two looked at each other. That's real love. You never looked at Luciano that way. Guiliana and I were just too blinded by our own selfishness to see that."

I feel the tears building in my eyes. "Well, that's in the past."

"It is? I read an article the other day, and I swear he was—"

"Please, Mom." I hold up my hands as I try to also hold in my tears. "I . . . I can't know about him. I can't read articles about him. I can't watch him. Nothing. This last month . . . it's been the hardest one of my life. This is the first time I've gone anywhere besides work, and Brenna had to drag me kicking and screaming. So, please, whatever you know or think you know about Bryce, please . . . just keep it to yourself."

"I understand," she says as Brenna comes back to the table. "Well, I'll let you two get back to dinner."

"Why don't you join us?" I say before I realize the words are coming out of my mouth. "Bring Dad over."

"Is that all right?" Mom asks, looking back and forth between Brenna and me.

"Of course," Brenna says as she slides in next to me. "The more the merrier."

For the next two hours, I sit with my best friend and my parents, eating and laughing and . . . just being normal. Yes, Bryce was accidentally brought up a few times, and while it hurt, it didn't kill me.

I might not be better yet, but I'm getting there. Slowly but surely, I'll get there.

BALL IS at the twenty-five-yard line, we have no more timeouts and we're down by four. I take a look up at the game clock and see there are ten seconds left.

Plenty of time.

"Fake seven power zero drag. Now, go win us a damn football game."

Davis slaps the top of my helmet before I run back onto the field, making sure my chin strap is adjusted as I head into the huddle.

"How about we win ourselves a football game today, boys?"

My words are met with a mixture of hell yeahs and other grunts of some sort.

"Fake seven power zero drag. Fake seven power zero drag on three. One, two, three, break!"

We turn and line up. I check to the right and then to the left. I always know my left is good. That's where Cole is. My right isn't so shabby either.

I look across the line to the defense. They are lined up exactly like the coaches thought they would be. All we need now is Dexter to do his job and for me to do mine.

"Red, twenty-two! Red, twenty-two! Set . . . hike!"

As soon as I feel the ball in my hands, the rest of my movements are on auto pilot. I block out everyone else and keep an eye on my receivers, trusting that my back is covered.

I roll out to my right, and waiting for me, exactly where I want him, is Dexter.

Pull back . . . launch . . . release . . .

Dexter plucks it out of the air as if the ball was drawn to his hands, and then he runs across the goal line for a touchdown. My haze goes away, and all I hear is the roar of the crowd as we celebrate our first win of the season. It wasn't as easy as we would have liked it to be, but a win is a win, and I'll take one of those any day of the week.

"Hell yeah!" Cole yells, picking me up like he has since high school. "Great game, man. Welcome back."

We give each other a few slaps on the back before I'm grabbed by the arm by one of the interns in the media department.

"Television wants to talk to you. You good?"

You good? Who knew that could be such a loaded question?

On the field? I'm great. I had a great preseason, have been having regular sessions with Malcolm and have been keeping my nose clean.

Off the field? Not so much. I miss her. I miss her every damn day. The only reason I'm not more of a mess is because she might think we're done, but I know we're not. And I'm doing everything in my power to show her that I'm worthy of her. Even if she doesn't know it yet.

"Bryce Donald. Three-hundred-and-six yards passing today and three touchdowns. What a return after last year. How did you feel out there today?"

I stare at the reporter who has a microphone two inches

from my face and contemplate how to answer this. I could answer with my canned media responses. The ones I've learned and perfected since I was in high school. Or I could say how I really feel.

Actions speak louder than words.

And just like that, I know what I need to do.

"Physically, I felt great. My arm strength is where it needs to be, and I've been making sure to keep up with my conditioning after last year. I couldn't have asked for a better first game on the field."

"I thought after your first win back you'd be livelier. Why isn't Bryce Donald jumping through the roof about his first win back with the Fury?"

Here goes nothing . . .

"WHY IS that on the television? You know the rule."

I don't mind that Brenna might as well live here with as much as she's over, but if she's going to be in my house, she's going to follow my rules.

And my rules are that we don't watch, talk, or read anything about Bryce Donald.

"In my defense, you were taking a nap and I wanted to watch his first game back."

"You know you could have watched him at your place. You remember? The one you couldn't wait to get so you could finally move out of your mom's house?"

"I don't have cable."

"Just turn it off please," I say as I walk through the living room to get a bottle of water from the kitchen.

I knew today was the first game of the season, that's why I've been hiding for the past three hours. I figured that, if I took a nap and ignored the world, I could wake up and pretend as if the game never happened.

Yes, one of these days I'll need to be able to hear his name without crying. I'm just not there yet.

"So, do you still want to go run errands today? Or are we putting that off again?"

Brenna doesn't answer, and when I walk back into my living room, I stop in my tracks. Not only is the game still on but also his stupidly handsome face is right there.

He's sweaty from the game, his hair all over the place from being in his helmet, and I can tell by the marks on his face that he got hit more than once. He's the most breathtaking man I've ever seen.

I allow myself to look at his eyes. Those have always been the gateway to his emotions. When he was at his lowest of lows last year, they were hollow. Now? They aren't as sparkling as I know they can be, but they aren't dead.

Good for him. At least one of us has been able to move on.

"I thought after your first win back you'd be ecstatic. Why isn't Bryce Donald jumping through the roof about his first win back with the Fury?"

"Turn it off, Brenna."

"You're going to hate me, but no."

I snap my head to her. "What do you mean no?"

"I mean that you have to hear him sometime. You can't ignore him forever. Consider this a test to see if you're any closer to doing that. The longer you ignore his existence, the harder it's going to be for you in the long run."

I start to argue back, but the sound of his voice silences me. God I've missed that. The way it was always so gravelly in the morning when he would whisper good morning to me. Or how excited it got when he would explain some football thing to me that I'd barely understand. Or when he told me he loved me.

I miss it all. I miss him.

"Don't get me wrong, I'm excited for this win today," Bryce starts, and as much as I want to walk away, I can't. "But it doesn't mean as much when you can't celebrate and be with the one you love. I let a lot of people down over the past year, but none more so than one woman in particular. She's the most amazing person I know, and I thought when I came back on the field, she'd be here with me. I thought after I did this interview, I'd run to the stands and find her waiting there for me. But that's not what happened, because . . . well, because I still have more work to do. Today might have looked like I was back, and maybe Bryce the quarterback is. But Bryce the man? He still has work to do. I only hope that I'm worthy of her sooner rather than later."

"Is this the same person you talked about in the *US Daily* article?"

He nods. "It is. I've learned that I can win all the football games I want, have all the money in the world or accolades I ever dreamed of, but if I don't have someone to share those experiences with, then what's the point? Football will only last for so long. But love? That one-of-a-kind love that only a select few ever know? That is what will last forever."

Bryce looks at the camera one last time, and I swear he is looking straight at me. I know that's not possible, but I swear that's what he's doing. His eyes are begging, no pleading, for another chance.

He said all the right things, but words have never been a problem for him. How do I know he's seriously changed?

"What article are they talking about?" I ask, vaguely remembering my mom also bringing up an article.

"Do you really want to know?" Brenna asks. Not because she doesn't want to show me but because she knows that if I read it, then there won't be any turning back. Everything I've done over the past month to ignore Bryce will be for nothing.

"Yes. I need to."

Brenna assesses me to make sure I mean it before bringing the article up on her phone. It was written by Sadie, his coach's fiancée and from what I've heard, a very well-respected national football writer.

Then I see the headline: "Bryce Donald ready to be a better man, on and off the field."

I think I read the article five times and then have to remind myself that Sadie wouldn't make things up for Bryce and everything in the article is true. They talk a lot about his mental health and how his problems began long before he stepped foot in Nashville. About how he didn't realize he had them because he had someone to confide in, but when that person wasn't in his life anymore, he didn't know how to process. He goes on to talk about how not many others have someone they can rely on in their life like he had, so his goal in the next year is to open an afterschool center for athletes. He wants it to be a safe place where high school athletes can get help with homework. Psychologists will be on hand to talk them through the trials and tribulations of their changing lives and help getting into college if they so wish.

"Oh, Bryce."

Then I get to the quote from Bryce that guts me. It's also likely that this is what my mother was talking about that night at dinner.

"I always thought I was just a football player. That I was put on this earth to throw around a football. And don't get me wrong, that's a large part of who I am. But some-one . . . someone so special that there aren't words adequate enough to describe how amazing she is, never thought of me as just a football player. She always thought I was so much more than a player. She believed in me from the very start. And everybody should have someone like that in their life. Someone who believes in them and makes them want to be a better man."

That's it. I can't hold them in anymore.

I collapse onto the couch, holding the phone to my chest.

He's saying all the right things, which he always does. But something about the way he spoke today, and something about this interview . . . they feel different.

I need to know. I need to know now.

"Are you okay?" Brenna asks, reaching for my hand.

I look up at her, and I don't know if this is a good idea, but I know I won't be able to do anything else until I do this.

"Call Bryce. I need to see him."

I KNOW I told Brenna I wanted to see him.

I know I *need* to see him regardless of if we work things out. Ignoring him was not helping me get over him. It was only making me more miserable by the day.

Now that I'm here, at Lake Laurel, because where else would he pick to meet me, I don't know if I can do it.

"You okay?" Brenna asks as we pull up to the lake. "You know you don't have to do this."

"No, I need to," I say, taking a few more deep breaths. "I don't like the way we ended things."

"Are you going to get back together with him?"

Well, that's the million-dollar question, isn't it?

"Honestly? I'm not sure. That's why I need to talk to him. I need to hear what he has to say and see if he's truly changed."

As soon as the words leave my mouth, Bryce walks from the back of his truck. And for a second, I stop breathing.

It's not because he's wearing a shirt that defines every muscle in his chest. It's not because his hair is crazy in that way I love so much.

It's because it's him. He's here. In Laurel Heights. During football season. To see me. Because I asked him to.

That, and I'm pretty sure the sight of Bryce Donald will always take my breath away.

"Listen to what he has to say," Brenna says. "If you still don't want anything to do with him, I'll be right around the corner ready with the getaway car."

Tears are already welling in my eyes as I slowly exit her car. As he walks closer, I can see he has his high school jacket over his arm, the one that I used to sleep in every night because I missed him so much. In the other hand, he's holding a piece of paper.

"Hey, Lulu," he says softly.

"Thanks for meeting me. I know you're busy—"

"No. I'm exactly where I need to be."

I'm speechless as he leads me back to the tailgate of his truck, which is down and covered in blankets. There's a bouquet of flowers sitting on top of a Tripoli's pizza box.

"Here, I believe this belongs to you," he says, holding open the jacket for me. Like I'm under some sort of hypnosis, I turn to let him put it on me before he lifts me up and sets me on the truck.

"What is all this?" I ask.

"This is the first of many things I do to make up for how bad I have messed up over the years. I figured I could start with your favorite pizza and flowers. The jacket is because, even after all these years, I still love it on you."

I bring it tighter around me, remembering everything this jacket once represented. It was his first promise to me. It was my memory of him. It was how I knew I wasn't supposed to marry Luciano.

"I remember when I first gave you that. I felt like the king of the world because the most amazing girl was wearing my jacket," he begins. "For years, I never thought of anything but football. It was my life, and my ticket out of this town. Then, one day, this girl walks up to me, wanting to teach me math. Her big brown eyes knocked me on my ass, and her smile took my breath away. It was the first time in my life that football left my brain and all I could think of was how to make her mine. I should have known then that you were going to be the only woman in my life I'd ever love."

I wipe the tears from my eyes but don't dare say anything.

"I worked hard to be the best at football, and that dream came true. Well, when I wasn't trying to destroy it. I haven't worked at all to be the man you deserve. In fact, I have epically failed at it. Yet, somehow, you gave me chance after chance. Chances I didn't deserve. Chances I didn't *earn*."

"Bryce—"

"No, Lucy. Let me finish," he says, unfolding the piece of paper he's been holding. "I've been thinking a lot about us. Not next offseason. Not when things settle down. Now because now is all we have. And this here is the list of things that I plan to do to be the best man for you."

I laugh. "You made a list?"

"Damn right I did." He smiles as he looks down at it. "Number one. We are going to talk every day. You will never not hear the words I love you every day from me."

"That's a good start."

"I thought so. Number two, every year on your birthday, I will take you wherever you want to go. You name it, it's done."

"Bryce, you don't need—"

"Shhh. I'm just getting started. Number three, I'm going keep my promises." His eyes lift and hold mine. "I know for years I have broken them, but not anymore. I promise that I will always put you first. I promise that, one day, when we have children, I'll never take the family you will have given me for granted. I promise that I will continue to work on myself because you deserve the best version of me."

A whole new batch of tears comes streaming at his words.

"And finally, I promise, that every day I will love you with my whole heart. Lucy Valenti, I am so sorry for taking this long to tell you all of this. I don't deserve you, but I want to. I want to deserve your love every day for the rest of my life."

I jump off the truck and take a deep breath. All I want to do is run and jump into his arms, but I can't.

Not yet.

"How do I know I can trust you this time?" I ask, crossing my arms as if to guard my heart. "I heard what you said after that game and I read the article. I heard about the things you wanted to do. How do I know it's not just to get me back? I have to know, Bryce. I know, deep down, even when we were miles apart, that you love me, and you know I love you, but how do I know this isn't the start of another cycle?"

Bryce walks toward me, reaching for both of my hands.

"Because now I know what it's truly like not to have you in my life, and it is absolute hell."

"You've not had me in your life before."

"This time was different. When we were young, we had the hope of us. It's what kept us afloat all those years. Then, these past few months, I had you. I knew what it was like to be with you. To kiss you. To hold you in my arms and know what it was like to have your love. It was better than anything I ever felt in my life. Then it was gone because of something I did. I've worked hard at football. I've never worked hard at being yours. Let me work my ass off to be the man you deserve."

One of the first things I ever noticed about Bryce was his eyes. I remember thinking that they could see through my soul.

Eight years later, as I look into his beautiful blues, it's as if he's begging me to look into his soul, to see how much he wants to change. He's laid bare, vulnerable, and telling me he wants to be a better version of himself.

That he wants to be better with me as well as for me.

All I've ever wanted was for Bryce to be the best version of himself. To be the man I always knew he could be.

"You know you'll have a lot of work to do," I say.

"I can't wait to get started," he says as he cracks a small smile before wrapping his arms around my waist, bringing his lips down to meet mine.

For the first time in what feels like months, everything is right in the world.

I know we have a lot to figure out, but we have love and a list. How can we go wrong?

FOR MY ENTIRE LIFE, when I had big decisions to be made, I didn't hesitate to call Lucy. When I was feeling nervous or overwhelmed, she was the only one who could clear my head.

That doesn't do me any good when I'm minutes away from asking her to marry me. I need my Lucy. I need her calm presence. I need her wisdom. I need her to make me a list.

Instead, I get Cole.

He might be good at keeping big ass defensive lineman from sacking me, but he's shit at love advice. I really need to find this guy a girlfriend, or at least finally force him to fess up about the owner of those panties I found in his couch.

"You sure you want to propose to her like this?" Cole asks for the fifteenth time. "Wouldn't you rather go someplace a little more . . . private?"

"Nope. This is it."

I look around at the field, which is currently being flooded by media, family, and a few rogue fans since we're not stopping anyone tonight.

We did it. After today's win, we're officially in the playoffs.

It has been a hell of a year. After a rocky start, it didn't take long for things to get back on track. I sobered up—for good this time. I started seeing Malcolm again and Lucy moved to Nashville with me. I meant what I said to her when I begged for forgiveness in Laurel Heights. I am committed on being the best man I know how to be. That includes therapy sessions, AA meetings, and anything else I can do to make sure I'm my best version of myself.

I'm trying to be the best brother. The best friend. The best teammate. I want to be a role model for the younger generation. More than any of those, I want to be the best forever for Lucy.

Am I there yet? Not even close, but every day I take another step. That's all you can ask of someone.

"She better say yes," Cole says as the intern who was tasked with holding on to the ring today sprints over to give it to me.

"Of course she's going to say yes. Why wouldn't she?"

"Let's see," Cole says as a group of fans attempt to push past him. "Maybe because you guys haven't been together for an entire year? Maybe because she wants to wait until your house is built? Or maybe she really doesn't love you like she says she does?"

I glare at Cole. "You're the worst future best man in the world."

"I'm just saying it's a possibility," he says as his eyes focus on something over my shoulder.

I glance back, and find my sister talking to Dexter.

"Oh shit," I say. "Does he not know about the rule not to fuck around with your quarterback's sister?"

"Maybe I need to remind him of that," Cole says, his voice dropping an octave.

I was over the moon for Lucy to move to Nashville, which she did as soon as we got back together.

What I didn't expect was for my sister to toss her bags into the moving truck and announce that she was coming too. I thought it was a joke until she showed up at my apartment and asked where she was going to sleep.

Our mother is not happy. I give her two years before she moves here as well.

"Not now, big guy," I say, holding him back as best I can. "As much as I'd love to see you scare a grown man until he wets himself, we have more important things to deal with. I need your tall ass to find Lucy for me."

Cole glares at Brenna and Dexter one more time before he starts looking for Lucy again. I figured she'd be here by now since it doesn't take that long to get from the wives' box to the field.

Wife.

The more I think about it, the more I like the idea of her becoming Mrs. Bryce Donald.

Luckily, Christmas fell on a weekday this year, allowing us to sneak up to Laurel Heights to spend Christmas with her family. When we were there, I was able to ask Mr. Valenti for his blessing. He said yes, but only if the Fury made the playoffs this year.

I'm still not sure if he was joking.

Either way, everything is exactly as it should be. Well, it will be in a few minutes.

"There she is," Cole says, pointing to the gate by the end zone. "Good luck."

He gives me a pat on the back and with one last, deep breath, I make my way to the love of my life.

"You did it!" she yells, running and jumping into my arms as I do my best to make sure the box in my hand doesn't press against her.

"We did," I say, giving her a kiss and lowering her back to the ground, quickly putting my right hand behind my back.

"You were amazing," she says. "I was keeping track of the other games today. It looks like you'll finish the regular season second in total passing yards but first in efficiency, which, to me, means more because quality over quantity, right?"

I laugh and lean in for another kiss. My girl will never not love math. Since she started attending games, she has found it to be her hobby to keep live updates of every quarterback in the league to see where I statistically rank against them. I think she's even made up new categories.

I love her so much.

"That's good to know," I say. "But I want to talk about something else."

She quirks a brow. "What else is there to talk about? It's a Sunday home game. You're going to go shower. Then you're going to go do your media interviews before coming home and eating pizza with me."

Yes, we already have a routine, and it's one I hope never goes away. It might not be Tripoli's pizza, but it will do.

And yes, I am trying to get Luciano and Celine to move down here and open a Lucine location. Plus, the guys in the Bachelor league really want to meet him after he won the league last season.

"Well yes, but I thought we could do one thing before that," I say as I get down on one knee.

"Oh my God," she says, covering her mouth as a hush falls around us.

"Many, many years ago I promised to ask you out on a date. I said that I'd wear a shirt with buttons and that you would wear a dress that drove me crazy. It took us a long time, but we finally got that date and many more after that. In that time, my love for you has grown in ways I didn't think possible. So now,

I ask you today on another date. Except, maybe this time, I'll wear a tuxedo and you'll wear a white dress that will bring me to my knees? What do you say Lucy Valenti? Will you marry me?"

I have never heard this stadium silent before. Especially after a win. But I swear I could hear a pin drop.

That makes it hard to ignore that Lucy isn't saying anything. She's biting her bottom lip and blinking frantically to keep from crying, but those tears could be bad or good for all I know.

Shit. Was Cole right?

Just when I'm about to figure out how to save face, she says the best word I will ever hear.

"Yes," Lucy says, her head nodding frantically. "Yes, I will marry you."

The stadium erupts in cheers. With weak legs, I stand, take the ring out of the box, and slide it onto her finger.

It's perfect. A round solitaire diamond that can be seen all the way back in Laurel Heights.

What's even more perfect is the feel of Lucy's lips on mine as she jumps back into my arms.

Over the years, I've often felt like the king of the world. In high school when we won the state title. In college when we won the national championship. Hearing my name picked first in the draft. Hell, even throwing my first professional touchdown.

None of those feelings compare to this.

Nothing compares to the love Lucy and I share.

And nothing ever will.

EPILOGUE
LUCY

THREE YEARS LATER...

THERE HAVE BEEN many times over the years when I have been proud of Bryce.

When he won the state title in high school. When his college career soared all the way to him being the top draft pick. When he battled his demons and came out the other side a better man.

None of those compare to tonight. When you watch your husband, the father of your unborn child and love of your life, win the championship and be named MVP in the process, it's a feeling like no other.

He did it. After years of hard work, tough times, near collapses, and a few missed opportunities here and there, he and the Fury can finally say they are the best in the league.

"Oh my God! They did it!" Brenna yells, nearly jumping on me as she gives me a hug. "Oh shit. Sorry. I'm just so excited I forgot that my nephew was there."

I laugh through the happy tears as I rest my hands on my very large stomach. "How could you forget? You already have three best-aunt-in-the-world shirts despite being his only aunt. You also organized the baby shower. How could you possibly forget that I'm about to have a baby?"

"I mean, can you blame me?" she asks, holding her hands in the air as she looks up at the confetti still raining from the rafters of the stadium. "I'm just . . . I'm just so proud of them, you know?"

I nod, fighting back another round of tears. "They really did it"

We link arms and watch our men, who are acting exactly like they should, as they hang out on the stage. Most of them have had their cell phones out the second the celebration started. They've already put on their league champion hats. Somehow, Dexter smuggled a bottle of champagne onto the stage and is dousing everyone with it.

In the middle of it all are Bryce and Cole, embracing like only best friends can. To think that they dreamed of this moment when they barely knew how to tie their cleats is almost unfathomable. They have been through so much together, and for a while, I didn't know if this dream would happen for them. Kind of hard to win a championship together when you aren't speaking.

Yet, here they are, celebrating this moment together, exactly how they should be.

"I'm going to go sneak on stage," Brenna says. "It's about time I show my man exactly how proud of him I am."

I laugh. "You go do that."

I look back to the stage, and Bryce has made his way behind Hunter, who is currently giving his speech as the youngest winning coach in league history. I'm too busy drinking in the moment happening behind him.

Bryce and Davis are in an embrace, and if I'm seeing things right, they both might be shedding tears. I don't blame them. If people only knew how much Davis has helped Bryce over the years, not only as a coach but also as a friend and mentor, they would realize what this moment means for them.

I look away and rest my hands back on my stomach as I make eye contact with Bethany. Neither of us say anything, yet we know exactly what each other are thinking. She's thanking me for coming back into Bryce's life, which coincided with the Fury's rise to the top of the league. I know this because she has told me it roughly a million times since I moved to Nashville.

I always play it off since no one woman is responsible for an entire team's turnaround.

Though, I have crunched the numbers, and the winning percentage of the team when I was in Bryce's life compared to when I wasn't is staggering.

"We'd now like to introduce, the most valuable player of tonight's game, quarterback Bryce Donald!" Coach Hunter announces.

The stadium erupts in cheers as Bryce steps up to the microphone, championship trophy in hand.

"There was a day I never thought this would happen. Hell, there were more than a few days. But here we are Nashville! At the top of the football world!"

The fans who made their way to Miami for the game go crazy in applause. As for me? It's all I can do to keep the tears at bay.

"I might be holding this MVP trophy, but one player isn't the team. I need to thank every single man who puts on the uniform with me every day. I'm not here without each one of you. I'd be remiss if I didn't give a special nod to Cole Campbell. My brother. My best friend. Who knew that what we dreamed of as kids would actually come true? And to my coaches. You never gave up on me, not even when I didn't give you any reason to believe in me. When you drafted me, I told you that we'd win a title.

Here we are. Thank you. Thank you for everything. And last but not least, I need to thank my wife, who is the love of my life and the woman who is about to give me a gift greater than this trophy. I love you, Lulu. We did it baby."

The crowd goes crazy again as Bryce holds up the trophy one more time before exiting the stage. I'm in full-blown tears and thinking about the road he referred to. It was long and hard, but it was worth every trial we faced to get to where we are now. Still, sometimes I wonder if I'd do it all again if I knew this was the only way we'd end up together.

Actually, that's not even a thought. I would in a second. Bryce's love is worth that. Our love is worth that.

That's how I know he and I have that once-in-a-lifetime love from fairy tales.

"He did it," Mrs. Donald says, putting her arm around my shoulders. "He really did it."

I lean my head onto her shoulder as we watch Bryce finish his speech and exit the stage. I'm so glad that everyone we love is here tonight able to share in this moment.

My parents are even here somewhere too. Dad and Mr. Tripoli are likely trying to sneak autographs, and my mother is probably still talking to Guiliana. Luciano and Celine left before the game was over because Celine wasn't feeling her best.

That's what happens to us super pregnant women.

Yes, she's also pregnant.

Yes, we're due days apart.

Yes, our mothers are thrilled.

And secretly, so are we.

"There are my girls," Bryce says, finally making his way to me and his mom. He wraps her in a hug that, once again, makes the tears start flowing.

No one should be this emotional when they are this pregnant. It's just not fair.

"Hey, Lulu," he says, bringing me in for a kiss I feel all the way to my toes. I thought that, after a few years of marriage, this feeling would lessen. That I wouldn't immediately feel his presence the second he walked into the room.

I was wrong. They are stronger.

The butterflies will never go away.

"I am so proud of you," I say, wrapping my arms around his neck. "How does it feel to be the best?"

He leans in for one more kiss, and I swear if we weren't surrounded by thousands of people, I'd be having my way with him right now.

Pregnancy sex is no joke. It's the best.

"It's the second best feeling in the world."

I lift an eyebrow. "Only the second?"

"Yup," he says, picking me up to bring me in for yet another kiss. "Best day of my life was when you became my wife. Then this. Though, I'm pretty sure when this little guy comes, today is going to get bumped again."

He leans down to press a kiss to my stomach, and I'm pretty sure he says something to his unborn son, though I can't hear it. It's probably something about how this is going to be him in twenty-five years.

The man is dead set on our baby coming out of me already being able to throw twenty-yard passes.

I joke and say that he's going to be doing calculus in the delivery room.

"You ready to get out of here?" he says. "I have to do a few interviews then we can get out of here."

"Sounds good," I say, taking his hand and turning to walk off the field. However, I don't get two steps before I feel something weird happening.

"What?" Bryce says, realizing I've stopped. "Lulu, what's the matter?"

I look back up to him, doing my best to stay calm.

"Want to ensure this day always stays number two? Then take me to the hospital. My water just broke."

Instead of going to Disney World, Bryce is going to the hospital after winning the championship, because it's baby time! Click here for the extended epilogue.

ACKNOWLEDGMENTS

When I say I never thought this book was going to come out, I truly mean that. This book was slated to come out in October, then November. And even until last week, I really didn't think it was going to happen.

But here we are, and I'm so glad Bryce and Lucy's story is finally out in the world. I hope you loved them as much as I do. Well now, I didn't love them for a minute around October of last year (that's author humor). And let's be real, Bryce made it really hard to love him.

This is without a doubt the hardest book I have ever written. Bryce and Lucy's story is so complicated. But it was *their* story. The angst. The push and pull. The almost and the almost nevers. I always knew their journey, but bringing it to life was a challenge I never saw coming. But I love it, and I hope you do too.

And for those who are wondering . . . yes, Brenna and Cole are next. And just you wait. Brenna, well, she is a handful. And Cole is just the man for the job.

As always, thank you to my parents. I've lost count of how many times I've come to you guys with a change in life plans, and never once have you tried to steer me toward a safe course. You've allowed me to follow my dreams and my path, and for that I am forever grateful.

To my family and friends: Your support has been amazing.

Many of you have no clue how I ended up here, but that doesn't mean the support hasn't been there. I love you all.

To Kelly. You've been with me on this book journey since day one. Not only are you an amazing alpha reader, but you are an amazing friend. Maybe one day we can go on a book trip again.

KKSB, thank you ladies for never letting me give up, when I wanted to so many times with this book. Julia, thank you for well, everything.

Kari March, another amazing cover. Thank you for making my books come to life.

To Jill, Kelly B., and Evie, thank you for your brutal honesty. This book is better because of you guys.

Oh Ashley. How you haven't fired met yet I'll never know. Thank you for making me better. Thank you for pushing me in ways I didn't think I could be pushed. I'm sorry I don't format correctly and I promise I'll work on the smut. Also, Chicago style sucks.

Michele and Angela, thank you for your keen eyes.

Michelle, thank you for keeping me organized and making sure I hit my word count for the day.

Corinne, I'm here because of you. If you wouldn't have given me a chance I wouldn't have started writing. You forever changed my life.

Adriana, thanks for always picking up the phone.

Last but not least: My Book Squad and my Thirst Squad on TikTok, thank you all for coming on this journey with me. I love all of you.

ABOUT THE AUTHOR

Known for her witty sense of humor, Chelle Sloan is a former sports editor who after years in the newspaper business, decided to become a romance author. You know, because that's the normal path to writing happily ever afters.

An Ohio native, she's fiercely loyal to Cleveland sports, is the owner of way too many tumblers and will be a New Kids on the Block fan for life. She does her best writing at Panera, or anywhere that's not her office.

When she's not writing, you can find her in the kitchen attempting to become a baker, fixing up her condo (badly and by watching YouTube videos), or falling in love with a book.

As for her own happily ever after? Maybe one day...

Stay up to date with all things Chelle & join the VIP Squad!

ALSO BY CHELLE SLOAN

THE NASHVILLE FURY, PRO FOOTBALL SERIES

Off the Record: A secret office romance

Off Track: A surprise pregnancy romance

Off Season: A second chance romance

Off Limits: A sibling's best friend romance

NASHVILLE FURY WORLD

Off the Market at Christmas: A childhood friends-to-lovers romance

LOVE ONLINE SERIES

Thirst Trap: A social media romance

Match Maker: A fake dating romance

Run Run Rudolph: A celebrity, holiday romance

ROLLING HILLS

The One I Want: A single dad/nanny romance

The One I Need: An accidental marriage romance

The One I Love: A friends to lovers romance

The One I Hate: An enemies to lovers romance

GUIDE TO LOVE SERIES

Runaway Bride's Guide to Love: A brother's best friend romance

Single Mom's Guide to Love: A marriage of convenience romance

Roommate's Guide to Love: A fling to forever, single dad, romance

Good Girl's Guide to Love: A fake dating, football romance